STEAMSHIP
to ZION

OTHER BOOKS AND AUDIO BOOKS
BY JERRY BORROWMAN:

Attack the Lusitania!

Stories from the Life of Porter Rockwell

Life and Death at Hoover Dam

'Til the Boys Come Home

Home Again at Last

I'll Be Seeing You

One Last Chance

A Distant Prayer (with Joseph Banks)

Three Against Hitler (with Rudi Wobbe)

STEAMSHIP
to ZION

a novel

JERRY
BORROWMAN

Covenant Communications, Inc.

Published by Covenant Communications, Inc.
American Fork, Utah

Printed in the United States of America
First Printing: April 2012

18 17 16 15 14 13 12   10 9 8 7 6 5 4 3 2 1

ISBN-13: 978-1-62108-017-6

ACKNOWLEDGMENTS

I'D LIKE TO THANK MY wife, Marcella, for her comments and critique of the story. Marcella has remarkable skill as an editor and she helps me to present more fully developed characters and a consistent storyline. I also had some great readers who dropped what they were doing to read the book when I was up against a submission deadline. They offered meaningful suggestions and needed corrections. Included in this group are Steve Jett, Norman Jenson, Reed Williams, Evan Rowley, and my mother, Geneva Borrowman, who at ninety-four years old remains my most enthusiastic reader.

Val Johnson, a professional editor, did a thorough edit for grammar and character consistency in just one weekend—and that in the middle of a hectic schedule of college teaching and work as senior editor of the *Ensign* and *New Era* magazines. He is a great friend and mentor.

I always appreciate the many people at Covenant Communications who get the book ready for printing and distribution, including those who design the cover and refine the story, especially my editor, Kirk Shaw, who has become one my closest friends.

I am blessed by the efforts of these people.

1—A FRESH START

"THIS IS OUTRAGEOUS! I WON'T stand for it!"

To observers standing nearby it appeared that Gloria Palmerston was going to strike Captain Edwards, and even he seemed to brace for the blow. But instead she abruptly turned on her heel and stormed off in the direction of the steamship ticket office.

"Hey, watch out there!" But it was too late. In her anger, Gloria ran directly into Marc Chandler, who had been standing patiently behind her on the pier studying a sheaf of papers—papers that went flying as he fell backward to the ground. "What's that, then? Are you really all that important that you can just bowl over anyone who gets in your way?"

"Hmmph!" was Gloria's response as she muscled her way through the crowd, some of whom were chasing down the scattered papers.

"Here, let me help you up." Henry Chandler stretched out his hand to his son and quickly pulled the twenty-two-year-old into a standing position.

Dusting himself off, Marc turned to the crowd. His grin showed that he was nonplussed by the whole thing, which allowed those standing nearby to laugh with him. Marc was one of those individuals who displayed natural charm. He had dark hair, brown eyes, a trim but athletic build, and a natural grace. As he accepted the last remnant of the papers from an elderly woman, he thanked her. "I hope it's not like this in America," Marc added.

"Look," said Alexandra Chandler, Marc's mother, "that young lady who bumped into Marcus is over there crying. Henry. We must do something."

"Do something? What can we do?"

"We can comfort her," said Alexandra, biting her lip. "And you can find out from the captain what all this fuss is about. No woman should be made to cry, let alone a highborn woman like that." Alexandra turned on her family with a stern gaze—a gaze they recognized very well. "So you go see the captain, and Honoria and I will go talk to the lady."

"Me?" said Honoria. "But why me? What would I say?" Honoria was the Chandlers' twenty-year-old daughter. Although quite attractive, with large dark eyes and beautiful dark brown hair, she was painfully shy and quiet, but her father preferred to call her "reserved."

"Just come with me, dear. You needn't say anything, but at times like this it helps to have more than one woman to offer comfort." With that, Alexandra started off toward the ticket office, pausing just long enough to momentarily return her gaze to Henry. "Well? You and Marcus should go talk to the captain right now."

Henry sighed, shook his head ever so slightly, but said nothing to his wife. "Come on, then, Marcus. Let's go see what we can do. Your mother will never let us rest until we do. Will you watch our things, Max?"

"Yes, sir," said Max, their fourteen-year-old son and the youngest member of the family.

"I don't know why we'd want to help her," said Marc. "She bowled me over with no hint of apology. It looks to me like just another spoiled, upper-crust brat."

"Now, Marc," said Henry, "she was obviously distressed and caught up in her own troubles."

Marc stifled a retort. He decided not to press it. This was too exciting of a day, and he wasn't going to let some overdressed debutante spoil it for the family. And, if truth be told, he found her one of the most strikingly beautiful women he had ever laid his eyes on, even if her perfume was so strong and fragrant that it could have knocked him down just as easily as the collision or her attitude did. His eyes wandered to the young lady at the ticket office.

"The lady is all right now that your mother is there, so you don't need to stare," said Henry with a touch of mischief.

"What?" Marc turned and glowered at his father. "I was just glancing that way to make sure she wasn't knocking Mum and Honoria down."

Henry laughed. Then he stuck his arm up in the air to signal the captain. "A short word with you, Captain Edwards?"

The captain saw him and said something to the other passengers he was talking with. Then he made his way over to Henry and Marc. Even though Henry was a relatively low-level employee with the Cunard Line, the captain had already made it a point to welcome him to the dock and to extend an invitation for at least one evening at the captain's table during the upcoming crossing.

"How may I help you, Mr. Chandler?"

"I'm sorry to bother you with something that is most likely none of our business, but my wife is quite concerned about that young woman who appeared to have an altercation with you. Is there anything we can do to help the situation?"

The captain sighed. "She's a sharp one, all right. A single woman who wants passage to America. But she has no chaperone and so of course it's impossible for us to transport her. That's why she was so hostile to me: I had to tell her no, and now I'm sure I'll hear about it from the company."

"Pardon my asking, but she appears to be a prominent person— how is it that she would be in a position to travel alone?"

"From what I can make out, she's the daughter of a nearby land-owner, the mayor of that town. So she's prosperous enough—she offered to pay her passage in cash. But why she wishes to make her way alone, to America of all places, is beyond my simple imagination. She acted quite anxious to get on board."

"She's a menace, if you ask me," said Marc.

"Perhaps . . ." replied the captain, "Ah, it seems as if she's enlisted the aid of your mother. Here they come."

Henry and Marc both turned to see Alexandra striding forcefully toward them, the young lady and Honoria hanging back by where young Max had positioned himself with the family's steamer trunks. "Right, then," said Henry, "you better prepare yourself, Captain. My wife has that determined look in her eye."

"Henry. Captain. I've learned something that may be of interest to the two of you. This young lady is very much in need of passage on this ship, and I think it unconscionable that she be refused."

Henry couldn't help but wonder how he'd become an obstacle to that plan but knew it foolish to intervene.

"I understand that, ma'am," said the captain respectfully, "but it's unthinkable for a young lady of such obvious breeding to travel unaccompanied on a voyage like this. That is a situation that virtually none of the respectable people on board would stand for. Nor will I stand for it. Someone has to be there to protect her, and my crew simply doesn't have time."

"That's what I thought," said Alexandra, a little softer. "It shows you to be a gentleman. But I believe we have an answer—if you still have a cabin."

"What have you planned, Alexandra?" asked Henry. "You know it can be unseemly to interfere in other people's affairs."

"I know it can be the Christian thing to do." Alexandra took a deep breath, knowing full well that what she was about to propose was questionable at best. But the young woman was so distressed and desirous of making passage that Alexandra had concluded she had to do something to help her. "I propose that we act as her chaperone. We are a respectable family, and she can come along as our guest. Between my husband and my sons, we can make certain she is protected."

"But, you don't even know her . . ."

"I know her well, enough, Captain Edwards. And I'd think you'd want the extra revenue that comes from a first-class cabin."

"But Mother, we really don't know anything about her—except that she is rude and impetuous and . . . I was looking forward to this crossing more than anything, and I'm not sure I want to do it standing guard over some princess."

"Quiet, Marcus. A woman is in need and we can help."

Marc inhaled sharply, forcing himself to keep quiet.

His mother had her hands on her hips and was standing squarely in front of the captain. "Well, Captain Edwards?"

The captain pursed his lips. Even though Alexandra was in command of the situation, the captain turned to Henry. "And what do you think, Mr. Chandler? Are you willing to vouch for this young woman and take her under your care?" No matter how forcefully a woman spoke, it was the head of the household who must make a decision such as this.

"You do have a suitable cabin?"

"We do."

"Then it is in the interest of the company to book it." Henry turned toward where the young woman was standing. She looked at him with a mixture of hope and scorn. Obviously she was not delighted with the thought of throwing herself at the mercy of strangers, even when they had reached out to her in kindness. "Let me have a few moments to talk with her, but go ahead and plan on her coming on board. We will act as chaperone if she's able to convince me that she's not running away from the law or some other entanglement."

"Henry, she's not running away from the law, for heaven's sake . . ."

"That's enough, dear. You've won the point, but I really do have to interview her first. It's the only prudent thing to do. We must take this responsibility on with full knowledge so it doesn't come back to haunt us later."

Alexandra hesitated and then relented. "Of course you're right, dear. Go talk to her and make the best decision. I hope it works out that we can help her."

"Is that acceptable, Captain?" asked Henry.

"I have no objection. We will plan on it, unless I hear otherwise."

Turning to Alexandra, Henry said softly, "I hope you haven't landed us in something troublesome. We have our own affairs to tend to, and they may become muddied enough as it is."

"That may be . . ." Alexandra's voice was more agitated now. "But how could I just stand there?"

"Others could, but you can't. No use fretting about it. Now I'll go talk to her." Turning, he said, "Marcus, why don't you go and organize things for the porters. And stand by to help Miss—whatever her name is—when the time comes."

"As long as she doesn't blast past me again . . ."

"Be nice to her," Alexandra scolded. "She may be our dinner companion for the next two weeks, so I don't want you nursing a grudge or teasing her. Do you understand?"

"Yes, ma'am."

As they busied themselves collecting the young woman's luggage and uniting it with their own, the family was surprised by how long their father's conversation lasted with her, particularly when they observed her face flush at one point.

"It's awfully hard to imagine Father saying something that would offend someone," whispered Honoria.

Alexandra smiled slightly. "She is a very strong-willed girl."

"And I've the bruises on my bottom to prove it," Marc added.

Alexandra rolled her eyes. "You're acting like a . . ." Before she could finish her sentence, her eyes widened and she whispered, "Quick, look away. They're coming."

"It's all settled, then," said Henry in a forced voice. "Miss Palmerston is an honorable lady from a prominent family who wishes to spend some time with relatives in New York City. She will be our guest for the crossing and then part company with us in New York." It seemed obvious to everyone concerned that there was more to the story than Henry was telling, but the terseness of his response and the set look on his face conveyed very clearly that he was not going to say anything more about it. "Now, Alexandra, perhaps you could see Miss Palmerston to her room."

"Perhaps you can formally introduce all of us first," said Alexandra.

"Yes," said Henry, looking around nervously, "of course. But we really should hurry. All of this excitement suggests that Miss Palmerston should lie down to calm herself." Through all of this, Gloria had stood by impassively, perfectly content to have Henry carry the burden of explaining what seemed inexplicable. "So allow me to introduce Miss Gloria Palmerston. This is my wife Alexandra, our daughter Honoria, and our two sons Marcus and Maximus."

"I prefer Max."

"Pleased to meet all of you," said Gloria quietly. Glancing at Marc, she added, "And I'm sorry for our . . . encounter."

Marc raised his head slightly as he considered the sincerity of her words. He found them lacking. "Of course. Apology accepted." His use of the word *apology* caused Miss Palmerston's eyes to narrow and her nostrils to flare slightly.

"Yes, well, then, if you'll see her on board the ship," said Henry to Alexandra in a hushed voice.

"But they've not even sounded the call for boarding . . ."

"I know that, dear, but I'll speak to the captain. It really *is* quite urgent that Miss Palmerston go aboard." Henry glanced around the docks with a furtive glance as he said this, which raised everyone's suspicion.

"Of course." Even though Alexandra lifted her right eyebrow—a sure sign that she was curious—she said nothing more. She held out her arm to Gloria, who stepped forward and accepted her companionship. Henry walked off to meet up with the captain as Alexandra and Gloria made their way to the gangplank, where the purser allowed them to pass after receiving a sign from the captain.

"What on earth is this all about," asked Marc when his father returned. "She is definitely not the type who needs to 'lie down because of all the excitement.' She's the cause of the excitement, for Pete's sake!"

"That's enough, Marcus. She needs our help. Just leave it at that." Just then Marc saw his father shrink back a bit. Following his gaze, he turned his eyes to the outer edge of the crowd, where he saw two rather rough-looking characters ride up on their horses, one putting a hand to his brow to shield his eyes from the sun as he looked over all of the people in the crowd, obviously searching for someone specific. When Henry saw Marc staring, he added, "Why don't we make our way toward the front of the line. The porter will take care of our luggage."

"Sure," said Marc, now very curious. Normally his father would have handled the luggage to save themselves precious money that would be needed once they reached America. But this was not the time to pursue it. "Come on, Max. Let's have a look at those side paddles before we get on board. I want to learn more about how this great ship works."

"Me, too," said Max excitedly.

"I'll take Honoria on board," said Henry.

As Marc and Max started toward the edge of the dock, Marc cast a quick glance to the side. The two figures on horses were gone. "It's going to be a very interesting voyage, Max."

2—WHERE IS SHE?

Catford, England—May 1850

"WELL?" THE TONE WAS ICY and hard.

"Ah, yes. Well, the truth is, ma'am, that we didn't find her."

The well-coifed woman, stern-looking in her black dress and high-necked collar, rolled her eyes. "Totally incompetent." Absolutely indifferent to the pained looks this brought to the two young men who had been up more than twenty-four hours searching every nook and cranny in Liverpool, she turned abruptly to her husband. "Well, what are you going to do about this? It will be a scandal. We'll never recover from it!"

He took a long draw on his pipe then released it slowly. "It's unforgiveable, really. After all we've done for her, it's unthinkable that she'd treat us this way . . ." He closed his eyes. At least that way he didn't have to see his wife scowling at him.

"Well?"

Opening his eyes slowly—a way to pretend that he was in charge—Gloria's father finally said, "We will tell the world that she's gone on a brief holiday to the Continent. Not Paris, because there might be some who have friends there." He tipped his head up as he searched his mind for a suitable place that a young woman of means might travel on a last overseas trip before her engagement. "Rome? No, too Catholic." He drummed his fingers. "Budapest . . ."

"Budapest!" His wife scoffed at that. "By herself? Really, where do you come off with such things?"

"Then where do you suggest we say she has gone?" He too was exhausted by the search. "It's an imaginary trip, so you might as well make it someplace desirable."

"Desirable, my eye! She's gone to Berlin. That's what we'll say. After all, the royal family has strong German ties—the Queen herself is of German descent, and Prince Albert is from Saxony. We'll tell everyone that she has gone to visit relatives there." She raised her hand when her husband started to protest. "Everyone has relatives in Germany, including us. You need to figure out their names." She was contemplative.

Her husband bit his lip. "Perhaps we could tell people she's gone to America."

"America! That *is* moronic—it would only add to the gossip. She is not a discreet young woman, and I fear she's already told some of our neighbors about her ridiculous feelings. A viscount, for heaven's sake, and she decides she 'doesn't like him.'" She shook her head. "As if being attracted to a person has anything whatsoever to do with marriage." She failed completely to see the irony of saying such a thing in front of her husband.

"Well, that provides momentary cover," he said, "but how do we find her? What if she never comes back?"

"Oh, she'll come back, all right." Gloria's mother turned to the two young men, also dressed in black. "You two will see to that."

"Ma'am?"

"Well, you must have some suspicion of where she is. You searched all of the docks?"

"Yes, ma'am. Of course." The irritation in the detective's voice was barely concealed. "Just as you ordered."

"Well, how did she get by you?"

"We believe she managed to board one of the ships before we got there." He suppressed the urge to say what he was thinking, *And we'd probably have made it on board had you not kept us waiting so long by talking us to death when you first learned of her disappearance.*

"And where were these ships going?"

"Ma'am?" It was an impossible question to answer. Liverpool was one of the busiest ports in the world, with steamships coming and going in every direction. France, Spain, the Mediterranean, South America, Canada. The list was endless.

She clenched her teeth. "Let me ask it differently. Where were those ships going that were prepared for immediate departure?"

The two men turned and whispered to each other for a few moments. "New York City on the Cunard Line, and Tenerife on a White Star ship."

"Well, then, you *better* be getting yourselves to New York. She most certainly wouldn't have gone to the Canary Islands—she's never particularly liked warm weather. Besides, we do have relatives in America, although they live in Boston, not New York City."

"But if she's already departed, how will they ever catch her?" asked her husband.

Once again she shook her head, astonished at men's ignorance. "They will find her because when her ship lands in New York City, she will have to take a few days to go shopping. She fled with virtually nothing, and she would not go on to Boston until she was properly prepared. All these two ninnies have to do is make it to New York within a few days of her and then watch the various lines that would take her to Boston."

One of the men nodded at this. "That is a workable idea. She could travel to Boston by railcar, but I'm sure it would be more fashionable to take a steam packet. We're lucky that Boston is not a stop on Cunard's Transatlantic service . . ."

"Yes, and even if she does get past them, it will be easy to pick the trail up in Boston. My understanding is that you've been to America and have connections there, Mr. Brandt?"

Geoffrey Brandt, the senior of the two investigators, nodded. "Many connections. I'll find her."

"Fine," said her husband laconically. "I'll make the arrangements. Now can you calm yourself, my dear, so that you are in good humor when our guests arrive? We need to put on a happy face as if all of this is an expected part of our plans for her."

"Really. You don't need to lecture me on how to behave in front of company. I will be a paragon of sociability." She dropped her gaze for a moment. Looking up, she noted, "Well, why are you two still here? Get yourselves to America!"

3—GETTING TO KNOW YOU

May 1850

"Please, be seated, Miss Palmerston." Captain Edwards himself held the chair for Gloria as Henry helped his wife into hers. "It's a delight to have you join me tonight."

Dinner at the captain's table was considered a singular honor in a first-class sailing vessel and far above the station which the Chandlers would normally enjoy. But Henry Chandler had been a senior clerk at the Cunard Line almost since its beginning in 1839, when Canadian-born Samuel Cunard was first awarded an Atlantic mail contract by the British government. Henry was hired by Cunard himself and had helped manage the remarkable growth of the company ever since.

As a staff officer, rather than line officer, he was responsible for documenting the proper transfer of Her Majesty's Mail Service, which was the single largest customer for Cunard at an annual subsidy of nearly £175,000 per year. Their main competitor was the American-owned Collins Line, which received a subsidy of $375,000 per year from the United States government. Now, for the first time, Henry was taking a transatlantic voyage as a gift from the company to him and Alexandra, with substantial discounts for their children.

"The *America* is a magnificent ship, Captain Edwards," said Alexandra. "And so comfortable and fast."

"We just took possession of the Blue Riband," Edwards replied with obvious satisfaction. "Cunard has held the record ever since the contest began."

"Blue Riband?" asked Gloria. "What on earth is a riband?"

Marc winced at the tone in her voice, concluding that she was even more pompous than he originally thought.

"Another way of saying *ribbon*," replied Henry. "The Blue Riband is simply a contest between all the great steamship companies to see who can achieve the fastest Atlantic crossing. It was originated by the Germans. And the *America* is currently the fastest on the ocean, with an average speed of ten knots. Winning a blue ribbon is the same as taking first place."

"Ah," said Gloria, as if this were the most *un*interesting thing she had ever heard.

"I believe I've met all of your family," said the captain graciously. "I can't say I've heard the name Honoria often before, although it certainly is lovely."

Honoria blushed and looked as if she'd give anything to run away and hide.

"Roman," said Marcus. "All our names are Roman because Father is a great admirer of the ancient Romans. Mother says it was the reason he was first attracted to her, since Alexandra is a distinguished Roman name."

"Now be serious, Marcus—" said Henry, but he was interrupted by Max.

"He's practically memorized Mr. Gibbon," said Max enthusiastically. Turning to his father, he added, "Quote the captain the line you like so much."

Max then withered under the glance he received from his mother.

"No," she said. "I'm sure the captain is already familiar with Mr. Gibbon's *Decline and Fall of the Roman Empire* and doesn't need that for his dinner conversation."

"I am indeed an admirer of that great book," said the captain. "I've had the good fortune to sail to Rome and to visit many of the sites of the ancient city. But please do me the honor of quoting your favorite passage. I'm curious about what you find interesting."

Captain Edwards was amused as each of the family members' lips moved in silent sync with Henry as he so seriously intoned, "The fidelity of the citizens to each other and to the state was confirmed by the habits of education and the prejudices of religion. Honour, as well as virtue, was the principle of the republic; the ambitious citizens laboured to deserve the solemn glories of a triumph; and the ardour of the Roman youth was kindled into active emulation as often as they beheld the domestic images of their ancestors." Henry cleared his throat and said, "It is after Honor that our daughter was named. Marcus was named for Marcus Aurelias, the last of the 'five good emperors' and author of the *Meditations,* a monumental essay to a government of service and duty."

"Very impressive," said the captain. "One of my heroes, as well."

"And Max?" asked Gloria, at last showing some interest in the conversation.

"For Claudius Maximus," replied Max. "He was the instructor and mentor of Marcus Aurelius and taught him all about devotion and honor." Obviously, by the way this description rolled so easily off his fourteen-year-old tongue, the family had held this discussion many times before.

"And yet in our present setting, Maximus is junior to Marcus," replied Gloria. Marc found it surprising that she would even make an attempt at humor.

"Not really," said Marc, joining the conversation. "I may be older than Max here in this life, but I'm sure he's older than me in heaven. He is far more serious about the great virtues than I am. I prefer to take life as it comes, rather than trying to force it. Things just seem to work out better that way." Marc was bound and determined not to be amused by Miss Palmerston.

Seeing that this interchange embarrassed Henry, the captain smiled. "You are a very interesting family. I'm afraid the names in my family are just those that my parents liked. Nothing so grand as great historical Roman figures."

"Gloria is a Roman name, you know," Henry said to Gloria. "A variation of Gloriana, meaning 'glory for one's country,' or, even more importantly, 'glory for God.'"

"It was a name thrust on me by my mother. Her mother was Gloria, so I had to be named Gloria. That I was too young to have any say in the matter . . ." she hesitated, forcing herself to calm her breathing. "I'm sorry, I . . ."

So much for her sense of humor, thought Marc. Still, he was surprised to see that she blushed a bit. It was one of the first signs of humanity he'd seen in her.

That ended this line of discussion, leaving one of those unplanned pauses in the conversation that make people feel uncomfortable, with no one knowing what to say next. Fortunately, the captain had discreetly caught the eye of the head steward, who came over to introduce the wait staff. Naturally they were the most experienced waiters on the ship, and who better to serve the captain's guests? As they reviewed the various beverages, wines, and entrées for the evening, one couldn't help but smile at the marvelous variety and sophistication of the menu.

If anyone hoped that in this "get acquainted" dinner they would learn anything new about their guest, Miss Palmerston, they were disappointed. Gloria alternated between animated conversation about political questions to brooding silence whenever the topic turned toward family. Fortunately, everyone in the party was tactful enough not to ask about her family, sensing that it was the cause of her bad mood. Even Max managed to strike the right balance in the modest comments he made. At fourteen he was no longer just a child to be seen and not heard, but he was also not old enough to add much to the discussion of world affairs, which were going quite nicely for Britain and America. But when the conversation turned to the ship, both he and Marc joined in enthusiastically.

At first, Alexandra sought to deflect the conversation, but when it was obvious that the captain relished the chance to boast about his ship, she demurred and allowed the boys to ask all the questions they had. "After all," she said to the group, "This is our best chance to get all these questions answered, since the captain will have many other guests to entertain in succeeding days." That led to an in-depth discussion of the ship and its functions.

"Will we still use sail?"

"Only if the wind serves us. The voyage can easily be completed using steam only."

"How much coal does it burn?"

"Sixty tons per day. We have four fire-tube boilers, fed by sixteen furnaces that consume all the coal we can carry." When Max whistled through his teeth at such an astonishing figure, the captain added, "It works out to one ton of coal for every 265 revolutions of the paddle wheel."

"My goodness," Gloria interjected, "How can you possibly carry enough coal to make it all the way to New York?"

"We can't, of course, which is one of the reasons we'll stop in Nova Scotia. While we have some Canadians on board who will disembark there, it's mainly a chance to restock our bunkers for the last leg of the journey south."

"About 120,000 pounds of coal per day—it seems impossible . . ." said Max. He was pleased to have the chance to show his skill at multiplication.

"Of course, it's costly," said Henry, ever the bookkeeper. "We strive constantly to find new and cheaper sources of coal. It's much to our advantage to have the Welsh coal mines within such close proximity to the Liverpool docks."

The captain was so pleased to have such an appreciative audience that he went on to describe exactly how the ship's two single steam engines used a reciprocating side-lever design to turn the massive crankshaft that in turn rotated the large thirty-six-foot-diameter paddle wheels to propel the ship through the water. "And if we have a favorable wind, we can add an extra two to three knots to our forward momentum." He motioned to one of the other officers standing nearby and had a quick, whispered conversation with him. "In fact, I'm told that if we can continue our present rate of speed, we'll arrive in New York City a day earlier than planned."

"Think of what the Romans could have done with a ship like this," said Henry. "Their empire might have lasted even longer than a thousand years."

"Think of what ships like this will do for the British Empire," replied Captain Edwards. "It is precisely because of our lead in naval affairs that Queen Victoria is hailed the world over. It is what gives truth to the phrase, 'The sun never sets on the British Empire.'"

"To the British Empire," said Henry just a bit nervously. He raised his glass a bit too quickly.

The captain pretended not to notice, yet he could see that something suddenly bothered this genial but serious man, and the captain made a note that he ought to try to find out what. But that would have to wait. The stewards ended the meal with a delicious choice of desserts, followed by a plate of petits fours.

"Tonight has been a refreshing break from the usual conversations of my dinner table. Thank you for a most delightful evening." The captain came from a modest family and had to adapt himself to the unthinking snobbery of his usual table guests—British aristocracy and occasional nobility, as well as aspiring Americans who relished the chance to show off their wealth. To share a dinner with a common family was an unusual delight for him.

As the family stood, the captain asked, "Perhaps you gentlemen would like to meet our chief engineer on the morrow." Of course this started the table buzzing yet again.

Each of the family members thanked the captain profusely, and Max noted that even Gloria finally found some courtesy, saying simply, "Thank you for a pleasant evening, Captain. You are a very gracious host."

"My pleasure," he replied.

"Allow us to accompany you to your room," said Alexandra. Gloria hesitated, but after seeing the look on the captain's face, she acceded to the invitation. It was clear that she was not free to roam about the ship and that she was expected to be accompanied at all times when in public places. It was also clear that she didn't care for that. To save her further embarrassment, Alexandra turned to Marc and added, "And why don't you take your brother on deck so you can watch the action of the paddle wheels in the dark. I'm sure that will be interesting."

"Yes," said Max, "and the fires in the boilers will shine more brightly. I hoped we'd get to see that."

Marc nodded and turned to Gloria. "Good night, then." They were the first civil words he'd spoken to her, and he could see that it almost unnerved her. *Good*, he thought to himself, not knowing why he would care.

4—ATLANTIC STORM

Late May 1850

THE GREAT STEAMSHIPS THAT NOW plied the waters of the world, particularly across the Atlantic, were really nothing more than very large sailing ships weighed down by the addition of massive quantities of coal and the boilers and engines needed to turn the side paddle wheels. The effect of the additional weight of the engines, centered at midship and in the upper decks, was to raise the center of gravity. In normal conditions this destabilizing effect was more than offset by the advantage of having a steady source of forward momentum that was not dependent on fickle winds. But in a storm, such as the one now gathering to the west, it had the potential to leave the ship floundering perilously in the water as one or the other of the paddle wheels was lifted up and out of the water by the rolling waves. The men running the engines had to be constantly on guard, because the temporary increase in the turning speed of the paddle wheel when it was freed from the resistance of the water could cause serious problems. So they had to be prepared to instantly react to the conditions, all the while struggling to keep their footing on the rain-soaked and tossing decks.

Captain Edwards wished that he could prepare his passengers for what was coming, but he knew that it wouldn't really help. You had to experience an Atlantic storm to fully understand it. Even so, what he could do was to order the passengers to their cabins, all of which were well equipped with chamber pots for the inevitable seasickness that was about to overtake them. Judging by the lightning that was flashing fiercely in the remarkably black clouds still some distance away, that order would come in another thirty minutes or so.

With all these thoughts bouncing around in his head, the captain came upon Marc Chandler, standing at the rail on the uppermost deck, looking intently out to sea. "Pardon me, Mr. Chandler. You'd do well to go below and prepare for a bit of a rough patch. Your steward will bring cold sandwiches for dinner if, by chance, you are hungry."

Marc, who was startled by the captain's voice, immediately turned to face him and quickly implored, "Can't I stay up here and watch the storm? I'd hate to miss the whole thing stuck down below. I've never seen anything like this." Casting a glance around at the ship's crew working furiously to furl all but the necessary sails that would be needed to maneuver the ship when the storm hit, he added, "It's a remarkable sight."

Edwards nodded. "There's nothing like it in my experience. The anticipation as we encounter the leading edge of the storm is energizing." He paused a moment to assess the approaching storm. Time was short. "But it held far less terror for me when I was just a member of the crew. Now that I am responsible for both the ship and the people on board, I don't enjoy it as much." He barked out an order to one of the crew members to check a hatch that he judged had been sloppily secured. Turning quickly to Marc, he said, "Do you have a pocket watch?" Marc nodded. "Then in fifteen minutes, down you go. You think it's a lark right now, but I can promise you that you'll be pleading for mercy before this is all over, and you'll have no other thought than a fervent prayer for it to end. Even if you were an experienced traveler, the decks would be too dangerous, so I must insist you go to your cabin."

"Yes, sir," replied Marc, his enthusiasm properly dampened.

The captain moved off quickly in the direction of the engine room. Ironically, the danger of a fire breaking out on the ship increased during a storm, since hot coals could be scattered far out onto the wooden deck by the roll of the waves. Even with the rainwater sloshing about the decks, hot coals had a way of finding a spot where dry tinder could ignite. So he had to make sure the crew was prepared to shut the furnaces down immediately if the order came. That's when they'd be in real trouble.

"Come on, then," said Henry urgently, coming up from behind Marc. He'd been on the port side of the ship and was now gathering the whole family together. The wind had come up alarmingly in just a matter of moments, and the sight of the storm front, all ablaze with lightning coming from deep within the bowels of the cloudbank, had rather unnerved him.

"The captain says I have another twelve minutes, and I don't want to miss a single minute of it."

Henry sputtered but knew it would be foolish to stand and argue. "Twelve minutes—don't make us come looking for you!"

"Yes, sir." At this point Marc found himself grasping the brass handrail so tightly that his hands ached. He forced himself to relax, knowing he should go below right now. But it was more than curiosity that kept him in his place—the thought of being trapped belowdecks in a storm was somehow unsettling, and now he felt trapped, unable to stay on deck but reluctant to go below.

"May I stay on deck with you?" asked Gloria, a request so unexpected that it took Marc completely by surprise, particularly since she had ignored him completely the first three days of the journey.

"What?"

"May I stay with you? You have eleven more minutes, I believe."

"Of course . . . if you want to . . . but it's dangerous."

"I'm sure I'll be fine."

That was more like it—the air of insufferable disdain had quickly returned to her voice. Marc pursed his lips and looked out to sea. The leading edges of the waves were now white-capped and undulating in a furious pattern.

"Amazing how the water takes on the color of the sky . . ."

"I beg your pardon?" Marc cast a sideward glance at Gloria. He really didn't care to discuss the color of the water, although it surprised him that she would even notice such a thing.

"I said it's interesting that the ocean takes on the color of the sky. On a cloudless day the ocean is brilliant blue. On a cloudy day it is the color of the gray clouds. And when that storm arrives it will be as dark as India ink."

"I guess that's right, isn't it? I hadn't thought about it."

Gloria took a slow breath. "I discovered it as I spent many a day looking out to sea." For just a moment she seemed vulnerable, and

Marc could imagine a lonely girl sitting on some isolated point above the ocean. But that image didn't last long as Gloria added, "I just wish this interminable voyage would end so I could disembark in New York City. The boredom is so tiring."

Marc bit his lip. The family had offered to play board or card games with her, to engage in conversation, and Henry had even offered to loan her some of his prized books. But she chose to sit in the first-class lounge instead, chatting idly with some of the other young women on board, or simply staring off into the distance. She'd even had the nerve to order dinner in her cabin the previous evening, which forced the family to explain her absence to everyone in the vicinity of their table.

"Well, the storm isn't boring. I believe we're in for a real row."

As if to emphasize his point, a giant wave crashed into the side of the ship, sending up a shower of spray that very nearly reached the deck where they were standing. A fine mist cascaded down on them, which caused Gloria to step back with a gasp—a big mistake, given the shudder to the deck that the wave had caused. Marc lunged to catch her before she lost her footing completely. He made it, barely, and the two of them very nearly tumbled to the ground. Fortunately, he was able to gain a footing at the last moment on some of the sand one of the sailors had strewn behind them, and he grabbed her by the waist just in time to prevent a fall. It was a very firm waist, and the warmth of her body sent an unexpected chill through Marc.

Gloria glanced up at Marc, a questioning look on her face, and continued to lie back in his arms, a little shocked.

He helped her to her feet and said simply, "Perhaps we had better go below. We're tempting fate." He had to raise his voice to be heard, given the strength of the wind and the unbelievable roar of the ocean. Never having been close to the water before, he was surprised at how quickly the water picked up the energy of the storm, whipping up the waves and batting the ship about. His father had tried to explain it all to them at lunch, when it had become clear that a storm was brewing.

Gloria, now on her feet again, huffed. "I suppose. But I hate the thought of being cooped up in a cabin like that. I enjoy the fresh air."

Marc smiled. "For once I might just agree with you."

She looked at him with searching eyes, and for just a moment Marc thought he saw a brief flicker of fear there—something that she had successfully masked until now. But she quickly regained her composure. "Still, this is dangerous. I suppose you'll have to accompany me to my door, otherwise the captain will throw me overboard for not being properly chaperoned." She rolled her eyes as she said this.

There was nothing for Marc to do but shake his head. That she could nurse a grudge against everyone—her family, the captain, and even the Chandlers, who had helped her solve her problem, was something he simply couldn't fathom. "I would be pleased to accompany you. There are better times than this to be thrown overboard."

Looking around, Marc could see that the nearest entrance to a passenger stairwell had been fully secured with a heavy stick shoved between the handles of the two doors. *If there's a problem, no one will be able to get the door open from the inside*, he thought. He considered removing it but feared the consequence if a member of the crew spied him. Looking around again, he tried to find a way to get belowdecks. Sleet was coming down at this point. Instinctively, he grabbed Gloria's wrist and started them toward the deck door at midship, near the paddle wheels. Marc realized that their situation had taken a terrible turn and that they were in real danger.

"Ow, you're hurting me!"

"There isn't time for this. We need to hurry." Marc didn't release his grip on Gloria's wrist. In fact, when the ship encountered a particularly violent wave, he put his arm around her waist to steady her. Neither one of them took time to comment at that point. Gloria at last sensed the danger of the situation.

"Where is the door?" she asked.

Marc was amazed that she'd been on the ship all this time without having figured such a thing out. He and Max had surveyed the whole ship from bow to stern and knew every doorway and porthole on the ship. It had seemed the only logical way to be prepared if something went wrong.

"The door is this way." While they'd be dry down below, the fury of the storm made him wonder at the ability of the ship to stay afloat. His mind told him it was foolish to worry since ships like this crossed the Atlantic in every conceivable type of weather, but the captain was certainly right that there was nothing like this in his previous experience. Just then a huge wave crashed into the port side of the ship, sending a cascade of water up and over the deck, drenching them from head to foot. Gloria slipped and Marc was unable to maintain his footing. The two of them went down on the deck, sliding in the water toward the deck door. Marc looked up at what had to be the most terrifying sight he'd ever seen. As the ship leaned to starboard the giant portside paddle wheel was lifted up and out of the water. Without the resistance of the water to slow it down, the wheel picked up noticeable speed. He was shocked to hear Gloria cry out in alarm, using some words that he thought inappropriate for a young woman to use.

Of course the effect of one wheel being lifted clear of the water is that the one on the opposite side was thrust far deeper into the water than it was designed to do, which put an incredible strain on the shaft and on the starboard engine. There was a terrible groaning sound as the paddle wheel bit deep into the water and Marc could feel the ship being pulled into a slight portside turn from the increased torque as the one paddle wheel churned the water without a corresponding thrust on the port side.

Gloria yelled out for Marc's help. In other circumstances Marc would have been surprised that Gloria would have asked for anyone's help, but he reached out and grabbed her just in time to keep her from sliding down and away from the housing. He barely kept his footing while holding on to her.

By that point the wave had rolled under the ship, and the starboard side was rising above them. Soon they would see that paddle wheel freewheeling in the air. Marc reached the door and did his best to pry it open. They had finally made it to safety. As he was opening the door, he saw something fly by him, sliding its way toward portside. A terrified shriek followed the movement and was quickly drowned out by the crash of thunder.

"That woman!" shouted Gloria, just as they watched the poor lady crash into the cowling next to the portside paddle wheel, which was churning the water into an even greater froth. She grabbed Marc's arm tightly.

"I've got to help her!" Marc said as he attempted to break free of Gloria's grasp to work his way over there.

"I know," Gloria said, shifting her grip from Marc's arm to the handrail next to the deck door. "I'll be fine. Go!" The wind drowned out the rest of what she said, although Marc thought he heard the word *fool* above the crash of the waves.

Marc felt bad leaving her in such terrible circumstances, but she was better off than the mystery woman. If the front of the ship rose to one of the tall waves, it could send the woman, whoever she was, right into the paddle wheel.

He subconsciously hoped that someone from the crew would show up because he really had no idea what to do. The ship was still rolling down into the trough—all of this had happened so quickly that he had simply reacted to it—and he was now slipping his way straight toward the maw of the giant paddle wheel. As he slid farther down, he heard some shouting behind him, and he managed to turn his head enough to see some of the engine crew signaling for him to stop. However, on a rain-soaked deck, gravity is king.

At this point the noise of the sea was almost overwhelmed by the sound of the machinery turning relentlessly above him. As he got closer to the side, he did his best to change the angle of his trajectory, and seeing that he would land directly next to the woman, who appeared to be holding on to a baluster for dear life, he put his feet out in front of him to absorb the blow. He hoped it wouldn't break his legs.

He closed his eyes, but to his surprise, he didn't feel the crunch of broken bone. Instead, just as he was ready to slam into the cowling, he felt the ship shudder beneath him and then start to rise up beneath him. The wave had passed under, and now the ship was following him.

"Oh, no!" he shouted, realizing that he was about to go sliding the other way. Desperately he reached out to grab something, but to no avail. The ship started its roll, and he began sliding in the opposite direction on the wet deck. His leather-soled shoes were completely soaked and offered no traction whatsoever. As the ship rose up above him, he went slamming into the port side of the outhouse-shaped entrance to the stairwell. As he did, he saw Gloria looking back at him with a worried but resolute expression. She looked exhausted, and he wasn't sure how much longer she could hold onto the rail by the door with the pitching of the deck.

Rolling to his back, Marc looked to see if someone had gone to rescue the woman, but she was still there, holding on with a terrified look in her eyes. Her position made it possible that if she let go, she would slide clear across the deck and into the water and paddle wheel on the other side, and it was obvious she recognized the danger. When Marc turned to see why no one from the crew was helping her, he could see that they were fully occupied by the engines. It looked as though fires had started up in the engines, and they were working furiously to extinguish them. From his fascination and study of ships of all types, Marc knew that if they didn't stop the paddle wheels, the torque on the paddle wheel in the water might wrench it loose from its mountings, which could damage the whole ship.

This time, because he was closer to the side when the roll started, he could see that he was going to crash, and he positioned himself as best he could to soften the blow. When his legs struck the cowling, the pain was so intense that he felt he must have broken one or both of them. His knees buckled, and he was almost made to stand upright against the cowling by the force of the fall. Gathering his wits, he quickly turned around, slumped down, and grabbed the same balustrade as the woman.

"It's going to be all right!" he shouted to her, even though he was doubtful of that promise. He was relieved when she nodded her head to indicate that she understood.

Marc thought furiously about how he was going to get both of them to the stairwell. He was sitting down on the deck near the woman. He could hear that the paddle wheel had started to slow, undoubtedly because the stokers had reduced the fires.

"Okay," he said to the woman as confidently as possible. "On the next roll, the two of us will lock arms and go."

Unfortunately, in order to explain this decision to his battered partner, he had to turn his head toward the back of the ship to get her attention. Which is why he was unaware of the danger at the front of the ship—a danger that quickly showed in her eyes. If he had been more of a seaman, he would have known this was coming. The captain, in order to stabilize the ship and save the paddle wheels from destruction, had slowly turned the ship directly into the waves so that the ship would hit them head-on. That would provide far greater stability. But in this case it meant that even as he was trying to shout out his plan, the front of the ship was being lifted in the beginning of a tremendous roll. This threw Marc toward the back of the ship and directly into the woman, who now lost her grip. In quick order the two of them were flying down the deck on a diagonal that led directly toward the paddle wheel, which was still turning slowly. There was enough of a sideward roll that unless something happened quickly, they were going to fly overboard and directly into the wheel.

Marc thrust his left arm out to grab her, while simultaneously grabbing something on the side of the ship to stop him. His right arm gripped the woman, his left arm grabbed the object, and the momentum of the woman now swung her away from the side of the ship toward the center. Realizing that she was now lined up with the housing of the stairwell, Marc timed his release so that she went swooshing off in the direction of the stairwell. "Grab on!" he shouted, hoping she would get the message and act quickly. Whether she heard him or not, he didn't know.

At just that moment, the wave rolled beneath him, and as the ship started down in the front Marc lost his grip and went frantically over the side. It was odd to hear himself screaming as the icy cold water swallowed him into its depths. His last conscious thought was of the terrific noise a paddle wheel makes as it churned in the already turbid water.

And did those feet in ancient time
Walk upon England's mountains green:
And was the holy Lamb of God
On England's pleasant pastures seen!

And did the Countenance Divine
Shine forth upon our clouded hills?
And was Jerusalem builded here,
Among these dark Satanic Mills?

Bring me my Bow of burning gold:
Bring me my Arrows of desire:
Bring me my Spear: O clouds unfold:
Bring me my Chariot of fire!

I will not cease from Mental Fight,
Nor shall my Sword sleep in my hand:
Till we have built Jerusalem,
In England's green & pleasant Land.

5—ENGLAND AND JERUSALEM

June 1, 1850

MARC WALKED THROUGH THE EFFERVESCENT green of the fields that surrounded Stonehenge, the ancient druid monument that Henry had insisted the family visit before their departure from Liverpool. It felt like heaven as he walked with the sun on his face, the ancient stones looming up around him.

William Blake had written a poem, now known throughout England as "Jerusalem," to suggest an apocryphal visit of the Resurrected Jesus to England to set it free from the "Satanic Mills" of the Industrial Revolution that blackened the skies in the cities and laid waste to the lush countryside where coal was stripped from the earth. Would the Great Salt Lake be as beautiful as his England? Would Father's intentions to visit that land prove to the family's benefit? Marc didn't have a clear picture of what this Great Salt Lake City would look like. If it was heaven, would the streets be paved in gold?

Something annoyed him—some kind of buzzing sound that was totally at odds with where he was walking and what he was feeling. The noise intruded even more forcefully than before, and the sky seemed to darken unnaturally.

Storm clouds! The thought suddenly brought on a terror unlike anything he'd ever felt before, and he tried desperately to fend off the unwanted thoughts of crashing waves and groaning steel. Straining his very hardest, he tried to force his mind back to thoughts of England but to no avail. The water was crashing around him, and he heard a woman screaming as he watched her helplessly crash into the housing of the stairwell, the force undoubtedly breaking both of her legs. Then he felt the ship heaving beneath him, and he clawed desperately as his grip was torn from the side of the ship. Suddenly there was a great clawlike wave above him, forcing him down and into the water. As his mind raced to reconstruct the scene, he felt himself going down deeper, and he knew he couldn't breathe but how much longer could he hold his breath?

Finally, as his lungs were about to burst, he took a great gasp and sat bolt upright in the bed, yelling in a strangled cry as he felt the urgency to survive. As he clawed with his arms, he felt something strong grab and steady him. Opening his eyes, he stared uncompre-hendingly until he saw his mother looking back at him. Turning to his right, he saw his father holding him, tears streaming down his face.

"You're all right, then!" said Henry.

"What?" he struggled for his breath. "What—what happened?"

"We nearly lost you," said his mother.

Now he saw Max standing by his mother, tears in his eyes, and Honoria behind them, sobbing openly. He allowed his head to be pulled against his father's shoulder, which was warm and dry.

"So, I went overboard, didn't I?"

Henry nodded.

"And the paddle wheel took me under."

"Fortunately, the ship was starting a roll to the starboard side. The paddle wheel lifted up, and you were able to come to the surface."

"The captain told us that the paddle wheel pulled you up," said Max, obviously still shaken but also interested by the adventure his older brother had survived. "It was turning very slowly and it caught your jacket. It probably saved your life!" Max sounded only a little jealous.

Marc shook his head. "That seems only right, given that it tried to kill me first." He hadn't intended that to be funny, but everyone let out a relieved laugh. The ship's surgeon had warned them that the concussion he'd suffered might have caused brain damage. Now that seemed less likely.

"The woman who was being thrown about . . . ?"

"She's fine," said Henry. "You saved her. Two members of the crew saw it all, and they said you are a hero. She was going over for sure when you reached out and grabbed her and then swung her toward the stairwell. She wants to see you when you're able." Henry hesitated. "She broke one of her legs . . ."

"I thought as much." The room around him suddenly started to spin, and he groaned as he fell back onto the pillow and shut his eyes.

Alexandra said, "The doctor says you're very likely to have vertigo for some time, so you better watch yourself." Then, in a softer voice, she said, "So just lie still."

"I can't entirely remember what happened . . ." Marc felt himself slipping—the spinning of the room, the warmth of the bed, the voice of his mother. "Gloria? What about Gloria?" When there was no response, he forced his eyes open and saw people shuffling uneasily. "Is she all right?"

"Yes. She's fine. You don't need to worry." The tone in Alexandra's voice was noticeably different this time—almost disapproving. "But—"

"You really should go to sleep, son. The doctor says you'll need a lot of rest."

"But the storm—" said Marc.

"Is over," replied Henry. "Twelve hours of violent weather with only sails to steady us. But the ship made it."

Marc nodded slowly, his eyes drifting closed again. "But are we on course?"

He heard his father chuckle. He realized he must sound a bit incoherent. But somehow it made sense to him—just like dreams always seem to make sense when you're having them. Even though he had a hundred more questions to ask, he couldn't fight off sleep, and before he knew it, he was back walking along the seacoast near the British town of Bath—another stop his father had insisted on so the family could see the ancient Roman ruins of that famed little place before they left England forever. "But if we leave forever we'll never get to heaven . . . not if heaven is in England . . . but maybe in Great Salt Lake City." He tried to manipulate his dream so that he would go to Salt Lake City, but never having been in a desert he really couldn't imagine such a place. *Is it covered in white salt?* The voices in the room faded.

6—A GOLDEN OPPORTUNITY

June 1850

"Mind if I take a look at those sketches?" Captain Edwards asked.

Marc was concentrating so deeply that the sound of the captain's voice startled him, causing him to jump, which set off a new round of vertigo. He was humiliated when the captain had to reach out to steady him on the stool he was sitting on.

"Very sorry to startle you like that . . ." said the captain.

Marc quickly responded, "Not a problem at all, sir." Marc stood up so he could talk to the captain at the same level.

The captain smiled. "I just asked if I might look at your drawings. I happened to see them over your shoulder as I walked by, and they look remarkable."

Marc blushed, since he hadn't really intended that the sketches of the boilers and reciprocating engine be seen by anyone but himself. But he handed his sketch pad over to the captain.

"Incredible!" Captain Edwards pulled an instrument of some kind out of his pocket that had marks on it that allowed it to double as a ruler. *Probably some kind of navigation aid*, thought Marc as he watched. The captain took some measurements on the sketch and appeared to make some calculations in his mind. "I think you've got the proportions of the flywheel absolutely perfect." Marc bit his lip so as not to smile. The captain looked up from the sketch. "How do you do that without first taking the measurement of the actual arms and levers?"

"I'm sure I'm not exactly right in the measurements, but you can get very close even using simple line-of-sight by paying attention to the relative proportions of the various elements you're sketching. To get things with full precision, I'd need coordinate paper, but this is more of an interpretation of the scene than a schematic."

"So are you more of an artist or an engineer?"

"I hadn't really thought of it like that," said Marc. "I suppose I'm more of an engineer or architect, at heart, since I doubt there's much of a market for sketches of steam machinery. But really I just draw because I like it."

"And why do you draw machines?"

"I don't know." Marc was a bit flustered—no one had ever taken an interest in his drawings before, aside from his parents' obligatory interest. "Because I like machines, I guess. The intricacy of their design is astonishing, particularly since they are really designed to do work, and yet there is a beauty in the logic of their design." He felt his face redden again. "Of course that all sounds very foolish, I'm sure."

"Not at all." The captain motioned for Marc to sit down again and then brought a deck chair where he could sit down with him as well. "The truth is, the future is in the hands of men like you—men who can design the great machines that allow difficult work to be done on a scale unheard of in earlier times."

"But I'm not—"

"What exactly are your plans for the future? I know your father is a clerk for Cunard, and he's highly respected. But what do *you* plan to do for your life's work?"

Yes, what are *you going to do with your life?* Marc thought. *At one point I thought I knew. Then the Mormon missionaries came to town . . .* Marc realized he had to reply to the captain. "I suppose like most men in England, I assumed I'd follow in my father's footsteps and be a scrivener or something."

"But that wouldn't take advantage of your skill in drawing. Have you ever thought of studying to be an engineer? It seems to me that you would do well at it."

Just then Henry happened to be coming by, and the captain motioned for him to join them. "I was just talking with your son about his career possibilities after taking a look at these sketches."

Henry pulled up a chair and sat down. "He's extremely talented at that, isn't he?" The pride in Henry's voice was obvious. "He and Max both love machinery. They are far more a part of this modern age than I am, I'm afraid."

"Yes, well that's the point I was trying to make. I asked if he had plans on becoming an engineer. Britain needs talented men to design and maintain all these great engines that now drive our society. If we are to stay at the top of the technological ladder, we need the best and the brightest among us to lead the way."

"But I could never get into an academic institution. The only thing that comes close to what I do is architecture, and it's not available to a boy from my social status. And I'm not that interested in the design of buildings, anyway."

Captain Edwards nodded. "But things are changing. While it's true that the traditional degrees of arts remain largely the purview of the upper classes, the introduction of polytechnic schools is changing things. The sciences must be dominated by those who have the most ability, not necessarily the best background."

"I've often thought Marcus should do something in the technical area," said Henry. "He's far too restless for the type of work I do. Yet he has never shown interest in seamanship, which is the usual route for a young man of our class to advance in the world."

"I do like what you do—" said Marc, but Captain Edwards held up his hand.

"It's all right. What your father said doesn't embarrass me. The sea is not for everyone. But a life at sea is not what it used to be, either. When I was a young midshipman, all vessels were powered by the wind and sail. The two most important men on board the ship were the captain and the carpenter since it was their combined skills that made the difference between life and death. But now that has changed, and it is the captain and his chief engineer. Mechanical ability is to be prized almost as much as leadership."

Marc nodded, not really knowing what all of this meant or how it applied to him. His curiosity was short lived, however. "Here's what all of this is about," said Captain Edwards. "But before I tell you what I'm thinking, do you mind if I ask a couple of questions?"

"Not at all," said Marc.

"How are your mathematical skills? Do you do well with the advanced forms of mathematics—algebra, geometry, and calculus?"

"He was a top scorer in his class," said Henry.

"Good." Edwards was thoughtful. "And do you feel you have the temperament for an advanced education? Your father said you are restless. Could you spend time in a classroom?"

Marc hurried to reply so that his father wouldn't have the chance. "I do. My father is an amateur scholar, and I've watched him study my whole life. While I am an outdoors sort of person, I can concentrate when I need to."

"Well said." Edwards looked directly at Marc. "Here is what I'm thinking. Your deportment during the recent storm was exemplary. It shows that you have courage and quick wits. Besides, as I learned of it afterward, I can see that you used this innate talent of yours to visualize things to effect the rescue of that woman. All of that recommends you as someone who is worth taking notice of."

"Thank you, but I acted more out of instinct than motive . . ."

"Which shows the true nature of your courage." Marc didn't respond to that. "At any rate, I would like to do something positive for you. I have a brother who is a professor at the University of Braunschweig in Lower Saxony, Germany. Perhaps you know that it is the oldest and most respected technical school in Germany, which makes it perhaps the leading technical institute in the world since there is no other nation that takes engineering as seriously as do the Germans."

"Of course we've heard of it," said Henry. "It is a great honor for you to have such a distinguished brother—"

"He was a miserable young man, as far as I was concerned," said Edwards. "Always serious and bookish. But he has made a name for himself."

"And how does that apply to me?" asked Marc, extremely interested in where he thought the conversation was leading.

"I'm thinking that you should go to Germany. Cunard is sponsoring a number of students at foreign universities to make certain that we stay in the forefront of technology. With my recommendation, and your father's years of devoted service, it may well be that you could gain a foothold in that world. Of course you would have to prove yourself equal to the challenge, but if you maintained respectable grades, perhaps you could make a whole new place for yourself in the world." He sat back in his chair. "What do you think of that?"

Marc had never been so sick to his stomach in his life. This was the opportunity of a lifetime—not something that he'd ever even dreamed of, because until this moment it had been impossible. But now all the ideas that bounced around in his head when he saw some great steam engine pumping water from a mine shaft, or being used to power the mills that were making central England so productive, now perhaps he could find a way to turn those thoughts into reality. But of course it couldn't be.

"I think it's a marvelous idea," said Henry. "What a great thing for you to do for my son."

Marc turned and looked at his father, the eternal optimist whose pride in his children sometimes overwhelmed his natural sense of modesty. In this case it was creating an impossible dilemma for both of them.

"Well, then," said the captain standing. "After you and your family have your holiday in America, perhaps you can look me up."

Captain Edwards extended his hand to Marc, and the young man shook it.

"Thank you, sir," said Marc, a little less enthusiastically than he would have liked. At this point he had to maintain the deception about their trip to America—the trip that would help his father realize *his* plans for the family. Edwards looked at him a little curiously, so Marc quickly added, "I can't imagine anything more exciting that what you have offered me."

Edwards nodded and then excused himself.

As they watched the captain make his way forward, Marc turned to see Henry smiling broadly. "A remarkable man, and what a grand offer. What he proposes could change your entire life."

They made their way in silence to an outside deck where they could speak privately. Marc turned to Henry. "Father, how can you even talk like this? You know I can't go to both Utah and Germany."

Henry's face fell immediately, which surprised and annoyed Marc, since it was Henry's plan, after all. "You're right, of course," said Henry. "You can't do both."

"No, I can't. Which means that while I can't say no to the captain's offer directly, since that would reveal our plan too early, it also means that I shouldn't act like it is something I want to do. It would be a betrayal of his goodwill to lead him on."

"Yes, of course." Henry was absolutely crestfallen. "But perhaps you could come back to Germany . . . ?"

Marc shook his head. "Father, the whole foundation of his offer is that you are an employee of Cunard; so I can't do this without you, and you don't plan on staying with the company." It was maddening how quickly Henry could forget the practicalities of a situation when his ego and hope became involved.

"What are you thinking?" asked Marc. He was already feeling quite bruised that this golden opportunity was to be sacrificed for the family's impending move to the great unknown desert of America.

Henry sat down heavily. "It's just that I don't see how I can ask you to give this up. This is the kind of opportunity that can change the entire future of a family. If you were to graduate from a German university, then your children would be entitled to go there as well. Or to a British university, for that matter. Think of how much that would change your life and the lives of your children. Perhaps we should return to England, for your sake."

Marc shook his head. "But you know that is impossible. You have staked all your hopes and dreams on joining the Church in Utah and meeting the living prophet. You know I could never ask you and mother to give that up."

"Yes." Henry bit his lip. "But the price is quite high, isn't it?"

Marc couldn't help but nod, even though it was almost unnoticeable. It was a price he'd questioned long before this opportunity came along.

"There's really no need to discuss it," said Marc. "The plan is set. I will not be going to Germany, so that's that."

He felt he should stand up to emphasize the point, but he felt wooden. The thought of attending a polytechnic institute was something unimaginable. That he could become an engineer, rather than just admire their work from afar, was a great temptation, and the prospect of losing the opportunity was painful.

"They call it the 'pearl of great price' for a reason," said Henry. "The merchant in the parable chose to sell everything he owned in order to purchase the one pearl of such great worth."

"Yes, and you yourself helped Elder Franklin D. Richards as he started to compile that little book that is to be published as the Pearl of Great Price, while he served in Liverpool. So you are willing to give up your career and your devotion to England to acquire it for yourself and our family."

"How do you see it?" asked Henry. "I really never sought your opinion, and you are too good a boy to offer it."

Marc sighed. "I don't mind not going to this university. It had never been a possibility before today, so it's not like I'm giving up something I've always dreamed of."

"But how do you see the gospel? What's its value?" Henry's voice had grown earnest. "I need to know before I ask you to make this sacrifice."

Marc tried to smile to reassure his father, but he couldn't. His own commitment to the Church was less certain than Henry's. "You have testified of an overwhelming spiritual confirmation when the missionaries bore their testimonies," said Marc.

Henry nodded and urged Marc to continue.

"But it has never been like that for me."

"I thought maybe it hasn't."

Marc tipped his head back against the chair and looked up at the black cloud of coal dust pouring out the great funnel in the center of the ship. "But I do feel at peace when I read the scriptures or attend church. And I'm not averse to going to America. It seems like there will be new opportunities there."

"I wish you could feel what I feel—that would make it easier for you."

Marc pursed his lips and nodded. "Perhaps I will, someday." He turned and looked at his father. "But it's all right if it doesn't happen right away. While I may not have your faith in things, I do have faith in you." Marc swallowed to force down the lump in his throat. He usually didn't brood over things, but having an opportunity like this come and go so quickly left him feeling ill.

"Well, if you are able to bear it, I would like to continue. Perhaps it's selfish of me . . ."

"It may be many things, Father, but it is not selfish. That is not in your nature."

"We will know more when we meet Elder Tyler in San Francisco. Once we make our way from there to Salt Lake City, I think it will all come clear."

Marc nodded. "I'm sure it will."

Henry had regained his hope, and Marc was glad for that. His father truly was a spiritual man, and Marc knew that he had to pursue this dream of his, no matter how impractical. *Off into the wilderness without adequate financial resources—there's no way I can leave you on your own.* Marc stood up. "We'll be all right. Captain Edwards's offer will give me something to daydream about in the hard times ahead."

"You are a good son," said Henry. "And God will bless you for it—of that I am certain."

We'll see. I hope it's true, if only for your sake, thought Marc.

7—SURVIVING GLORIA

Halifax, Nova Scotia—June 1850

"We're stuck here for two days? How is this possible?" Gloria said to Marc, annoyed but also with a tone of fearfulness.

Marc turned so quickly at the sound of Gloria's voice that he felt dizzy for a moment. The doctor said this would eventually pass, but it was certainly disorienting in the meantime.

If Gloria noticed him stagger, she didn't say anything. In the days that had passed since he regained consciousness, Gloria had kept entirely to her room. The trauma of nearly being dragged into the ocean had upset her tremendously. In fact, this was the first time she had come on deck since that night, and only then because of the announcement that the voyage would be delayed for two or three days while the damage to *America* was repaired.

Most of the passengers were all right with that, since the thought of spending a few days on dry land was appealing, but obviously it did not suit Miss Palmerston. For his part Marc thought Halifax a rather interesting place, with high hills stretching down to the waterfront and the locals speaking in their rather odd-sounding Canadian accent. The vegetation seemed sparse compared to England, and he hoped he would have the opportunity to get off the ship and go exploring.

But he was not up to a confrontation with Gloria, so he turned away, subconsciously shaking his head as he did so.

"Are you shaking your head at me?" she demanded.

In his usual quick-witted fashion when it came to Gloria, he turned and said, "What?" Then he braced himself as she strode directly for him. "You shook your head at me because you think I'm unreasonable, don't you." It was an accusation, not a question.

"I have nothing to say about you, Gloria," replied Marc as evenly as possible. "Your reaction to the news of the ship being out of service—news that we are all subject to—is entirely your own business."

"And you think I shouldn't be upset that our plans have been waylaid in this heaven-forsaken place? People make plans based on a ship's timetables, you know, and reputable companies stick to those schedules."

Marc debated in his mind how to respond to this: Should he counter by telling her how immature she was, particularly since it was the crew of this very ship that had saved her life? Should he be patient, trying to explain that the vicissitudes of sea travel make timetables more of a hope than a promise, since no one can control the weather? Or should he just throw her over the rail and be done with it?

His final option seemed to be that he should just turn and walk away. It was this last option that seemed most appealing. But he steadied himself with a deep breath and, choosing none of these options, replied calmly, "I'm told that Nova Scotia is a very pleasant place and that the residents here are well known for their generosity in helping those who are shipwrecked or are visiting. I look forward to a few days with them." *That ought to rankle her!*

"Oh," she said, a note of cunning in her voice, "you are a clever one. You always find a way to put me in the wrong. No matter what I say, you have a skill for making it seem selfish and arrogant, don't you?"

Marc's eyes widened—both at the thought that she had even noticed his replies and more to the point that she was, in some ways, right. But that didn't change the fact that she *was* selfish and arrogant. "Perhaps it seems that way to you, but to me it is the way that people ought to behave. I see no sense in railing against the captain and his crew for something that is out of their control. I can't understand how you would even think that we should proceed with a damaged ship. I would think that you, of all people, would appreciate the dangers of the open ocean, particularly if a new storm arises." It irritated him mightily that his voice had risen in both pitch and volume as he said this.

"I'm not the only one to feel the way I do—I'm just one of the few who expresses herself. Because of this delay, weddings will be missed, business meetings cancelled, and connections forfeited. And not because of significant damage to the ship but incidental. So you can sit there and judge me all you like, but at least you know where I stand."

Marc was amazed—somehow she had managed to put him in the wrong. *You are the one with a talent*, he thought. *A conniving, guileful talent*. He wanted to say that but again chose wisdom over valor, biting his own lip instead.

For her part, Gloria looked as if she was going to cry—whether out of anger or disappointment, Marc couldn't tell. Nor did he care. He was angry that she'd worked him up to such an ill temper. "I don't have time to debate this with you, Gloria, particularly since our opinions make no difference whatsoever—the ship will be here the next two or three days *no matter what*. So if you'll excuse me . . ."

He attempted to turn quickly so as to not give her a chance to reply, but the wave of nausea this motion caused forced him to hesitate just long enough to see a stricken look on Gloria's face—which was not at all what he expected. Whatever it was, it almost made him feel sorry for her. But he was far too indignant just now to feel much empathy, so he continued his turn and marched off to the door that would take him down to his cabin.

She's the one who should be embarrassed . . . Reaching his door, he turned the handle with some violence, which, of course, sent yet another searing pain through his arm and shoulder. *Why do I let this woman get such a hold on me! Argggh! If only she would just . . .* He lay down in his bed to settle his aching head. He fell asleep wondering what that forlorn look on her face had been all about.

* * *

New York City—June 6, 1850

The excitement in the air was palpable as the *America* rounded the point of the Narrows between Staten Island and Brooklyn that signaled the entrance to New York Harbor. The short trip from Nova Scotia to Long Island was uneventful, perhaps even anticlimactic after the storm at sea, and everyone on board knew that they would be telling the story of that storm for many years to come. The captain had even told Henry in confidence that the storm was much worse than he and the crew had let on to the passengers and that they had been in very real danger of foundering in the ocean. That his crew had been able to rescue Marc was something of a miracle that left even the experienced seamen on board slightly astonished. Now the voyage was about to come to an end, and they were to disembark into the frenzied world of 1850 New York City. Henry, who wore his feelings on his sleeve, seemed overcome by a wave of melancholy, which was very much at odds with the excitement of the other passengers.

"You really should try to look cheerful," whispered Alexandra. "People will wonder what's wrong with you. We do not need any suspicion at this point."

Henry sighed. "I know. It's just that this is where our connection to England really ends. We'll transfer to an American ship and then be off to the Caribbean, never to return to Britain again."

"You don't know that, dear. You may be called on a mission, for heaven's sake." She straightened up, obviously more concerned about their plans than she wanted to show. "Besides, we discussed all of this before, and we believe it's the right thing to do." She looked at him squarely. "At least I believe it's the right thing to do, and I think you do as well."

Henry smiled. His wife knew exactly what he needed. When his courage wavered, she willingly stepped forward to bolster his confidence.

"You are absolutely right, my dear. This is a time for new beginnings, not good-byes. We've already said those, haven't we?" He was aggravated that his voice choked up ever so slightly on the last two words.

"Papa! Do you see those buildings? There must be a million of them!" Max was clearly not suffering from melancholy.

"You shouldn't exaggerate, Max. There are not a million buildings. But New York does have more than half a million residents, so it's the largest city any of us have ever visited. And I'm told that it's a virtual melting pot of nationalities, so we're likely to encounter people from all over the world."

Marc nodded slowly. "We're going to have to learn a whole new way of saying things, aren't we?"

"I'm sure it will be easier for those of us for whom English is our natural language than it is for those from other nations with different mother tongues," Alexandra said.

Marc laughed. "I'm not sure, Mother. Have you heard the Americans on board? I can hardly understand a word they say. I would hardly say that what they're speaking is English."

Max thought that was funny, which earned him a reproving glance from Alexandra. But even she had to admit that the Americans were sometimes difficult to follow.

"It's as if they speak in slow motion," said Honoria quietly. "I like it, because it's easier for me to follow . . ."

It was just about now that their ship was pulling up to their assigned pier on the Hudson River side of Manhattan Island, and everyone crowded to the port side. The view was magnificent, with the New Jersey Palisades framing the west side of the river and the church steeples in Manhattan the east side.

"Seventeen days, including three at Nova Scotia. That's not so bad a crossing time," said Henry—always the loyal Cunard employee.

"The captain said we were on track to make a much faster than usual crossing until the storm came up," said Max dejectedly. It was typical of a boy his age that he would want both the excitement of the storm *and* the thrill of a Blue Riband speed crossing, not realizing that the two were mutually incompatible.

Henry nodded, and then the family stood silently looking at the city that was about to become the jumping off point for their real adventure. They were startled by a voice from behind.

"Excuse me . . ." Gloria said in a more subdued tone.

"Oh, Gloria," said Alexandra. "How nice to see you." Her words were not entirely sincere. After all, Gloria had been a stranger to them for many days, ever since the storm, and for Alexandra that was a sign of rudeness.

"Yes. I'm sure it's been very impolite of me to stay in my cabin so much, but I just haven't felt up to socializing."

That is an understatement, thought Marc.

"Still, you have all been so very kind to me, and now the journey is about to end. I will be on my way to Boston—"

"Boston!" exclaimed Alexandra. "I thought you had relatives in New York City." She was genuinely indignant at the idea that she had been misled, particularly if it meant the family would have to divert from their plans to see her safely to Massachusetts.

"It's fine, dear," said Henry quickly. "Gloria made it clear to me from the beginning that Boston was her ultimate destination. For reasons that really shouldn't be shared, she didn't want anyone else to know about it, but she will be safely escorted by a friend who lives in New York City. Much of the journey can be made by railway train, from what I understand, so we'll see her safely to her New York City friends and then be on our way."

"No! That won't be necessary," Gloria interjected.

Marc puzzled over this. Her words were certainly firm and commanding, as was typical of Gloria, but not in her usual arrogant way—rather more of a . . . frightened way, as if she didn't want anyone to go with her once she left the ship.

"Well," said Alexandra, "we certainly won't let you out of our sight until you meet up with your hosts. From what I can see of this place, it is simply unfit for an unaccompanied woman."

Gloria frowned. "But not all of you, certainly. That makes no sense—my, er, friends would be overwhelmed. Perhaps Mr. Chandler could accompany me."

"No, we need Henry to make arrangements for the rest of our journey. Marc will go with you."

"What?" exclaimed Marc and Gloria simultaneously. "Not me," mixed with "Not him," but Alexandra waved their objections away. "You need Marc, and that's all there is to it. Now I think you two should get ready to disembark first. I believe Henry wants to be one of the last off the ship so he can talk with the agent when things aren't so hectic." Henry nodded at this, recognizing that Alexandra's natural skills for organization had taken control of the situation.

"Yes. Well, I better get ready, then," said Gloria, resigned to this adjustment to her plans. "Perhaps you could help me arrange for a porter."

"Marc will do that," Alexandra offered.

Marc shook his head and turned to go find a porter.

"Marc!" said Alexandra firmly. "First accompany Gloria to her room so she can gather her things."

Marc inhaled sharply but nodded. "Of course. How thoughtless of me."

"Well, then, Gloria, this is good-bye. I'm glad we could help you. Children, please tell Gloria good-bye."

Honoria stepped forward and took Gloria's hand. "It was very nice to meet you . . ." She hesitated before adding, "I think you are a very interesting person." That made Marc smile. His sister was able to say everything while saying nothing. Max responded with a more simple, "Good-bye." And with that Marc extended his arm to escort Gloria to her room.

"Once we get on shore, you can help me find a cab and then leave me. I really don't need you to accompany me anywhere . . ." The saucy tone had found its way back into Gloria's voice.

"That, unfortunately, is impossible. My mother will expect a detailed report of exactly where I take you, the people who meet you, and the safety and security of the journey. While I'd be perfectly content to let you fend for yourself, I am not willing to risk her censure on your behalf. If I tried, she'd simply insist that we find you, and that would slow us down. So I'm afraid you'll have to put up with me for another hour or so. Then you will be free." He tried to match the fire of her tone as he said this.

"Fine. Now, at the very least you can let me find my way to my own cabin. I'm not as helpless as everyone thinks me to be."

Marc withdrew his arm. "I'll be back to meet you just as soon as the bells sound for the initial disembarkation. I'm sure the captain and crew will be more than pleased to let you off the ship first." He was delighted at the huff that this prompted. Without another word, he left her.

* * *

"All right, children, we need to have everything packed and in good order. With any luck we'll spend just one or two nights here before connecting to a Caribbean packet."

"I can't wait to see the Caribbean," said Max. "I've always wanted to see where the pirates hide themselves."

"Max! There will be no pirates in the Caribbean. They were done away with years ago!" In spite of how emphatically she said this, there was an uncertain tone to Alexandra's voice.

Henry laughed. "Yes, I'm afraid there will be no pirates. But there are always tropical diseases and lightly clad natives to contend with . . ."

"Henry, you are as bad as he is." Alexandra tried to be stern, but she couldn't help but feel lighter with Henry's humor.

"I'm looking forward to seeing palm trees," said Honoria. "The pictures I've seen look wonderful and exotic. It must be beautiful to see all that sun." A dreamy look came over her face. She was more the inheritor of her father's imagination than her mother's practicality.

"Well, we're not likely to see anything if we don't get our trunks and luggage packed. We have to get off this ship before we can get on another one!" The family knew very well that this was their cue to go to work.

8—THE FRIENDLY PART OF TOWN

June 1850

AS GLORIA AND MARC MADE their way from the luggage terminal, they were confronted with a cacophony of noise, dust, and odors that nearly overwhelmed them.

"I didn't realize how lucky we were at sea—no horse manure to contend with," said Marc. It was true: living with animals was a part of modern life, and the stench of sewage was ever present in cities everywhere, including Liverpool and New York. But after more than two weeks at sea, their noses had adapted to a constant clean sea breeze.

As they made their way to the line of waiting cabs, Marc asked Gloria what their destination was.

"I don't know," was her reply.

Marc stopped short. "What?"

"You always say that when you talk to me. It's annoying."

Marc caught himself just in time to not say "What?" again, but he did manage an incredulous, "Excuse me—but you're the one who doesn't know where she's going. *That's* annoying."

"I'm going to Boston. I have to figure out how to get there."

"But the friends you told my mother about—"

"Are purely fictional."

Marc inhaled deeply. "Would you please tell me what's going on?"

Gloria looked squarely at him. "No. It is none of your business. What is your business is to help me figure out how to make my way to Boston. I do have friends there, and that's where I intend to take up residence."

"But why would you make up a story like that?"

Gloria shook her head. "You are so naive for an otherwise bright and intelligent and attrac . . . man who is quick-witted and genial. Yet you miss the obvious."

"Which is . . ."

"Which is, if you'll exercise your mental faculties, quite obvious."

When he stood there saying nothing, she added, "Consider how we met: I am demanding passage as a single woman on a ship and am quite in a hurry to do so. You spot a number of men in black hoods but fail to notice that I step behind your father. I am nervous as a cat on hot cobblestone until we are safely on board and the ship is underway. Now what does all of that suggest to you?"

"That you are . . ." he furrowed his brow. "That you are anxious not to be seen." She shook her head ever so slightly in disappointment. "That you are nervous that those men will find you . . ." And then his face lit up. "That you are running away! That's it!"

"Brilliant. I am running away."

"But from what?"

"The better question would be from whom, but that isn't really your concern. The point is that I am going to Boston to take up residence, I had to leave in a hurry, and it is infuriating that the only ship available at the time was one that bypassed Boston on its way to New York. Most transatlantic steamers would have made a port of call in Boston, but instead this ship gets stuck in Halifax, of all places, and you and your dad get to go sightseeing." She took a deep breath.

"I don't think it's fair of you to make light of my father. He was your only friend when you needed one."

Gloria's face colored, and she turned away for a while. "Your dad is a good man and much kinder to me than I deserved. It's just that you can see my predicament. I needed help to get out of there in a hurry, and your family was the only way I could make it happen—but on a ship that was going to the wrong port in this very foreign land of America."

"But I thought . . ."

"You thought I wanted to come here? I wanted to get away—it had nothing to do with the destination . . . only the escape. If there had been a ship heading to Southern France, I would have been much happier. At least I know French. I can hardly understand a word these Americans are saying!"

Marc laughed, having some empathy on that point, at least.

"But . . ." He was going to ask more questions about why she was running away but decided that it really was none of his business. Rather than argue with her anymore, Marc said, "Then we ought to make our way to the train station. I studied various maps and timetables on the ship since people connect up from here in New York to all sorts of places on the Eastern Seaboard. North to Massachusetts and Maine, south to Philadelphia and Washington DC. Trains, coaches, and packet steamers make it possible to get from New York City to anywhere else in the country, but the vast majority of business takes place on the Eastern Seaboard."

"But what about Boston?"

"Yes, I know. But I'm not sure of the best way. I know there is locomotive service to a place called New Haven—there was a timetable for it on the ship. But that is only part of the way to Boston. I'm not sure if you have a connecting train there, or if you need to go by horse-drawn coach or take a steamship. But I do know that you have to make your way there first."

Gloria nodded. "That's good enough. Now how do we find a train station to this . . . ?"

"New Haven. It's in Connecticut." Marc pronounced the word as connect-i-cut, not knowing how Americans pronounced it. "The way we find the train station is to hire a cab and ask him to take us to the appropriate terminal for the New York and New Haven Railroad. I know it's in downtown Manhattan, so it must be nearby."

"Well, then." She hesitated. "I appreciate your helping me. My situation is quite urgent, and I do appreciate having someone to help me sort it out."

Marc recognized what an effort this was for her to say, so rather than respond with sarcasm, as was his style, he replied simply, "I'm pleased to be of service." With that he motioned to the porter who had been waiting impatiently with Gloria's bags. "We need to find a cab to take us to the New York and New Haven Railway Terminal."

"Yes, sir. It will be that line over there."

An odd thing happened as they made their way past the various lines of cabs. They were surprised to find that more than a few of the coachmen seemed to take notice of them, with some pointing and others nodding.

"Very odd," said Marc. "Does it seem to you that they are taking special notice of us?"

"Perhaps you are the *only* one who fails to realize that you are with a young beauty," Gloria said with a sly smile, which caught Marc so totally by surprise that he blushed. This seemed to please her.

"No, that's not true. They're not the only ones. Still . . ."

Just then three coachmen from their intended line approached them, which caused quite a stir, given that the cabs were supposed to be taken in an orderly succession.

"Get out of the way!" said the lead driver, physically shoving the other two. "You know that this is my fare."

"But you know who this is," said one of the displaced drivers. "It's not fair!"

"I know who it is," growled the first, "and I'll see to it. Now you two keep your mouths closed while I help this lady and her gentleman." Marc felt very anxious, since it was impossible for anyone to know their identities given their recent arrival. But Gloria took no notice and quickly engaged the coachman in a conversation. He assured her that he knew the way to the proper railway terminal.

"I'm not sure about this," said Marc before they stepped up into the cab. "Something doesn't seem right."

"Hush. I'm in a hurry. If you want to help me, then do so. If not, I'll make my own way."

Marc bit his lip. He looked around one last time and was still alarmed by the look in the eyes of the coachman, but he extended his arm to help Gloria step into the cab. Tipping the porter, he then pulled himself into the cab, knowing that at this point their fate was in the hands of the driver.

* * *

"Welcome to New York City, Mr. Chandler. It's a distinct pleasure to meet you. I've seen your name on many an invoice and voucher."

"Thank you," said Henry, slightly flattered. "And I recognize your name as well, Mr. Kingman." Kingman looked expectantly toward the rest of the family. "Ah, yes," said Henry, a bit too nervously, "allow me to introduce my family." He proceeded to introduce each in turn. "My oldest son, Marcus, has already disembarked to help another passenger find her way to friends in New York City. He will join us shortly."

"Yes. I met him briefly earlier, and the lovely young woman he was traveling with."

"Not traveling with—simply escorting. This is her first time to America, as well."

Kingman nodded absentmindedly, not really paying attention as he checked their tickets one last time.

"Well, perhaps you can direct us to our hotel. We're looking forward to seeing your city."

"It's just that your ticket doesn't make sense," said Kingman. "All I show is a one-way ticket for each of you, but of course that's got to be an error. I'm surprised you didn't check that."

"Ah, yes," said Henry, the pitch of his voice tightening. "We booked it one-way since we're not entirely sure how long we'll stay. We may take some other travels while here in America and wouldn't want to be tied down to a fixed schedule. We'll book return passage when we get back to the city."

Kingman looked up, his demeanor very changed. "I understand that, but it's certainly not standard policy. Your travel is complimentary, but we have to be reimbursed from London and the cost will be much greater for one-way tickets rather than a combined outbound and return. We can always change the return date if you get held up."

Henry took a shallow breath. "I'm sure all this can be worked out at a more leisurely time, Mr. Kingman. We've been at sea a dreadfully long time, and we're anxious to get some rest. Perhaps you could consider this tomorrow . . ."

"You are scheduled to stay at the Excelsior Hotel. The company has a contract there, and you will find it to be one of the best in New York City."

Henry relaxed noticeably. "Yes. That would be wonderful." Kingman was just about to stamp their documents when something caught his eye. Naturally the family's bags were being searched by customs officials.

"What's this?" said Kingman, annoyed at the inspector. "You should show some respect for my colleague's things." He strode over to where the inspector was rummaging through one of Henry's bags. At first Henry was not alarmed, since there was nothing he was carrying that could be considered contraband. But when he saw Kingman suddenly step between him and the bags, obviously shielding them from whatever it was he'd taken an interest in, he glanced nervously toward Alexandra. Even she looked nervous, but everyone did their best to remain composed.

In a few moments, Kingman turned and strode directly toward them, holding something in his hand. "And just what is this doing in your luggage, Mr. Chandler?" He held out a small leather-bound book. Henry's face flushed immediately.

"That's a personal item of mine, thank you."

"I've seen this before. We sometimes have dozens of immigrants coming through who have this book. But they all tell us that they are migrating to the West. To the Mormon territory. You're not a Mormon, are you, Mr. Chandler?"

"I don't see how that would be any of your business. I—"

"It *is* my business if you intend to come as immigrants rather than as a guest of the company for a holiday."

Henry stood stiffly and struggled to clear his throat. "I . . . I find this . . . very impertinent of you, Mr. Kingman. I do hold a senior position, you know."

"I know that you are in America, now, Mr. Chandler. And your ultimate destination is of concern to me. If you tell me that you intend to return to England, that will be fine. I've heard nothing good about the Mormons, but it means nothing to me if you've chosen to join some obscure sect. But if you intend to abandon your duties and set off for the West, then I must take a stand. To abandon us here would violate the trust the company has put in you."

At this point Henry was ashen, and Alexandra had instinctively drawn Max and Honoria close to her. This was their greatest fear, now realized.

Henry took a deep breath to steady his breathing, and then leaned his hands on the counter that separated him from Kingman. He debated whether to come on forcefully to Kingman, essentially accusing him of insubordination, or whether to approach him in a conciliatory tone, hoping they could work things out. In the end he decided that, given his personality and temperament, the only thing he could do was to tell the truth and hope for the best outcome. Taking another breath, Henry leaned forward and said sincerely, "I am more than willing to discuss this with you, but it's quite embarrassing in front of my family, particularly with other people behind us. Perhaps we could meet privately . . ."

"No. That will not do. We will discuss this now until I find out your intentions. If you have defrauded the company, I shall have to take action."

Henry stiffened, his idealism offended. "Defraud the company—how dare you accuse me of such a thing! For your information, I have qualified for at least four of these excursions in the years of my service, but I have never taken one since I had no desire to spend company money needlessly. Virtually everyone in the London office will attest to my honesty and integrity!"

Henry was so forceful in this retort that Kingman backed away. "Of course you are right—fraud is too strong a word to say, I'm sure. But the fact is that you intended to deceive the company—at least that's what it appears now . . ."

"For your information, my family and I are Mormons. And it is our intention to migrate to the city of San Francisco. There's talk that the Church will establish itself there. But wherever we wind up, San Francisco or Salt Lake City, there will be no damage to the line. Besides, the time spent in transit and while we are here in New York is my holiday time. I have not resigned, nor do I intend to do so until I have used my time appropriately. So you have no standing whatsoever to trouble me like this. Now please return my property and certify our documents."

Alexandra would later say that Henry was quite magnificent when he did this, but of course she realized the terrible emotional price it demanded of him. For someone to even suggest that Henry Chandler was unscrupulous in any way was as hurtful to him as any dagger that could be thrust into his heart. Kingman looked around nervously, recognizing the electrical charge in the air. After taking a moment to compose himself, he stepped forward to deliver his response to Henry's demands.

* * *

"This doesn't feel right to me," Marc said. "The railway terminal is supposed to be in lower Manhattan, and yet I'm quite sure that we are headed north."

"How can you know such a thing, as we've never been here before?"

"I know that the sun is to my right and that it's three o'clock in the afternoon. And since I'm facing the back of the coach, that pretty well tells me that we're going north. There are fewer and fewer commercial buildings the farther we go. I don't suspect we'll find a bustling train station on the outskirts of the city."

Gloria finally looked out the window, and what she saw did shake her confidence. It seemed as if they'd entered a rather seedy neighborhood that did not at all reflect the prosperous scene where they had started their journey.

"Listen," said Marc. "You hear the men shouting over there on that corner?"

"They're shouting at each other. Why should that be of interest to me?"

"Listen to their voices."

Gloria strained, and then her cheeks flushed. "They're Irish. But why should that matter?"

"It matters because with the great famine last year, nearly twenty-five percent of the people in New York City are from Ireland. But none of them live in the old city—we are in an Irish enclave, and that makes no sense if we are going to a railway terminal."

"Perhaps the driver is taking us to a less-crowded terminal farther to the north. Boston is to the north of New York City, is it not?" This time there was nothing but sincerity in her voice.

"I doubt it. If he is, then it means he's trying to run the fare up on us. But I'm sure there's something else going on. When we were back there it was as if the various coachmen recognized us."

"That's impossible . . ." Gloria's voice was weak.

"Gloria—you know something that I don't. You've got to tell me. If we are in danger, I deserve to know the source."

"It's nothing. I'm sure that—"

"Gloria! We're slowing down! You've got to tell me what you know." He waited, but she said nothing. The blood had drained from her face. "Those men in black cloaks—who were they? What did they want with you?"

"They were—"

"They were what? Quick, please tell me!" Marc felt desperate. If he were on his own, he would have leaped from the carriage, but he had Gloria to consider.

"They were private detectives hired by Mother! She had arranged a marriage with a perfectly horrible man—but he was a noble, so they wouldn't listen to my protests. He was the ugliest creature imaginable, and everyone knew that he had been cruel to his first wife. She died in childbirth, leaving him without an heir. So he went looking for a bride."

"And he found you?"

"He found my mother. He lusted after me."

"But why would she—"

"Oh, Marc," said Gloria furiously. "You know perfectly well why she would consent to such a horrible thing. He is a viscount!"

Marc sat back heavily against the seat. "And to bring both the wealth and prestige of an aristocratic marriage into your family is simply more temptation than an aspiring mother can resist."

"I told her I wouldn't marry him, and she slapped me. My father stood by doing nothing—he's a genial but ineffective man. My mother drove him to be mayor because of the prestige, even though he's ill suited to it. When she told me I had no choice in the matter, I resolved to run away." She looked up at him. "I do have friends in Boston, and they will take me in. I was sure that I could reach them before anyone found me. And then I would have had residency so that Mother's thugs couldn't take me." She looked at him desperately. "How can it be those men, though? How could they be here? We left directly and on the fastest ship on the ocean. It must be something else."

Marc felt a sinking feeling in his stomach. "It was Halifax. If those men boarded the next available ship, they would normally have been at least two to three days behind us. But with the delays we had in the storm and then again in Halifax, they could easily have steamed right past us. They must have promised the coachmen in New York City a bribe if they spotted you and brought you to them."

"How would they recognize me?" she asked incredulously.

Marc smiled a humorless smile. "You are a beaut . . . er . . . you have recognizable features, and you're looking to board a train to Boston and just happened to arrive on the *America.* Those men could have passed word all up and down the pier."

"Why wouldn't they simply have been there to meet me?"

"Because you would have recognized them and cause a scene. By letting you get quietly in a cab, they can control the situation."

"What do we do?"

Marc shook his head. "I don't know. We need to get out, but if we alert the driver, he'll simply speed up. Still, perhaps we should prepare ourselves."

"But all my money is in the luggage, and that's on top of the coach."

"Better to be without money than kidnapped . . ."

It turned out that all of this was nothing more than an academic exercise, since just as Marc was working through an escape plan in his mind, the coach jolted suddenly to a stop. "We're in for it now," he said quietly.

Gloria nodded in despair.

9—THE BEST-LAID PLANS

June 1850

HENRY RECOILED, AS IF STRICKEN. "Surely you wouldn't do that to us?"

Kingman straightened up. "But I would. You have convinced me that you are entitled to this trip. But if it is your intention to leave the employ of the line, then I will initiate your termination immediately. Your reservation at the Excelsior will be cancelled, and you will be on your own."

"But I shared with you in confidence our plans to use our privileges to gain passage on a Panama-bound ship. If you terminate my employment, we shall not be given the courtesy fare, which would bankrupt us. That's hardly fair, in view of my years of service."

"Listen, Mr. Chandler. I have told you that I have great regard for your work, and if you will assure me that you will return to England and take it up again then I will honor all commitments made to you, including return passage. But if you insist on joining this wild religious sect, then I feel no obligation to you whatsoever. It will bring discredit to the line and to you personally."

"But I prepared a successor. The books are in good order, and there will be no interruption in the work to be done at our Liverpool office. No one is harmed except my family and me."

Kingman leaned forward. "Can't you see that I'm doing this for your own good? You are an Englishman. The Mormons have been thoroughly discredited here in New York, where they were founded, by the way. I urge you to return home and enjoy your family in familiar circumstances."

Henry sighed. He knew he was defeated. He could argue his point on moral grounds, but he could never overcome prejudice.

"Thank you for your concern for our welfare, Mr. Kingman," said Henry sincerely. His anger had melted away like frost in the morning sun. "I know that you believe you're trying to help me. But I am convinced in my heart that this is the right course for me and my family. So with or without your help, we must make our way to California."

"I'm sorry to hear that. I must withdraw all benefits from you immediately, as I believe that's what my superiors would demand of me. In the meantime, I hope you'll change your mind. If you come back to me any time within the next week, I will see to it that all record of this exchange is expunged. No one in England will ever know. If I don't see you in a week, I will notify my superiors of your actions."

Henry nodded. "Thank you for the offer. Can you suggest someplace for my wife and I to stay while we try to figure out how to proceed?"

"Of course, you can keep your reservation at the Excelsior, but without a company voucher, it will be quite expensive."

"No, I'm sure that is not our best course."

Kingman paused for a moment then motioned for one of his assistants, whispering something in his ear. "Mr. Bell here will take you to a less expensive but still reputable hotel. We send a lot of business their way, so they will give you the best price possible. You can stay as long as you like."

"Why, thank you. That's very generous, all things considered."

"I hope you stay with them for less than a week and that I will have the honor of making your acquaintance again."

Henry bowed slightly. Motioning to Alexandra and the children, he made his way to the door. As he turned to leave the room, he caught Kingman's eye one last time. He saw sorrow there. "What have I done to my family?" he said softly to himself. "How shall we ever make this work?"

* * *

"Out you go, then, Miss Palmerston." If looks could kill, then the black-shirted detective who opened the door would have been dead, felled by the contempt in Gloria's eyes.

"How dare you kidnap me! This is the United States, and people are free here. I demand you return me to the ship at once." Marc thought it clever that she didn't give away her ultimate destination.

"Ah, yes, but you are a British citizen, and there's a missing persons warrant out on you which we are duty bound to honor."

"You take your hands off of me—" But Gloria was destined to lose that battle, as the fellow reached in and forcefully pulled her from the wagon. Marc did his best to resist but not for long, since a blackjack club smacked him on the head from the other side of the wagon. The crack made his head feel like it had been struck by a large bolt of lightning. He had no time to react before passing out.

As they dragged his unconscious body from the wagon, it appeared as if one of the guards was going to kick him, but Gloria intervened. "He's done nothing to you. Leave him alone."

The second guard, the one who had hit Marc, was not impressed until the other said, "That's right. We are to treat Miss Palmerston with respect. Leave that fellow alone. We want this to go along nicely."

Gloria took a breath to steady herself.

"Now, then. You need to pay the driver for his trouble, ma'am, and then we'll move you into the apartment we've reserved until the next ship sets sail for Liverpool." The fellow's voice was very grating, even when he was forcing himself to be polite, and it infuriated Gloria.

"Pay the driver!? You want me to pay the driver when he kidnapped me! You happen to be the dumbest lout in this whole city."

"Yes, ma'am, and you've got all the money. Your mother is not particularly generous in her expense allowance, which may be a foolish thing, given the level of discretion required by all of this. The last thing she would want is for word to get back to that aristocratic suitor of yours that you tried to escape. I can't imagine that would go well for either of you. So from now on we'll operate from your funds, if you get my drift." Gloria was repulsed by the blackened teeth behind his disgusting smile.

But she was at a disadvantage and knew perfectly well that this fellow could steal all of her money if he chose, so she rightly decided to pay. "And just how much is the fare, you common highwayman?" she demanded of the coachman.

"Ah, for a ride as long as this it's two bits, ma'am. Plus a dime for the risk I took. That's what was promised to me by this fine gentleman." The driver's smile was just as crooked and grotesque as the detective's.

"Bits? Dime? I have no idea what you are talking about. I have no American money."

"A shilling, then, ma'am. Give the driver a shilling, and he'll be fairly treated."

"A shilling! That's downright robbery!" Gloria glowered. Opening her purse she pulled out a shilling, realizing the high cost of collusion. "I'll report you to the authorities," she said fiercely as she threw the money at the driver. "Kidnapping is a capital offense, even in America, I'm quite certain!"

The driver laughed as he stooped down to pick up the coin. "You do that, ma'am. I'm sure they'll be interested. Of course, the problem is trying to find an official who cares." With that he mounted the seat atop the cab, clicked his tongue while shaking the reins, and away he and the horses went.

Gloria watched for a moment, trying to orient herself to where they were. But it was no use. Unlike Marc, she had studied no maps and she had no idea how Manhattan was laid out.

Turning to her abductor, she demanded, "What are you going to do now?" She didn't like what she saw in his eye. Before he could reply, Marc started to stir.

"Good, wake him up, Tom. I want this man, whoever he is, to hear what I have to say to the lady. But inside. We don't need no Irish ears listening in on our business."

Tom stuck his toe into Marc's ribs and pushed him until Marc sat up, rubbing his head.

"What is going on?" he asked, before scowling. It seemed that Gloria was destined to bring Marc even more trouble than her usual quota.

"Get him on his feet. Let's move inside," the fellow in charge said as he picked up Gloria's bags and motioned for her to go before him into a flimsy little tenement building. Even though the construction was new, the place already reeked of human odors, and Gloria was grateful that she'd used some French perfume that morning. By keeping her head down, she smelled that more than the odors around her. Once into the hallway of the building, the fellow motioned for her to open the door to what turned out to be a one-room apartment with a bed by the window. The thought of spending even a single night there was repulsive to someone who had grown up in a respectable house like Gloria had.

Before moving inside, Marc did his best to make a mental map of where they might be. The front of the door faced into the sun, which meant that was west. He knew they'd headed north from the city, which meant that Manhattan proper was now to their right. If they could attempt an escape, it would be to the south, so he glanced down that way. The streets were crowded, which was good. They could more easily disappear into the crowd. But it didn't look as if they were filled with the type of people who were likely to offer help. While relations between the citizens of Liverpool and the Irish were better than between most Englishmen, since they shared the Irish Sea and engaged in extensive trade between Liverpool and Dublin, the Irish still hated the English and would not look favorably on their accent. That was all he had time to conclude before he was muscled into the hallway, being pushed from behind by Tom, with an occasional kick to his butt.

"Now, then. You may sit and sleep on the bed, Miss Palmerston. Your gentleman friend will sit on the floor over there but only after we've tied his hands. It will be up to you whether or not we tie you up, as well. It looks like the next ship out is in two days, so we'll be here for a bit. You can sit quietly or you can get yourself bound . . . Your choice."

"I will not sit by idly. You have no right to do this to me. I will pay you whatever my mother offered to pay you for my return if you let me go. You can keep what she's given you plus what I give you." Gloria was irritated that tears started to flow down her cheeks, but she was also indignant. "It should be of no concern to you whether or not I marry, nor whom I marry. Please, just let me go!"

"I can't do that." The fellow who had not yet given his name motioned for her to sit down. When she resisted, he forced her.

"Now let me make things very clear for you. I don't want any misunderstanding, because your position is precarious. I run a respectable agency in Liverpool, and my clients know that they can depend on me. Were I to abscond with your money and fail to deliver you to your mother, my reputation would be dead. So my first preference is to fulfill my duty. But if you give me trouble, there are alternatives." His face grew very dark. "For example, I can steal all of your money and leave you with nothing. More than that, there are people here in America who will pay for attractive young women to work in the gentlemen's clubs of the city. We could simply take all your things and receive a bounty for bringing you to the right people's attention. But that's not a place for a woman like you, now is it?"

"How dare you!" shouted Marc. "How dare you threaten her with *that*!" He made a move toward the detective, but Tom suckerpunched him in the gut, sending Marc sprawling to the floor.

"As to your friend, here," the fellow in charge continued, "we have no gripes with him. I assume he's someone from the ship who was simply helping you." Then he smiled something of a wicked smile. "Or perhaps he's your lover and the reason you are trying to escape . . ."

"He is NOT my lover! What a ridiculous thing to say. He is a gentleman—unlike the two of you."

Marc wasn't sure that she needed to say *ridiculous* with so much certainty. Would it be such a bad thing for him to be her forbidden love?

"Fine. He is not our problem, and we will let him go once we have you safely on board. But until then . . ." The man turned and looked directly at Marc. "Until then, you better not cause us any trouble, because there are other men in this city who are looking for hard laborers to build railroads in the West. They too are willing to pay a bounty."

"They do not have white slaves in America!" said Marc, stepping back slightly to prevent another blow.

"Says you. It's true that there are no white slaves, officially, but Americans seem to have no problem with the idea of slavery in any form. So what they do with a fellow like you is I bring you to them, they give you something that knocks you out cold, and the next time you wake up you are in the back of a cattle car on a railway train in Ohio or Nebraska. You say you want to get out, but you find you have no money and no shoes. You are in the middle of a wilderness—a wilderness so forlorn that there is nothing like it in England. No food, no people, nothing. So you ask them for shoes—it's the only way you can survive. They agree to give them to you, but to do so you have to sign a credit slip. And that's how it begins. You are a freewill laborer, but because you are always in debt for food, clothing, and shelter, you have no choice but to do the work they tell you." The fellow walked over and forced Marc to extend his hands. "These don't look like the hands of a laborer, do they? You're more the clerk type, aren't you."

"What I am is none of your business."

"I'm just saying, with hands like these, lifting railroad ties and steel rails is likely to break your health in no time. You seem athletic enough, but they'll soon use that up. The casualty rate is very high here in America. A city dweller on the open plains doesn't always last so long."

"You are a cruel and unfeeling brute," interrupted Gloria. "You know that I have no desire to go back to England and that it may put me in the way of danger, yet you still force your will upon me. How can you live with yourself?"

The fellow cocked his head to the side as he pondered the question. After a moment's reflection he replied, "I am a man who cannot afford to consider morals. I've told you already the arithmetic involved."

Gloria opened her mouth to accuse him further but realized it was of absolutely no use whatsoever. So she sat back on the bed, miserable and forlorn.

Marc was next to receive advice. "Now, you've heard your fate, mister. If you'll sit quietly for two days, you'll be out on the street just where you want to be, completely free to go about your life. But if you cause trouble, you'll either be dead in New York or alive in Nebraska." He paused. "And I don't know which would be worse."

"And just how is it you know so much about America?" asked Marc. "You can't have gotten here more than a day or two ahead of us."

The fellow grinned. "I'm a detective, aren't I? And besides, what makes you think this is my first trip to America? Perhaps I speak from experience when I tell you the various alternatives available to an enterprising man such as myself."

A cold chill of dread ran up Marcus's neck and spine. This fellow had been here before, and he had done exactly what he threatened. Marc sat down and put his back against the wall. Closing his eyes, he could picture the desperate men who even now were effective prisoners in the West, their life force seeping away as they labored from sunup to sundown with inadequate food and drink. If he weren't careful, that could be his fate.

* * *

"What are we going to do, Henry?" Alexandra shivered, even though the room they'd secured wasn't cold. At the Excelsior they had planned on two rooms, but in their new circumstances they had opted for a single room. Even at that they were lucky, since most travelers lived in a communal setting when living on a tight budget. At least this way they had some degree of privacy.

"I don't know. Our resources are far too meager to afford passage by way of Panama, as we planned. Yet I have no idea how to make our way to the West on an overland route. I'm not at all suited to such things."

"I think we could make it," Max offered. "Marc and I are strong, and we'll help you."

Henry cast a kindly glance toward Max. "I'm sure you are right . . ."

"He is generous but wrong," said Alexandra firmly. "Our only answer is to find a way to get to San Francisco where we can meet Elder Tyler. He made it very clear that he can lead us to Salt Lake City more economically and safely than by any other means. He's the only American we know, and I believe that he is the only one whom God would have us follow. This is a setback but not the end of our plans."

"And you are undoubtedly right, as well, my dear." Henry rubbed the temples of his forehead, a sure sign that he was feeling stressed. "I wish Marcus would return. It's hard to make plans without him, since we need his strength."

"It does seem late. You left word at the Excelsior, since I'm sure that's where he'll go to find us?"

"I did. It's just down the street, you know, just up past the next square. He should have been here by now."

"I'm feeling kind of hungry," said Honoria, joining the conversation for the first time. "Have we enough money for some simple food?"

Henry's voice caught as he replied. "My anxiety has caused you children unnecessary worry. We have more than adequate money for the moment. We'll have food and shelter. We just need to figure out how to earn the additional money needed to make the journey to the

West. Perhaps Marcus and I can get a job for some time in order to save. Besides, we should at least investigate traveling by way of the Great Plains."

"I just don't feel good about that. Walking all those miles, buying a wagon, living out in the open." Alexandra shivered as she thought of it. "We have no experience in such living at all. But we do know ships and cities. We must go to San Francisco and meet up with the Saints who are there."

"And if San Francisco isn't the place of refuge—we'd then be faced with crossing what might prove an even more hostile wilderness through the mountains."

Alexandra inhaled deeply. "You are the leader of this family, Henry, but I have told you how I feel."

Henry slumped. There were no good options. So the best was undoubtedly to proceed as they had originally planned, by way of Panama to California. But how they could afford it, he did not know. Honoria started whimpering, which was understandable. The family was facing their worst crisis ever.

"God will hear our prayers," said Henry, at last realizing that it was his responsibility to lead. "So let's kneel by this bed and open our hearts to His inspiration."

* * *

"May I ask why you won't tell us your name?"

"Why would it matter?"

"If I am to spend the next three weeks with you, it would be less noticeable. I'm sure the captain of whatever ship we board will be curious."

"Ah, yes. We should talk about that. Occasionally one of my runaways tries to seek outside assistance while traveling, to somehow communicate that he or she is in distress."

"Very wise of them, I would think."

"Very foolish. It forces me to make up stories, you see. Which is why when the time comes, you will have your choice of four stories. First is that you have a rare disorder that, while not on the quarantine list, is rather dangerous to a person's health, with one of the symptoms being delusions. The second story we can tell is that you are a prisoner, a young woman who murdered her husband and then escaped from England on a cargo packet. I like that one because it puts me in the role of bounty hunter, which tends to keep people away. The third is that you are a lunatic, given to violent outbursts and outrageous claims. In this version Tom and I are your brothers, taking you home to our grandparents in England in hopes that their mature company can have a calming effect on your nerves. I think these are all rather interesting roles to play, don't you?"

Gloria fumed. "And what if I don't like any of your stories."

"That's your fourth option: you can make one up yourself, and we both play our roles accordingly. One young lady came up with the idea that as my charge she was very shy and didn't care to talk. Perhaps not surprisingly, that is the one that gives you the greatest freedom on board, since you can join communal dinners and stand on the deck occasionally. Of course, at the first sign of trouble, I pull out one of the other three and instantly destroy your credibility."

"And you think no one would believe a lady of obvious breeding more than you?" asked Marc.

The fellow laughed. "Once again you misjudge me. You've never seen me dressed in an evening jacket with top hat and cane. I rather tend to exude the charm of an English gentleman. Everything in life is an act, you know, and I can assume whatever character suits the occasion." The fellow smiled serenely. "My experience tells me that there are no *gentle*men. Just men. The chivalrous ideal you hold in your mind of men who sacrifice for their ladies and who do what's right for its own sake does not exist in my experience."

"Then you've never met my father. He is a gentleman in the finest sense of the word. It was he who stepped up to Miss Palmerston's defense and who insisted that we treat her with respect, even when she showed contempt for us." Marc was surprised at what he'd said and glanced quickly over to Gloria, who looked as if she had been struck. "I'm didn't mean . . ."

The fellow laughed. "Oh, I believe you did. I know many of these brats of privilege. They carry on with great airs, looking down on everyone around them. But when they try to stray from their closeted little worlds, they run into men like me, and then their innocence quickly gives way to reality."

"And just what is your reality?" asked Gloria. "What does the world look like from your sordid place in it?"

"My world looks just like yours. Your own mother so desperately wants respectability and money that she sells her own daughter into an inconvenient marriage. Your father stands by doing nothing to defend you. You show pluck and courage in trying to escape but learn the hard way that life is difficult and unyielding. Can you tell me how that is so very much different from what I see?" Not waiting for a response, he continued. "It is, in the end, for all of us, about money."

Marc bit his lip to stifle his response and was about to speak when his face suddenly changed. Instead of pressing the discussion, he changed the topic. "But you never told Miss Palmerston your name."

"I don't know why that's important. Today it is Frank Shelby. Tonight it may be Geoffrey Brandt. Who knows what I may use tomorrow? Names are very much like costumes—you change them frequently to match the role you are playing."

"But what did your mother call you?" Marc did his very best to make this sound casual.

"My mother still calls me Jonny." He laughed. "Or maybe it's Geoffy. But that doesn't inspire a lot of fear, does it? So I don't wear that particular name very often."

Marc found it remarkable that Geoffrey Brandt—the name he assumed came closest to the truth—was so talkative. He'd always imagined kidnappers to be tight-lipped. But Brandt was rather open. They did have two days to pass, and perhaps he enjoyed the chance to brag about the nefarious work he did. *Perhaps that can be turned to our advantage.* So Marc started asking seemingly innocuous questions, like who Brandt had captured, who he had worked for, and how much he got paid. When he asked the question, "And just who have you given to the press gangs of the Western railroads," Brandt finally bristled.

"That's none of your business."

"But you have done it—it's not just an idle threat?"

"An idle threat?" Brandt contemplated for a moment. "An idle threat—well, that's what Billy Call said. He was the youngest son of Lord Call from Somerset. He ran off to America, which was fine with his noble father. But not his mother. She sent me to bring him home. But when Billy gave me trouble, he woke to a train whistle."

"And what did you tell his parents back in England?"

"I told them how their son had met an untimely death in a carriage accident. I told them how dangerous the streets of New York City are, with all kinds of ruffians overturning cabs right in the middle of Fifth Avenue. Naturally they believed me, since the English are anxious to believe anything negative about America. I told them I'd arranged for a proper burial for their poor boy—which I did, by the way: there's a headstone and a body in a grave down by Trinity Church. They were so grateful that they paid my bounty anyway."

"You blaggard," said Gloria. "That's an awful story. I hope it's not true. A body in the ground and this Call boy in the West. It's preposterous!"

Marc chose to ignore Gloria's remark, because he was very interested in this story and wanted to hear how it ended. "But how could you convince them? Surely they wouldn't just take your word for it."

"Of course not. But they did believe the combined weight of an official coroner's report, stamped with the seal of the City of Manhattan, as well as the newspaper article that talked about the awful tragedy."

"But there is no 'City of Manhattan,'" said Marc. "It's a borough of New York City."

Brandt grinned. "You know that, and I know that. But unfortunately my forger didn't know that. Fortunately, neither did his lordship or ladyship."

"Well," said Marc. "I suspect you found some drunk to fill the casket. Someone who would never be missed."

Brandt nodded. "You are smarter than you look, Mr. . . . ."

"Johnson. Marcus Johnson." Marc didn't dare turn to Gloria for fear their exchanged glances would give away his deception. Apparently she played it right, since neither Tom nor Geoffrey reacted.

"You will be very wise to remember the lengths I will go to in order to complete my business, Mr. Johnson."

* * *

As Henry made his way back to the hotel from the local greengrocer with some fresh vegetables for a stew that Alexandra hoped to make, he was distracted by the noise of a large crowd gathered down by one of the piers. Responding to the distinct impression that he should find out what it was all about, he veered from his course and came to stand at the edge of the crowd. The scene was familiar enough to one who had worked in Liverpool for many years, with a well-dressed gentleman standing on a large wooden crate while facing an angry crowd of disgruntled workers. As Henry listened, an idea formed in his mind.

"There will be no compromise on wages! That is final. The pay is what I have said it is, and if you go on strike, you will all be fired and replaced. Can I make it any clearer than that?"

The crowd roared angrily, but it had little effect on Mr. William H. Aspinwall. He was one of the wealthiest men in America and was a force to be reckoned with in the world of steamships. Having started out as a merchant who branched out into shipping, he gained his great fame from the magnificent clipper ships his firm, Howland & Aspinwall, commissioned in the 1840s. These uniquely American sailing ships set speed records all around the world and shortened the time for multi-ocean commerce dramatically. Howland and Aspinwall were among the first to see the commercial opportunities of ocean-going steamships, and Aspinwall had helped found the Pacific Mail Steamship Company in 1848 to provide mail service to California after the war with Mexico brought that new territory into the Union. Now, with the gold rush underway, demand was constant and urgent for transport to the California gold fields, and travel by steamship via Panama was a matter of perhaps six weeks versus nearly nine months to a year by pack train or wagon train across the continent. The discovery of gold by Mormon workers at Sutter's Mill in 1848 had enriched the company considerably.

"But these wages can't even support a single man, let alone a family! We give our lives to you, and you treat us with contempt!" This came from one of the agitators who had whipped the crew of Aspinwall's ship into open rebellion. The irony was that Aspinwall was a far better employer than his rival, Cornelius Vanderbilt, who held monopolies on steamship traffic in New York, New Jersey, and up the Hudson River.

"These wages support the competition that is needed to win passengers' money. If I raise the fare, your men will have no work since no one will travel on our line. The choice is yours—accept these wages, or I will find replacements. You have one day to decide!" Aspinwall strode to his cabriolet carriage, pulled by some of the finest horses in the world. Stepping up into his carriage, he turned to the mob for a final glance.

Someone shouted, "You won't find any blacklegs to do your dirty work!" Aspinwall turned a cold eye on the man.

"You have twenty-four hours, then you are out of work!" He tapped his lead horse gently with the whip, and his carriage lurched out and onto the main thoroughfare.

10—NEW PLANS

June 1850

"CAN YOU GIVE US SOMETHING to drink?"

"Get it yourself," said Tom.

"I would, but I'm rather tied up."

Tom expressed himself with a grunt.

"Where did Mr. Brandt go?" asked Gloria. It was now at least 9:00 p.m., and the city street was getting dark. Brandt had left a few hours ago.

"I don't see how that's any of your business!" said Tom.

"He's probably off to visit one of those gentlemen's clubs he spoke of," said Marc.

"And if he was, what is that to you?"

"Nothing. It just seems unfair that he gets to go out and have a great time while you are stuck here guarding us."

Tom straightened up. "I get my share of the take to do this. He's the boss, and I do what he says. Don't you go talking bad about Brandt."

Tom started to pour some water. "Not water!" said Marc quickly. "I'm sure I saw some rum over there. Or is that for Brandt, as well?"

Gloria looked at him curiously. She had never seen Marc drink wine or any alcohol in the time they'd been together.

"That rum is for me!" Tom grumbled. "At least I think it is. Geoffrey didn't say nothin' about it."

"Well, I think you should share it with us. Who knows what's in this American water that will make us sick. You need some good alcohol on the first day in a place until you get used to the local water. At least that's what I've always been told."

"Really, Marc. I don't know that we need to go drinking—" She stopped when Marc shot her a sharp glance. Not knowing what he was thinking, she did have the good sense to quiet down.

"Well, if you are any kind of a decent fellow, you wouldn't leave me thirsty here. I've been drawn into this whole thing as a total innocent. You could at least be hospitable."

"Well, it is a big jug."

"Exactly," said Marc. "And it will never be missed."

"But Geoffrey doesn't like it when I drink. He says it makes me thick-headed . . .'"

"So not only does he go out to a fine evening on the town, but he tells you what to do while you are here with us."

"Nobody tells me what to do," growled Tom. "I'm a made man, and I can do what I please."

"It's awfully hot . . .'"

"Fine, just one drink for you and one for me." Tom found a chipped glass which he brought over to Marc. Even though Marc's hands had been tied up, he had just enough maneuver room to manipulate some rough bread to his face during what had passed as supper and again now as the glass was placed in his cupped hands. The other end of the rope around his hands was secured to a heavy beam, which made escape impossible.

"Thank you," said Marc gratefully as he took the glass. "Bottoms up, then." Tom raised his glass and started slurping it noisily. Gloria watched as Marc first held the glass up to his face then brought his hands down and emptied the contents of the glass into a hole in the floorboards. By the time Tom brought his glass down, Marc had already raised his again as if to his face. Bringing it down empty, he said, "Oh, but that hits the spot."

"It does indeed!" Tom cracked a smile for the first time. "Nothing like a little rum to put fire in your belly."

"I don't suppose I could have another?"

"What? No! I promised you just one, and now you've had it."

"But one was just enough to whet my whistle. Surely you'd like another . . .'"

Tom looked around, as if Brandt might be watching.

"Besides," said Marc. "It's going to be a long night, and you need something to bolster your strength. Rum will give you a sugar boost."

Gloria had to stifle a laugh. While it was true that rum was flavored with molasses, the alcohol made you sleepy, of course.

"Oh, all right, then," Tom said. "It can't do no harm." So he poured Marc another glass, and they went through the same ritual again. By the time they made it to the fourth glass, Tom was pretty happy.

"Why don't you sing something for us," said Marc cheerfully. "It would do our spirits good."

"My mom always did say I was a good singer."

"Well, let's hear it, then." With that, Tom started into an exuberant, if disgusting, set of songs that would have been appropriate on a sailing ship but not in front of a lady. Every so often, Marc would raise his empty glass, which Tom now cheerfully filled, along with his own. When Marc happened to glance over at Gloria, she shook her head at him, wise to what he was doing and surprised at his ingenuity.

* * *

"He should be here," Alexandra said with alarm. "Henry, you've got to go find him."

"I'll go to the railway depot immediately." Henry stood up and pulled on his light wool coat. The humid air of New York City turned cold when the sun went down.

"Take Max with you—I don't want you out there by yourself."

"I don't want you and Honoria here by yourself." When Alexandra started to protest, Henry added, "I am a man, Alexandra, and can take care of myself and my family. I will go to the railroad station alone." Alexandra nodded, ashamed that she'd embarrassed him.

* * *

"So now the big oaf's asleep. What do you propose we do?" Gloria asked.

"First, you sneak over and see just how soundly he's asleep. If it's as deep as I think it is, then I propose that we get out of here."

Gloria got up quietly, as Marc recommended, and sneaked over to the sleeping detective. She was able to wave her hands furiously in front of his face without a stir. It startled her when Tom rolled slightly, increasing the growling of his snoring. But it was obvious that they could do whatever they wanted with no problem from Tom.

"All right, then. Let's get out of here," said Marc a little more forcefully. He was the one tied up, which meant any action to be taken had to be initiated by Gloria.

"And get recaptured by Geoffrey Brandt? You heard what he'll do to us—what he'll do to you."

"I don't think he's above making good on his threats to you too. And even if he doesn't, you might end up with a man who will beat you down until you are broken. So I don't propose we get captured. Now hurry over here and untie me. We may not have a lot of time."

A sickened look came across Gloria's face, and she got up from the bed but hesitated for a moment.

"Marc, it's not that I don't admire what you're trying to do. But we are in a strange city in a strange country, and it may be even worse out there than in here. Mr. Brandt really would sell you into servitude if he caught you . . ."

Marc was surprised that Gloria seemed interested in what would happen to him. But this was no time to think of that.

"Listen, Gloria. This man is capable of anything. I don't trust his intentions with you, nor will I stand for you to be alone with these two for the sixteen or seventeen days of the crossing. My father put me in charge of seeing you to safety, and you are anything but safe here. So we're leaving, and I am getting you back to our hotel. Father will know people at the shipping line who can protect us until you decide what to do."

"And just what will I do? You and your parents will protect me while you are here, but then you'll leave for England. And then this man will hunt me down, even if I go to Boston." This wasn't spoken in her usual accusing way.

"I've thought about that. And I don't have a good answer."

"Then maybe I should go back to England."

He looked up. "You, Gloria Palmerston, giving up? That's not like you."

"Being afraid is like me." She dropped her gaze. "You were there when I had a shadow of a doubt about rescuing the woman in the storm. I've not told anyone about this, for shame, but I almost told you to forget about her. To stay with me and save ourselves. For all my bluster, perhaps I am a coward and deserve what I get back in England."

"I don't know what it meant that night. Maybe you were frightened. But you *did* let me go save that woman. You *were* courageous and held on for dear life, even when you could have let go and it would have all ended. If you don't want to marry the viscount, you shouldn't. You have the strength in you to say no a hundred times over." Mark's words tumbled from him like an avalanche started from a pebble.

"But that still doesn't answer what happens after you leave. I could go to the authorities, but they can't protect me around the clock. And I believe that this man is cruel enough that if I defy him, he'll do what he said he'd do. And he'll probably come looking for you as well, just out of spite."

Marc hesitated, debating what to say. Finally he said, "You . . . you could come with me and my family. We're not going back to England—not ever. We're going to San Francisco and then to Salt Lake City. This detective fellow won't follow you there—to quote him, 'The arithmetic doesn't make it worth his trouble.' Besides, when we get to San Francisco, we'll have friends to meet us—friends who know the West and who can stand up to men like him." He looked away. "I'd be glad to have you come along . . ."

"San Francisco? Salt Lake City? But I thought you were just on a family holiday. Where is Salt Lake City?"

Marc caught his breath. She hadn't said no to the idea outright. For all the trouble that seemed to follow her, he was still very attracted to her and found himself hoping that she would continue with them farther on their journey.

"We're going to San Francisco by steamship via Panama. It's the fastest way to get there." He chewed his lip, not knowing what to say next. "Salt Lake City is in the middle of the Western mountains from what I can find out about it. It's where our church is. We're moving there to join our people."

"Your people? What people? What kind of church is in the moun-tains of America?"

Marc took a breath. It almost sounded foolish when you told people about where you were going before they knew anything about the Church. But this was the only way. If Gloria didn't come with them, then she should go back to England. "We're Mormons. Our church is The Church of Jesus Christ of Latter-day Saints. We believe that God has called a new prophet and that he gave us a new book of scripture—not to replace the Bible but to go along with it."

Gloria almost staggered. "A new Bible? A prophet? You can't be serious. Prophets lived in ancient times. There are no prophets today."

Marc shook his head. This was going nowhere, and it was using up valuable time. "It's now or never. If you want to make a new life in America, you can come with us. If you don't want to go to Salt Lake City, then you can make a life for yourself in San Francisco. Our friends tell us that more than 30,000 people live there, maybe even more. They tell us that the climate is wonderful and the bay is spec-tacular. More than 100,000 people have come through the port on their way to the gold fields. So for people looking for a new start in life, it's the perfect place."

Gloria was as thoughtful as a person in their predicament could be. "I never thought of myself as a pioneer, but there really is nothing for me in England. My mother clearly doesn't care about me." She furrowed her brow. "But Mormons. Why are they called that?"

"It's too long to tell right now. It's a nickname, after the book I told you about—the Book of Mormon."

"It must be a powerful book to influence someone like your father."

"It is." Marc smiled. "In fact, it's where I got the idea to get Tom drunk. Now are you going to untie me, or are you going to take your chances with Geoffrey Brandt?"

She moved quickly to untie his hands, which were quite swollen by this point. "If he captures us, he'll be ruthless."

"I know. That's why he can't capture us. But even if he does, I have an idea."

* * *

"Still no news of Marc?" Alexandra Chandler was desperate by now. Her husband had been out until after midnight, and there was still nothing about their son. Someone on the ship said he thought he saw him get into a cab, but that was the last of it. "None of the coachmen could tell you anything?"

"It was very odd. No one would tell me anything, but as I talked with a couple of them, the others seemed to look at each other with furtive glances, as if they knew something they weren't telling me."

"And no one at the shipping line?"

"No, but Mr. Kingman promised me he'd send word if he did hear about Marc. He is a decent fellow, you know."

Alexandra shook her head. This was the man who had cut off their salary, and Henry was speaking kindly of him. "And the police?"

"Not a word. Not that they'd be a lot of help. It looks to me like there are very few police for the number of people who live here." Anticipating her next question, he said, "And no, they haven't heard of him at the Excelsior."

Alexandra sat down heavily. "He's fallen into some kind of trouble. Hopefully he's not been murdered. Who knows what to expect here in America."

"I'm sure he'll be all right," said Honoria, her eyes watering up again.

"Yeah, he's a fighter," said Max.

The family sat in silence for a time. Finally, Henry spoke up. "I did hear about something that may be useful to all of us when Marcus returns—there seems to be a labor action against a Mr. Aspinwall, the proprietor of the steamship line that goes to Panama. The colliers on his steamships to Panama are threatening to strike. He has a full complement of passengers awaiting passage, so people on the street are all saying that he'll either break the strike or bring in blacklegs."

"What are blacklegs?" asked Max.

"Blacklegs are strikebreakers. The men whose jobs are on the line hate them, but it gives people who need employment a chance."

"And what does that have to do with us?" asked Alexandra.

"What it has to do with us is that the ship is going to Panama. If the strike continues, I believe Marc and I could apply as replacements. There's a chance that we could get our passage, maybe even yours, in exchange for our labor. That would get us to San Francisco after all."

"Oh, dear Henry," said Alexandra. "You are a strong and good man. But you are in no condition to fire the boilers on an oceangoing steamship." When Henry reacted, she added, "I'm not being cruel, I'm thinking of your health. This is not a good idea."

"Well, it may be the only idea," said Henry firmly. He stewed for a bit, debating whether he should point out that it was she who insisted on the passage by way of Panama rather than exploring the option of a land crossing by way of wagons and oxen. But he knew that it would do no good—she was well motivated in both her arguments: for San Francisco and against his working as a laborer. But they couldn't have it both ways. "We have to gain extra money if we are going to make it."

"I'm sure you are right, but right now I'd prefer to discuss it after we find Marcus," said Alexandra. "Obviously we can't do anything until we know what's happened to him."

Henry nodded. "Of course that's right. We'll discuss it then. In the meantime you need to rest for a bit. You were up all night."

"You are the one who was out all night looking for Marc . . ."

"Yes, and you were the one who was up worrying about both of us." Alexandra smiled. "We'll all get some rest . . ."

"And then I'll go looking for him again in another hour or so."

11—A RACE AGAINST THE CLOCK

June 1850

"You'd think it would be easy to hide in a city of half a million people!" Gloria vented.

Marc glanced at Gloria and smiled. Her attempt at humor was a relief, given that their situation felt so desperate. Marc had insisted that they walk at least a dozen city blocks before they attempted to hail a cab. The fact that the earlier cabdriver had been in collusion with Geoffrey Brandt made Marc nervous at the thought of even attempting to get a cab. Had he been on his own, he may have chanced walking all the way back to the dock. But Gloria was tired, and at this late hour he just didn't feel it was safe for her to walk any farther—not with all the drunken men who staggered into the street from the many saloons in that neighborhood.

"There—there's a cab!" Marc stepped out into the street from the dim corner and shouted for the cab. At first it appeared that he hadn't been heard, but then the cab lurched to a stop. "Let's go!" Gloria stepped forward in as dignified a manner as she could muster. "No— don't walk like that—muss up your hair," Marc said urgently. "And act a little tipsy."

"I beg your pardon! What on earth are you talking about?"

"We don't want them thinking that a highborn lady is in these parts. If that cabdriver knows Geoffrey Brandt, he'll suspect us for sure. You need to look like a local girl."

Instinctively Marc bent down quickly, scooped some of the filthy ooze that passed as a street in this part of town, and smeared some of the grime on Gloria's cheeks and dress. The look of sheer fury on her face would have made him shrink away at any other moment, but there was no time.

"Come on—let's go!"

"But the driver should come back here for us, not expect us to tramp up the middle of the street in this filth!"

"Are you going to quibble when it's nearly midnight and this is the only cab we've seen?"

Gloria bit her lip but picked up her dress and stepped out into the street. She still looked dangerously well-dressed until, in their hurry, both Marc and Gloria tripped over each other and fell face-first into the muck. Marc quickly pulled himself up, motioned to the cabdriver that they were all right and that he should keep waiting, and then reached down for Gloria. At this point she'd brought herself to her knees and she took his hand reluctantly.

"This really is outrageous! Are you sure this is necessary?"

"Come on! We've got to hurry." In a way, Marc was relieved at how they looked, because no one would ever recognize them now.

"Bit of a mess for my cab!"

"Sorry about that," said Marc, doing his best to imitate Tom's very peculiar American accent. "We'll make it up to you in a tip."

"Where you off to, then?"

"Downtown. The Excelsior Hotel."

The fellow laughed. "They're not likely to let you into the Excelsior dressed like that."

"You let us worry about that," said Gloria indignantly.

"Ah, an uppity one."

"And a bit drunk, I'm afraid," said Marc. "We have friends who plan to meet us there. We're not going in. We'll ask the bellman for help."

"Well, up you go, then."

"What? You should help us into your—"

Marc grabbed Gloria's arm so hard that she let out a small yelp.

"We'll be fine," he said to the coachman. "Glad you'll take us this late at night."

"It is awfully late. The missus is going to be sore at me, that's for sure. I really should head for home, which is the other way from where you want to go . . ."

"As I said, we'll make it up to you in our tip." Marc reached in his pocket and pulled out some coins to show that he had the means.

"All right, then, off we go."

Marc, having already helped Gloria get into the cab, pulled himself up and into the coach and then pulled the door closed. The driver snapped the reins, and the coach lurched forward—which brought another indignant gasp from Gloria.

"I know, I know," she said through clenched teeth. "I'll mind my manners. But this is the worst experience of my life."

"Let's just hope it doesn't get any worse. I'll be relieved beyond measure when we reach the Excelsior and make it safely inside."

Marc allowed himself a quick glance out the window. The gas lamps flickered in the night, briefly illuminating the faces of those who were still out enjoying the evening. Ladies in long gowns chatting up their male customers, drunks staggering or being thrown from the swinging doors of the saloons, and tightly knit crowds of men who Marc suspected were part of the infamous Irish gangs that fought each other at the least provocation. The great famine in Ireland, which had been ignored by their British overlords, had led to mass starvation and forced emigration, mostly to Boston, New York, and Philadelphia. Marc was glad they did not have to walk past these ruffians. Settling his head back against the leather cushion, he closed his eyes. He had to quickly open them again to ward off the involuntary image of Geoffrey Brandt standing on one of those corners recognizing them.

"Are you all right?" asked Gloria. "You're breathing funny."

Marc forced himself to calm down. "I'm all right. In fact, I'm getting better with every rotation of the wheels beneath us."

* * *

"What's this?" said Geoffrey Brandt as he mounted the keep to the door. "There's no need for a light at this hour. What is Tom up to?" Stepping inside, he grunted in disgust. Tom was splayed out on the floor like a slumbering walrus, and the Palmerston brat and her young man were nowhere to be seen. Cursing, he stormed across the room and kicked Tom in the side.

"Wake up, you idiot!" The big man simply groaned and rolled from his back to his side. The smell of rum was heavy in the air.

Striding over to the chair where Marc had been tied up, Geoffrey noted the empty glass and a dark stain around a hole in the floorboards. Kneeling down, he sniffed the spot.

"He poured it all out! The blaggard got Tom to drinkin' while he poured his out. They've made an escape!" Standing up quickly, he cursed again. Then he pounded one gloved hand into the fist of his other hand.

"It's a smaller town than you might think, Mr. Marcus Johnson. This isn't over yet—not by a long shot!"

With that, Brandt tried to wake Tom a second time, but to no avail. When the big man was drunk, he was out, and no amount of kicking would change that.

"All right then, I'll do it myself." Brandt grabbed a truncheon—a very useful handheld stick that came in handy when needing to knock someone's brains out—and made his way out into the night air.

"No cabs this time of night." He scowled. "I should have bought a horse." But he hadn't and he couldn't find one at this time of night. "Ah! There's always Joe. He owes me a big one." He smiled, knowing that it was very unlikely that Joe would be asleep at this hour. "All right, then, Miss Gloria Palmerston. We could have done this the easy way, but now you're going to make it more interesting."

* * *

"Clothes make the man. Naked people have little or no influence on society." Marc shook his head as he recalled this odd quote. *Where did I hear it?* He realized it was from the American missionaries quoting some American author by the improbable name of Mark Twain. Although it seemed foolish to think of something humorous, it made sense that this would come to mind just now, given that they had just been rebuffed by the doorman at the Excelsior Hotel. "Really, my family is supposed to have registered here earlier today. Are you certain?"

"There is no Chandler family," sniffed the doorman. "And as I said earlier, we simply couldn't admit anyone dressed as you are anyway."

"We're dressed this way because we fell in your mud-filled streets," said Gloria firmly. "If you were as civilized as you appear to believe you are, you'd have cobblestone. As it is, I'm filthy, cold, and tired, and I demand a room."

Rather than being offended by this tirade, the doorman stiffened his back respectfully. He recognized the absolute arrogance with which Gloria addressed him, and it resonated as authentic. "Perhaps I could check with the desk again." Still leaving them outside, which made Marc extremely nervous, the man went inside for what seemed an interminable amount of time. Finally, just when Marc was about to bolt for a hidden crevice in the side of a building to get out of the light, the fellow returned. "As it turns out, there is a message for you, Mr. Chandler. Your family has relocated to the Kimball. You are to meet them there."

"The Kimball? Where is that—why would they have moved?"

"I have no idea why they changed their reservation. The Kimball is a respectable but more modest establishment than the Excelsior. It's located three blocks from here—two streets down on this same avenue, and then one block to the east on Fulton Street. It's that direction." The fellow pointed to the north.

"Why would they do that—" Marc started to say.

"But what of me?" Gloria interjected. "Your parents thought I was going to stay with friends, so they have no room. What shall I do?"

Marc shook his head to clear it. "Yes, what about Miss Palmerston? She is a respected lady from England who, through a series of mishaps, was unable to connect with a Boston-bound train. Do you have room for her here?"

"Unfortunately, we do not." The doorman remained aloof. Marc suspected it was because he still doubted the veracity of their story and the worthiness of Gloria to occupy one of the rooms in their exalted hotel.

"What shall I do?" The fear from before had returned to Gloria's voice.

"You will come with me," said Marc. "We will find my parents, and you will spend the night with us."

"But, there may not be room . . ."

Marc cast a quick sideways glance at the pompous doorman. "Apparently there's more room there than in this place and probably better accommodations, anyway."

The doorman merely sniffed and turned away.

"But whatever we do," he said in a whisper, "let's do it quickly. If Brandt has figured out that we're missing, he could very easily be searching for us this very moment."

"Tell me again how to find this place," Marc asked again, partially to confirm his understanding but mostly to annoy the doorman one last time.

"That way—two blocks, then one block to your right." With that the doorman turned without a word and disappeared into the lobby of the Excelsior.

"We're on our own again." Marc struck out in the direction he'd been given.

"And somehow I don't mind that so much," Gloria whispered.

* * *

Geoffrey Brandt sat next to the driver of the cab as the horse clopped along. "Where does Cunard usually put up its people?" Brandt asked Joe, a cabdriver who often helped Brandt out when he needed special transportation arrangements. Joe had been found at his favorite pub, his cab parked back around the corner in the dark, the horses hungry and neglected. Joe wasn't exactly a well-esteemed driver.

"The Hotel Strand is the usual place. Sometimes the Grand or the Greenwich. For really important guests they put people up at the Excelsior."

"No, not the Excelsior. The way that fellow was dressed, he was not suited to the Excelsior." Brandt leaned out the window, straining his eyes to see any sign of the two escapees. By now they'd reached downtown. The gas lamps were closer together there so that the area had a much brighter and welcoming feel to it. Out of the corner of his eye, he spotted a couple walking huddled against a wall.

"It might be them," he muttered. But when he turned to look again they were gone. "I'm hallucinating. It couldn't have been them. They wouldn't be out walking at this hour. They'd be smart enough to go straight to a hotel. It's no use," he said caustically as he turned to Joe. "They've either been mugged or found themselves somewhere safe to stay. We'll find them tomorrow. Will you put the word out to the other coachmen to see if they picked a couple up near my apartment?"

"Of course," said Joe, knowing very well that he'd be rewarded for doing so. "If they took a cab, we'll find them."

"And if they didn't, we'll find their bodies." Brandt smiled. "That would be a tragedy, wouldn't it?" The thought of their getting what they deserved was almost satisfying enough to overcome the sense of loss he felt in not getting his bounty.

* * *

The hotel clerk at the Kimball Hotel had been annoyed when Marc and Gloria showed up. But he'd been alerted to watch out for Marc, so he said he'd take them up to the Chandlers' room.

"Don't know where they plan to put you—they already have four people in there as it is."

"Do you have a second room?" asked Gloria. "I would like my own room."

"It's not on the same floor, but we do have a nice room for a single lady."

Gloria signed the register with relief.

"Do you want to go talk with Mother and Father so we can figure out what to do with you tomorrow?"

"I'm so very tired." She looked at Marc for a moment. "Besides, you said you have something in mind."

Marc nodded. "I do have a thought—but it will hinge on whether you decide to go to San Francisco with us or go to Boston. I'm sure I can keep you safe if you come with us, but I'm not as confident about your trip to Boston."

Gloria looked dazed. "I just don't know. I'm so tired."

"Then we'll decide tomorrow. But I don't think there's much time. Brandt is a detective by trade, and he will have contacts who will spot us in no time. We have to move quickly."

Gloria nodded. Turning to the clerk, she asked, "Can you have someone come knock on my door at 7:30?"

The clerk nodded.

"Good. Then if you'll see me to my room, Mr. Chandler can find his way to his."

"Do you have any luggage, ma'am?"

Gloria shook her head, and Marc felt the distress she must be in. They'd had to leave her luggage in Brandt's apartment—to have dragged it out onto the street in the middle of the night would have attracted bandits. So she had quickly unpacked a few essential things, including her money, placed everything in an overstuffed handbag, and then abandoned all her other worldly goods. Marc had been impressed that she could do so and told her as much on the cab ride down to the city.

"I'm afraid I'll need to buy clothes tomorrow," she said sadly to the clerk. "I met with some misfortune today." Her voice was subdued now, and even the tired night clerk recognized that she was almost at a breaking point.

"I'm sorry to hear that, ma'am. Let me show you to your room now so you can get some rest." The clerk looked at both of them and, with a subtle sniff, continued. "We can draw baths if you like. My wife could help you get the things you need tomorrow."

Gloria smiled and nodded at the man. As the clerk left to instruct one of the staff members to prepare baths and a new room, she turned to Marc. "Thank you for helping me. I'm sorry I've gotten you all messed up in this. I wish I could undo it."

"But you can't, and if I hadn't been with you, your future would have been lost. Things turned out all right tonight, and they wouldn't have without both of us doing our part."

"True." Gloria lingered. Beneath the fatigue in her countenance there was a glimmer of light. "Good night, then . . ."

Marc was wise enough not to say anything. He just looked at her, through the grime and wear-and-tear, thinking about how his opinion about her had changed in such a short time since they started their voyage from Liverpool.

Finally Gloria's train of thought ended, and she spoke. "You were brave tonight. You saved me. Thank you." Before he could reply, she looked toward the returning hotel clerk, and they made their way toward the stairs.

Twenty minutes later, after Marc had gone to men's bathroom to cleanse himself of the dirt and worry of the evening, the pall that had hung over the Chandlers was suddenly and happily lifted as Marc knocked quietly on the door.

12—INEVITABILITIES

June 1850

"I'm sure it was him," Marc said to his father. "He was sitting next to the driver of a cab, just two blocks from where we are now. With his connections, he'll find us in no time. I've got to go see Mr. Kingman." They had stayed up until nearly 3:00 a.m. talking about their situation—the Chandlers cast adrift with inadequate money, Gloria fleeing from detectives, and now the very real threat that Marc could be caught up in the violence.

"We should go to the police," said Alexandra.

"If we were in England, I'd agree. But this man Brandt seems to have connections. I wouldn't be surprised if the police betrayed us, if given enough incentive," said Henry.

"Why don't you want me to go to Mr. Kingman?" asked Marc. "Cunard bears responsibility for Gloria's safety as much as we do."

"It's just that it ended so badly with him." Henry coughed nervously. "I hardly feel we're in a position to ask for a favor."

Before Marc could respond, Alexandra said quietly, "Henry, this is not a favor. It's a necessity. And Marc's right—Cunard is Gloria's best hope."

Henry nodded. "All right, then. Hopefully he's there this early." He rubbed his eyes. It was now barely 6:30 a.m., so they'd had very little sleep. "Let's go."

"Can you find your way there along the backstreets?" asked Marc.

"I'm sure we'll be safe. Why don't you wear that hat that comes down around your ears? I'll walk very close to you. This Mr. Brandt has never seen me, so he might not make a connection."

"Will you go wake Gloria and tell her to stay here with you, Mother? She's so impetuous that I can imagine her going out for a breath of fresh air, only to be snatched away."

"Of course. We'll take good care of her." She paused expectantly. "So go, already."

The two hurried out the door.

* * *

"The Excelsior? I'll be hanged. I didn't think she was up to that, not from what her mother told me. She must have brought more money with her than I thought. Probably stole her mother's jewelry."

The cabdriver who had driven Marc and Gloria to the Excelsior the night before waited patiently. This had turned out to be the most profitable pickup ever—the couple last night tipping him generously for transporting them so late at night, and now Geoffrey Brandt about to tip him for ratting on them.

Not really fair on my part, he thought. *One or the both of them is in trouble if Brandt is involved.* But as Brandt tossed him a quarter, his eyes widened in delight. "I'd sell out my own mother for that," he said.

"What was that?"

"Oh, nothin', Mr. Brandt. I'm just grateful for your generosity."

"You better be telling the truth or you'll regret my generosity . . ."

"No need to worry about that, sir. I'm sure I took the people you're after. The Excelsior it is. You can count on it."

Brandt didn't reply. He simply whipped the horse he'd hired and started riding south toward the city.

* * *

"This is all very disturbing, Mr. Chandler. I really should report this to the police."

"After we're gone, maybe," replied Marc urgently. "But it just seems the risk is too great of Brandt having corrupted someone at police headquarters. At least that's how it seems to me."

Kingman nodded. "You're possibly right. Still, it's a mighty temptation to look in this letter and discover the details about what you've written."

"The letter only has power over Geoffrey Brandt if you don't open it. If he thinks you know what is written therein, then he may come after you, as well."

"I can take care of myself," said Kingman sternly, but he hesitated. "Still, it does seem to be the best way to protect you and Miss Palmerston." He furrowed his forehead. "But you want me to destroy it after you depart?"

"I'm convinced it's the only way to keep him from following us."

"All right. I will go to the pier when you depart. Once you're safely at sea, I'll either give the letter to Brandt if he approaches me or destroy it within his eyesight."

"Perfect. That's perfect. Now I feel like we've got some insurance for when he finds us," Marc noted.

"*If* he finds us," corrected Henry.

Marc shook his head. "No matter how fast we get out of New York, he will find us. Of that I'm sure."

"Thank you, Mr. Kingman," said Henry formally. "I know you are angry with me, so I am grateful that you would do this anyway."

"Not angry, Mr. Chandler. Puzzled and concerned. I think you're making a mistake. But that is your business, not mine. I'm happy to do this small thing for you—although I wish I could do more to this Geoffrey Brandt. I've heard rumors of him for a number of years. Now it seems they are true at least in part."

A thoughtful look crossed Henry's face. "Maybe there is something. After he departs for England the next time, perhaps you could send word by packet steamer that he should be placed on a travel blacklist. I added the names of a number of scoundrels to that list myself. It might prevent him from traveling so easily between the two countries to wreak his mischief. At least it will keep him off Cunard ships."

Kingman smiled. "A very good idea. We really will miss your experience."

Somehow it relieved Henry immeasurably to think that this man still respected him. "Well, then, we'll be off to arrange the next leg in our travel."

As they reached the door, Marc hesitated then turned and came back to Kingman. "One more thing. I'm sorry to burden you, but this is really vital. After we're safely on our way, will you send this money to the New York and Erie Railroad, even though I don't have the name of an agent? It's to pay the debts of a man named Billy Call. He is the younger son of Lord Call from Somerset. He is one of Brandt's victims, and this may save his life."

"But doesn't this leave you with precious little money for your own needs?" asked a very subdued Kingman.

Marc couldn't hide his concern but still set the money into Kingman's hands. "It's up to you to save the lad."

Kingman shook his head and then glanced at Henry, who nodded in support of Marc.

"All right, then. You can count on me. Good luck to both of you." He cleared his throat. "I will put in a good word for you when I report your termination to the company. Not that it will mean that much . . ."

"It means everything to me," said Henry. Were he not an Englishman, he would have stepped forward and hugged Kingman. Instead he extended his hand, which Kingman took.

"Now you best be on your way. You have arrangements to make."

Marc and Henry soon managed to sign a contract with William Aspinwall for passage on his steamship to Panama, but at the price of a rigorous work schedule. Aspinwall required them the next day. They had no time to waste.

* * *

A number of things conspired to make it difficult for Geoffrey Brandt to find Gloria and Marc. Difficult, but not impossible. The first was that Marc had given his name as Marcus Johnson but when talking to the doorman at the Excelsior, he'd only used the family's last name— never Marcus. The second was that the doorman wasn't on duty that next evening and no one in the hotel recognized the name Johnson. And of course the hotel staff had no idea about Gloria since she had never been a registered guest. The third problem was that when he did finally track down the doorman who had been on duty, he found that he was the type of man who took his responsibilities to his guests very seriously and would never violate their privacy.

It took a lot of money for Brandt to first remind the doorman that neither the man he was seeking nor the young woman who accompanied him were guests of the hotel. Once they got past that obstacle, it took even more money to recall that, yes, there was a young couple who had come by at an indecent hour, dressed very shabbily, but the name was not Johnson. Finally, the poor man had to be convinced that it was all right to give out the correct name, Chandler, and the fact that the family were likely staying at the Kimball.

"You're very lucky that I'm on an expense allowance," Brandt had said as he handed over the final banknote. The bribe had escalated past the usefulness of coins to paper script, and it was extremely unusual for Brandt to pay that much for information. Except that this time he had a grudge to settle—no one had successfully escaped from him before, and he didn't want it to spoil his reputation.

But it was the third day after their escape before Brandt put all the pieces together. By then the Chandlers had been very busy.

* * *

The confrontation came unexpectedly when Marc was sucker-punched in the gut as he rounded a corner by the Kimball Hotel on their way back from making arrangements for their trip to Panama.

"*No one* escapes from me. I thought I had explained that to you both so clearly the other night." He said the words with the dark anger of a professional killer—not yelling but shooting each word off like a bullet storm. Marc took a swing at Brandt, but Brandt's thugs quickly brought him to his knees where they kicked him in the ribs. Henry tried to intervene but was quickly leveled to the ground.

When Marc was pinned down and unable to mount any further defense, Brandt said, "Look, Chandler—I'm not really interested in you. You've crossed me and I ought to make you disappear. But I think we can come to a quick understanding." He spat a black load of chewing tobacco at Henry's feet.

"What do you want, then?"asked Marc, stalling for time. His ribs ached and his anger burned, ready to spill out. But he and his father were no match for this group.

"You know what I want. The lady. She needs to be taught a lesson. So tell me where she's at, maybe even arrange a rendezvous where she isn't suspecting us, and we'll make it easier for you and your family to go to Panama. I'm a generous man who is *always* willing to pay for information . . ."

"How do you know about Panama?" asked Henry, speaking for the first time.

Brandt smiled. "It's my job to know everything about my marks, Henry, good fellow. Like the fact that you've been an exemplary clerk for Cunard, but you have now jumped ship because you're off to the West. Adventure! I also know that you have a determined wife, a frail daughter, and a fourteen-year-old son who you really should watch out for. After all, they're your blood—not some highborn chit who happened to string you along."

Marc's blood ran chill. Somehow Brandt knew everything. Well, maybe everything. Marc had to find out if Brandt knew the one key thing before he decided what to do next. He tried to think of some clever way to ask, but his thoughts failed him. So he just asked. "And who told you about us and our plans for Panama?"

"Right. I'm going to just up and tell you my source so that they'll never work with me again. You really can't be all that dim."

Marc nodded. "You're right. I am stupid. Someone like you is probably connected at the highest level with the local Cunard office. The only people who would know about us and our plans would be the senior officers—maybe the top man himself." Marc ignored Henry's warning glance. He could see in his father's eyes that he thought Marc must have lost his mind.

"Clever," said Brandt. "You get me to bragging about my contacts and you're able to guess who it is. Then, assuming I leave you alive, you blackmail that person for giving out confidential information."

"Say what you will . . . it has to be a top person. No one else knows about us."

"It may be someone at the top, maybe not." He shrugged. "But not for the likes of you—why waste my money at that level when it could be anyone: a junior clerk who overhears a conversation, a dock worker who gets word to send your bags to the Kimball instead of the Excelsior, or a cleaning woman who finds the paperwork."

"I underestimated you," said Marc, doing his best to mask the relief he felt. Brandt had unknowingly just confirmed that his contact was most likely not Kingman. And that was exactly what Marc needed to know so he could safely play the next card in his hand. "Help me up, will you, and we'll talk."

"Marcus! You can't be serious. I forbid you to talk to this man! Let him do what he will to us, we will not betray Gloria! I forbid it!" Henry played his role perfectly, albeit unknowingly.

"Be quiet, Father. Mr. Brandt will find Gloria with or without us. Maybe we can make things easier for her. But I need to talk with him privately for a moment." The fury in Henry Chandler's eyes was so intense that Marc winced as his father struck him. That had never happened before in his life, and it was unnerving. Still, Marc had to proceed. He had to think of the family.

As the two of them stepped to the side, Brandt had a smug look on his face. Then, as Marc kept talking, Brandt's look faltered and then his face flushed. When Henry saw him shove Marc against the wall, he tried to intervene, but Brandt's men restrained him.

Marc shoved back against Brandt and repeated more loudly what he had said the first time. The look of pure fury on Brandt's face made Henry think that Brandt might kill Marc right on the spot.

* * *

Gloria and Mrs. Headly, the night clerk's wife, returned from their clothes shopping trip at 3:00 p.m. as promised. Gloria was no longer without suitable clothes, and she had picked a wardrobe fit for travel and for the warm weather of the Caribbean and California. She was surprised that Marcus and Henry weren't there, since it had been agreed that as soon as she returned, the family would make its way to the pier, where the men would board as strikebreakers and then the women and Max would come on board as if they were passengers. Gloria had been led to believe that the timing was critical, which is why she had hurried.

"Where are they?"

"I don't know," Alexandra replied, the anxiety evident in her voice.

"I would have stayed out shopping if I knew they weren't really serious about being on a schedule . . ." Gloria's voice trailed off. "Do you think *he* might have found—?"

"That's what I've been worrying about," said Alexandra, with a stricken look.

Gloria glanced at Honoria, whose face was as white as a sheet.

"What should we do, Mother?" asked Max. "Should I go look for them?"

"No, Max!" Alexandra calmed her voice. "No. Whatever has happened, we must not get separated. It's most likely that they were delayed in getting the things they needed, that's all. I don't want you to be out running around on the streets when they return."

Max set his jaw so as to not show any emotion, but the tension in the room was worse than anything he'd ever experienced.

13—GETTING HIS DUES

Pacific Mail and Steamship Pier—June 1850

"FILTHY SCUM!" ONE OF THE strikers yelled at Henry.

Henry flinched as this striker came menacingly close to hitting him. One of the hired security guards intervened to protect him.

Henry started to apologize to one of the strikers before Marc cut him off.

"Don't say anything or you'll just make them even angrier. If we're really going to do this, we have to go on board right now!"

"Do you think we should go? Perhaps we should just return to England so you can go to that school in Germany and I can retain my position with Cunard."

Marc shook his head. His father could be so infuriating. At Henry's urging the family would make a decision, Henry would confirm it, and then at the crucial moment he'd question it.

"You're the head of the house—but make up your mind right now. If we're going back to England, we need to come up with another plan to protect Gloria." The exasperation in his voice was obvious.

"No, no. You're right. Let's go on board." It was Marc's idea to have the women board separately, as if they were passengers, even though both Alexandra and Honoria would be expected to help in the kitchen. Gloria somehow had enough money to buy passage for herself but not enough for the whole family.

Making their way through a cordoned-off area while strikers spit on them and cursed them was the most humiliating ordeal ever endured by a man of Henry Chandler's disposition.

"Keep your chin up, Father. We're doing this for our convictions." Henry nodded and forged ahead. Once they were on board, the purser was waiting for them.

"What on earth are you two supposed to be doing on the ship?" the purser asked with incredulity.

"We're stokers. Mr. Aspinwall hired us."

"Stokers! With those scrawny bodies! This must be a joke." Henry was about to respond indignantly when the man suddenly came abruptly to attention.

"Is there a problem here?" The voice of William Aspinwall was confident and strong.

"No, sir, Mr. Aspinwall. I was just expressing my concern that the work may be too difficult for these men. They look more like clerks than stokers." The purser wiped his brow. "But if you hired them, then it's all right, of course."

Aspinwall looked over Henry and Marc like he was assessing a new team of horses. *It wouldn't surprise me if he wanted to see our teeth*, thought Marc. This was more humiliating to him than passing through the strikers.

"My purser may be right, gentlemen. This is filthy, backbreaking work. Are you sure you want to do this?"

"As long as you promise us passage all the way to San Francisco."

"You'll have to work all the way to San Francisco for that."

"Then tell us where to go, and let us get to work."

Aspinwall shook his head. "I'd make you a clerk if I needed one, but I don't. Ships travel by steam nowadays, but it takes human muscle to feed the boilers. Report over there."

As Henry and Marc disappeared belowdecks, Aspinwall turned to the purser. "You're right, of course, John. Neither one of them is up to this. But they are desperate enough to give it a try. I don't know what's so important that they have to get to San Francisco, but we'll use them for as long as they hold out."

"Yes, sir. Of course. I'm sure they'll toughen up after a few days."

Aspinwall nodded vacantly. "Try to take it a little easy on the old man, at least at first. Put him on the auxiliary boiler—the one for running the pumps—it doesn't draw as much."

"We usually rotate the men into that."

Aspinwall glared. "Do what I say. Put him on the auxiliary boiler and leave him there."

"Yes, sir!" As Aspinwall walked away, the man found himself surprised. This was the first time he'd ever heard of Aspinwall showing what might be construed as compassion.

* * *

"It's just a few moments before we go on board," said Alexandra.

"I can only imagine how difficult it was for Mr. Chandler and Marc to go through that crowd. Look how they are treating those men . . ." Gloria said.

Alexandra and Max turned toward the direction of their ship and saw a group of strikers spit on some men who were attempting to get through the strike line. Alexandra shook her head. "This is ugly business, and I worry about Henry doing that kind of work."

"Isn't that the man . . . ?" asked Max.

"What man?" asked Alexandra, but before she could receive an answer, she heard Gloria gasp in alarm. "What is it, dear?" she asked.

Gloria seemed to shrink behind Alexandra. "It's Brandt."

"Over there," said Max. "He's getting on that ship." Before Gloria could tell Max not to point, which would possibly draw attention, Brandt turned in their direction and clearly saw them. At this point he stepped on board the ship docked next to their Panama-bound steamship. Brandt glowered at them for a moment then raised his hand, tipped slightly to the side, and then he sneered. While far enough away that it was difficult to make out his expression, the act of putting his finger to the rim of his hat was more than enough to signal that he had seen them. And the look of sheer contempt in his eyes made it plain that he was not happy to be there. Gloria put her arms on Alexandra's shoulders to support herself.

"I thought we were done with him," said Alexandra in a subdued voice.

"I don't know what happened with him and Marc," replied Gloria. "But Marc assured me that he wouldn't bother us."

Just then the deep, sonorous sound of the ship's horn rolled out across the harbor, sending a chill up their necks. Their involuntary response was to shut their eyes while the horn sounded. When the sound stopped, Gloria opened her eyes and said, "But the ship is leaving. And Brandt is on it!"

"It's true," said Max. "It's leaving!"

"Quick, Max," said Alexandra, "run over to that dock worker and ask him where that ship is bound. We must know!" The thought that Brandt was on a competing ship to Panama was almost more than any of them could bear. Max tore off at top speed.

"I don't know what I'll do. If he's figured out where we're going . . ."

"Then we will change our plans. We can always go overland to Utah. We'll need to alert Henry and Marcus, but . . ." Her voice caught.

"But what?" asked Gloria.

Alexandra shook her head. "But now that Henry has given his word that he'll serve on this particular ship, I can't imagine that his conscience would allow him to back out of his contract."

"Oh, dear," said Gloria.

"I'm afraid I have quite a pit in my stomach," replied Alexandra.

Then Max came running up to them. "It's going to England. I asked the man twice! He said it's going to to Liverpool!"

"To Liverpool!" shouted Gloria. "He really is leaving!" The relief and joy in her voice was boundless, and without thinking she put her arms around Alexandra and hugged her.

"It is good news," said Alexandra with a sigh, as she untangled herself from the unexpected hug.

"It's Marc," said Gloria quietly. "I don't know how he did it, but he arranged for this. What a curious man . . ."

* * *

After their encounter with Aspinwall, Henry and Marcus found their way down into the pit where the furnaces and boilers were located. The heat coming off the furnaces was incredible—it seemed impossible that it wouldn't catch the ship on fire simply from the ferocity of the radiant heat.

"You the two replacements?" the man in charge asked them.

"Yes, sir. Henry Chandler, and this is my son Marcus." Marc was surprised at the confidence in his father's voice. It seemed as if he'd adapted very quickly to the demands of the situation.

Sizing them up, the fellow said, "George Connolly. You'll report to me. From the looks of you two, you're going to have a tough go of it for a few days until you get used to this."

"We're up to whatever you demand." A little less confidence in Henry's voice, perhaps a result of the unrelenting noise and incredible heat that was broiling them.

"For now, just sit over there and watch. There's a rhythm to all this that you have to learn quickly. If you don't do it right, hot coals will come sliding out of the furnace when the ship rises and falls to the waves, and then we've got a real problem. So just watch. These two still have two hours on their shift."

Connolly looked them over a second time. "Listen, this can all be a bit much, at first. When it's time to leave port, you can go up on deck and get some air."

"Thank you. My wife and other children are coming on board. They'll be working too, but it would be good to help them get settled."

Connolly nodded. "Just be sure you're back in two hours. That's when you'll really start your training."

As Marc sat down, Henry leaned over. "So tell me again how you did it." Before Marc could reply, Henry added, "And I'm sorry I doubted you."

"It was better that you did doubt me—it made it more authentic when I talked with Brandt. Your role was pivotal, and you pulled it off." Marc took a breath. The heat was stifling, and he was really becoming frightened at the thought of doing this in two-hour shifts on and off throughout the day and night. He worried even more for Henry. But now they were committed.

"Brandt is a braggart. He's good at what he does, but he wants people to know about it. While holding Gloria and me captive, he started bragging about some of his exploits and all the rotten things he's done to people. What he didn't even think about was the possibility that I would ever get away or even if I did that I would remember what he told me."

"His mistake, for sure."

Marc nodded. What Brandt had thought of as idle chatter, Marc had memorized as material for potential blackmail.

"I just started reciting back to Geoffrey Brandt all the things he'd told me, including things about the men whom he had kidnapped and others whom he has hurt."

"That's when he shoved you?"

"I thought he was going to kill me, which is why I quickly added that I'd taken the time to write it all down and seal it in a letter that I had taken to the Cunard offices."

"Your conversation with Kingman makes sense now."

"I explained the deal I'd made with Kingman—that if he saw us safely off to Panama and then saw Brandt get on a ship bound for England, he would tear the unopened letter up and drop the pieces into the ocean by the pier in Brandt's view. But if Brandt tried to follow us or failed to board the ship to England, then Kingman would take the letter to policemen he trusted."

"Which is the point in the conversation where Brandt blanched and looked as if he was going to throw up."

"He said that if all that were true, he'd just arrange for something bad to happen to Kingman, to which I replied that Kingman had already taken steps to protect himself, both physically and by having an unnamed subordinate who would follow through on turning Brandt in to the law should anything bad happen to Kingman. I then reminded Brandt that at the very least, anything done to Kingman would get Brandt permanently barred from entry to the United States, which would cost him a great deal of business, at the best, and at the worst he'd go to jail. He might even be hanged if the authorities found out that any of the people he'd abducted into servitude had died as a result of it."

"And that's when he capitulated and said that we and Gloria could leave the country."

Marc nodded. "That is when he threatened to kill me and you on the spot out of pure vengeance."

"You didn't tell me that part . . ."

"I didn't need to, because I simply added to what I'd already told him—that my arrangement with Kingman also included a clause that if either you or I turned up missing, he would follow through with the plan."

Henry shook his head and smiled while taking out a handkerchief to wipe his brow. "I had no idea you were so clever or devious. You undoubtedly saved our lives and protected Gloria in the process." Henry smiled. "It was very good thinking on your part, and you turned an ugly situation into one that still has hope. I'm very grateful . . ."

Their conversation came to a quick end when George Connolly shouted at them to pay attention.

"One last question," Henry said quietly to Marc while looking straight ahead. "How will we know that it worked?"

"As a matter of fact, it probably already has. When Brandt confirmed all this with Kingman, he was told he had to board that ship right next to us. It departs for England within minutes of our scheduled departure. I suspect that the ship's horn that just sounded was Brandt's ship pulling away from the pier. Brandt's little crime wave will come to an end, at least for the time being. And Gloria will find her way to San Francisco without interference."

A contented silence settled over father and son. The noise and acrid smell of the coal burning furiously in the boilers was overwhelming, but that was a challenge they would face when it was their time to work. For the moment they were content that they'd done what they could. "The women and Max should be coming on board right about now."

Henry stole a quick glance up to the deck and was pleased to see Alexandra wave at him.

"They're all on board. Another hour and this chapter of our lives will be over."

14—FIRES OF THE UNDERWORLD

Off the Coast of South Carolina—June 15, 1850

"CHANDLER! YOU'VE DONE IT AGAIN! Put those fires out!" George Connolly was a decent man, but Henry's lack of skill in the coal room would try the patience of a saint—and Connolly, by his own admission, was anything but a saint.

"Yes, sir!" Henry scrambled to stamp out the fires of the lumps of coal that had spilled from the furnace. Marc reached over and did his best to help him while trying to shield his efforts from Connolly so he wouldn't be yelled at for neglecting his own furnace. Marc's was the hungry one—a furnace that was crucial to powering the giant paddle wheels. Henry was on the auxiliary boiler, as promised to William Aspinwall, but even that was proving extremely taxing for him. Sweat dripped down his face, in spite of the relatively cool breeze blowing through their work area. His cheeks were flushed under the grime of coal dust that had been attracted to his sweaty face.

Paddle wheel steamships were really nothing more than converted sailing ships, with the same sharp bow and rakish decks but outfitted with huge paddle wheels on each side. The sheer size of the wheels required that the massive capstans completed their rotation far above the waterline. With so much weight towering above the sea, the ships had to carry a substantial load of ballast to keep them settled firmly in the water. Even with that it was impossible to eliminate the natural motion of the sea, the rising and falling of the bow and stern in response to the waves, and even the unmonitored shifting of passengers from side to side and forward to aft. For the passengers who traveled on the ships, all this motion was nothing but an inconvenience, at worst a possible source of seasickness. But for the men laboring furiously in the boiler area, it was a constant enemy as they strove to shovel their heavy loads of coal into the furnace at just the right time in order to avoid having a cascade of glowing coals come flying back out of the furnace into the work area, where it could catch the dark new coal on fire around their feet. Most who worked there had spent their lives in physical pursuits, thus acquiring a natural feel for the uneven motion of a ship at sea and the corresponding agility required to react appropriately to it. Marc's natural athleticism helped him adjust very quickly. But for a man like Henry, whose only experience with coal was to occasionally open the door of the small iron heater in his clerk's office at Cunard, and who lacked any natural physical grace whatsoever, it was hopelessly challenging. His initial days in the furnace room were like a living nightmare directly out of the pages of Dante's *Inferno*.

"Back to your own boiler, Chandler Two!" barked Connolly, and Marc stepped away. At this point, the coals with flames had been stamped out, and Henry was hurriedly trying to shovel the rest into the open door of the furnace. Covered in soot from head to toe, he looked more like a tall and slender stick figure than a man, with gangly legs and arms flailing in an uncoordinated fashion each time he tried to shovel the coal. Marc had to look away or he thought he might throw up from the anxiety.

Fortunately, after perhaps another fifteen minutes of Henry struggling against the heaving deck, the ship steadied as the wind died down and Henry was at last able to get into a rhythm that was adequate to keep the auxiliary boiler at the correct pressure.

"Are you all right?" asked Marc in what in other circumstances would have been a regular voice. Down here the incredible noise of the reciprocating engine made a shout more difficult to hear than a whisper would be in a normal conversation. He glanced to his side and saw his father nod, but everything about his appearance belied that assessment. "Just another twenty minutes to go. Keep a nice steady pace . . ."

Henry nodded a bit more furiously as if to indicate that he didn't need the encouragement. Marc found it every bit as uncomfortable as Henry did that their roles had reversed, and it was now Marc who was the one doing the most to provide for the family.

"Chandler!"

Henry jumped at the sound of his name but quickly turned to see what George Connolly wanted. Connolly was biting his lower lip.

"Stand down, Chandler. Schiller here reported early. He'll take over." Henry started to protest that he was more than able to finish out his own shift, but Connolly simply waved him aside. Henry nodded and staggered over to the side, where a fifty-gallon oak barrel of water was available. Henry drew a large draft and started swallowing as fast as he could.

"Slow down, Chandler," said Connolly, moving toward Henry. "You'll kill yourself if you drink too much too fast."

Henry nodded and started taking smaller sips, but it was obvious that he would have stuck his head face-first into the barrel if it was up to him.

"Go ahead and sit over there." Connolly motioned to a stool next to the coal chute.

After another ten minutes, Connolly moved over toward one of the boilers, where he pulled on a long cord, sounding a shrill whistle that signaled the end of the shift. Of course, they weren't the only ones affected by the whistle; stewards, cooks, waiters, and other staff undoubtedly rotated out of work at this major shift change. The firemen had more frequent shift changes, because the work was simply too difficult for a man to last an eight-hour shift, but the off-hours shift changes were handled by a shout and hand gestures.

Marc stepped back from the furnace gratefully, handing his shovel to the fellow who was to succeed him, and then made his way with the others to the water barrel. His mouth felt as if he'd just crossed the entire Sahara Desert without finding a single oasis along the way. When it was his turn, he drank greedily, waiting to be yelled at for drinking too fast, but no one said anything.

Extending a hand to his father, Henry waved him off, struggled to stand, tottered, but then slumped back down. Henry cast a quick sideways glance and saw Connolly shake his head and look away. This time he accepted Marc's hand.

"You've got to put an end to this," said Marc as he helped Henry up the stairs and out into the open air.

"I don't want to talk about it. It's difficult work, but I'll be fine."

"No, you won't. It's backbreaking work, and the heat is going to kill you. There isn't another man your age who would go anywhere near those furnaces."

Marc came to an abrupt stop as Henry whirled on him. "And just what do you expect me to do? We're at sea! It's not like we can change our mind and go back ashore. They are not going to turn the ship around for me, and out here in the open ocean they don't have anyone to replace me." Henry's eyes flashed, and Marc could only assume that his face had reddened even more.

"I just worry about you. There are times I think that I can't take it. There was one moment today when I felt like tearing off all of my clothes and running for the side of the ship to jump in the ocean. I thought I was going crazy."

Henry smiled weakly. "I know what you mean." By now they had reached the ship's railing on a service deck where the passengers couldn't see them. Marc leaned over the rail to feel the rush of air that came up from the ocean as the ship made its way forward. He knew his father was next to him but didn't turn to look until he heard the tortured sound of Henry retching into the water. The last thing Henry needed was to lose food and moisture. Marc wanted to help, but what could he do? So he continued to look out to sea until Henry calmed down. Marc turned and smiled at him, and Henry shrugged.

After a brief pause to cool down, they made their way to a small lavatory where they could scrub off at least some of the grimy soot. But when they got there, Henry said, "You go ahead. I don't have the energy. I'm going straight to our cabin to lie on the floor. I need to get some sleep before the next go-around."

Marc nodded even as his stomach twisted uncomfortably. He'd never known his father to present himself to his mother in any other fashion than absolutely clean and scrubbed. That he would forgo that most basic demonstration of manners showed how exhausted he was.

"Sure. I'll be there in a bit. Be sure you take some more water before you lie down." Henry nodded and shuffled off toward their little cabin. Marc wanted to walk with him to steady him but knew that gesture would only make things worse.

* * *

The ship's laundry was the second-hottest place on the ship.

"How can you do that?"

"Do what, dear?"

"Sing. I'm exhausted, and this work is tedious."

Alexandra Chandler smiled at Honoria. "It is hard, isn't it?"

Honoria nodded. That she verbalized a complaint made it clear that she was struggling. Complaining was simply not a part of her nature.

"But we'll be done in a few minutes, and we should find your father and Marc waiting for us in the cabin. Then everything will be all right, at least for a while."

"But how do you sing? Aren't you tired?"

Alexandra nodded. "More tired than I've been in years. But somehow I enjoy this work." When she saw Honoria's eyes widen, she hurried to add, "I know you've never seen me in a role like this because your father has been a good provider. But at heart I really am a common girl who grew up doing laundry. We all had to work, and laundry somehow appealed to me. I like the idea that I make things clean and bright. It is one of the few activities where you can tell you've made a difference."

"I wish I were as positive as you. But I find the work very tiring."

That's because you are so frail, thought Alexandra, but she didn't say it. "I'm sure it will just take some getting used to. Besides, we should be in Panama in just ten days, so this will be just a short time in passing."

Honoria smiled and nodded.

"I hope that Max is all right. He must get lonely," said Alexandra.

"I'm sure he's having a wonderful time—he always does. He is so curious and energetic."

The exact opposite of his older sister . . . Alexandra chided herself for thinking such a thought. But Honoria felt things deeply and worried incessantly. She had nearly collapsed from the strain of having Marcus lost in New York City, and Alexandra knew that the thought of Henry working in the boiler room had left Honoria almost frantic. It seemed so unfair that such a beautiful young girl should have to bear up under such great emotional burdens.

At the sound of the whistle, Alexandra pulled her hands from the soapy water and began cleaning up. "Well—that's it! We made it through another day."

"And in spite of how hard this is, we're still far better off than Father was yesterday." Honoria wiped her hands and face. She too had been sweating as a result of all the work.

"Yes, but he'll make it through." Alexandra struggled to control the panic that she felt rising. The main reason she'd enjoyed working in the laundry is that it had fully occupied her thoughts, and for a few moments she could forget about the impossible challenge that Henry had set out for himself. She had found him twitching on the floor when she arrived at their cabin the previous evening, sound asleep, but his muscles convulsing involuntarily from the strain. Her heart had ached when he had to get up early in the morning for his next shift and watched with even more dread when Marcus had helped him back to the room later that morning. Now he was finishing up yet another shift, and she could not bring herself to even try to imagine what she would find.

"You're crying, Mama. Did I do that to you? I'm sorry . . ."

Alexandra bit her lower lip. "It's fine, dear." Her voice caught. "In retrospect, I wished we'd stayed in New York for some time so that your father and Marc could have earned enough money for us to pay our way on this part of the journey." Alexandra took a couple of deep breaths to steady her voice. "But your father was insistent, and it will all work out in the end. You'll see."

"Gloria would have been captured by those awful men if we had stayed."

"Yes, we never would have left her to those men." Alexandra said this with an air of resignation. "It was the right thing to do. Still, I can't help but feel that if we'd never met her, things would have . . ."

Honoria instantly regretted that she'd brought this up.

But Alexandra recovered quickly and smiled at her daughter. "Well, the least we can do is return to the cabin with a cheerful face. For what those men of ours have been through, they deserve that."

Honoria tried to return the smile, but failing that, she reached out and took her mother's arm.

* * *

"The catch of the day is excellent, madam. I was allowed a sample and recommend it most highly. It's served with what our chef calls Caribbean spiced rice. I think you will find it an entirely new experience for your palate."

Gloria looked up from the menu in the dining salon.

"I'm in the mood for an adventure—perhaps I'll give it a try." She smiled at the waiter, who nodded appreciatively at having his recommendation accepted. Gloria was an attractive woman, and she was pleased that the men on the crew were happy to flatter her.

"Are you from London?" one of the ladies at her table asked once they'd received their entrées and had begun their meal. "I've always wanted to go to London, but my husband says it's foolishness. Now he's taking me on this awful adventure to California." The woman's eyes misted up, and Gloria quickly responded to avoid the melodrama.

"I'm not from London, although my father has a townhouse there. He's been admitted to Court and so has a chance to mingle with some of the highborn people on occasion."

"Oh, my . . ." said the ladies. Their exclamations of admiration surprised Gloria. It established her preeminence at the table, even though she was quite certain that some of the women came from much greater wealth than she did. But even so, there were still many Americans who were caught up in the trappings of royalty, even though it had been nearly seventy-five years since they fought for independence. *Perhaps it is a false sense of inferiority born of America's very short history as a nation*, she thought to herself. *If only they knew the truth of old families like mine.*

Not wanting all of this to get out of hand, she added, "Of course, the rest of the year we live quite modestly. The most excitement we have is when my father, the mayor of the township where we live, is called upon to host some event and my mother gets to act as hostess. But even then, it's hardly fancy." That was a small lie, since her mother relished her role as hostess and inevitably turned even the smallest of events into lavish affairs. But Gloria desperately wanted to draw attention away from her to someone else in the group.

Instead, one of the ladies responded with, "It must all be very exciting . . ."

Shaking her head ever so slightly, Gloria then nodded pleasantly but said nothing. As the other young women chattered on, she reflected on just how delightful the Caribbean air was to breathe. The sky was blue and the air was heavy with cool moisture. Of course, it was a very different story when they ventured close to some island—then the air grew heavy and hot. But out here in the open, she found herself lulled by the constant splashing of the paddle wheels and the throb of the great engines as they worked untiringly around the clock. Her thoughts turned to Marc and the hard labor he and his kind father were performing to keep this ship headed toward a new life. Those who had saved her from kidnapping and eventual forced marriage and misery.

"Perhaps you dear ladies will excuse me. I think I'd like to take some air on the deck." She was genuinely moved by their looks of disappointment. "Of course any or all of you are welcome to join me, if you like . . ." Again, she found herself quite flabbergasted that virtually all of them arose from the table with her. In some ways it was nice to be the center of attention, once again, so delightfully different from the journey across the Atlantic where she'd been viewed with such suspicion. But this leg of the journey was leading to an unknown and wild destination, and it came at such great personal expense to the Chandlers that it was difficult to enjoy it without the weight of guilt.

* * *

"Oh, Henry. This has got to stop. We've got to call the ship's doctor. Surely he'll write a note excusing you . . ." They had reached their seventh day at sea.

Henry tried to hold up his hand to shush his wife but immediately started coughing again, his handkerchief turning a deep crimson as he coughed up blood, darkened by coal dust. His face was flushed beyond recognition, and Alexandra realized that he was very likely, suffering from heatstroke.

"Quick! We need ice."

"Ice—they'll never give the likes of us any ice—" Marc started to protest, but Alexandra flashed him a look that sent him scampering down to the galley. One of the great miracles of the mid-1800s was that ice cultivated in the lakes and ponds of New England in the winter could be cut into large blocks and stored in sawdust through the summer. New England ice was shipped as far away as Saudi Arabia in the summer, with only minimal loss to melting. This phenomenon was attributed to Yankee ingenuity and was envied the world over. Of course, on a trip like this, the ice was reserved for first-class passengers, so Marc had to plead his case with great vigor before he was able to return to the room with a bucket full of the precious frozen liquid. "This will help," said Alexandra as she started bathing Henry's face and shoulders.

"I can't let him go back down there," said Marc darkly. "He can't take another day. I'm sure of that."

"Of course," replied Alexandra.

Honoria sat on the edge of the bed, stricken. All color had drained from her face.

"I'll tell them that I'll do double shifts. That way they can't be angry at us. They'll get everything they asked for."

"But you can't do double shifts. You are in almost as much trouble as he is."

Marc shook his head furiously. "I am not. I'm doing fine." The truth is that he wasn't doing fine. Nothing in his experience had prepared him for an ordeal like this. Sometimes he was so unbearably hot toward the end of a shift that the image of jumping overboard into the cool waters of the ocean was almost hypnotic, and he had to force himself to stay at his post. "But there's no other way. They won't let us out of the contract—they can't, not out here in the middle of the ocean. So I have to do it. There's no other way."

Marc hated the pained look on his mother's face. She was now in the most impossible situation a woman could face—having to choose between the health of her husband or her child. The sheer agony she felt was evident in every wrinkle on her face.

"I . . . I . . . I don't know what to do," she said.

Henry moaned as she withdrew the cold rag from his face. "There is nothing to do but for me to do my duty," Henry said quietly. The sound of his voice startled nearly everyone in the room since they thought he'd been asleep. "We are nearly halfway there, and I will simply have to bear up. Once we get to Panama, we'll take time off to recover. As Marcus said, there is no other way."

The hopelessness of the situation left everyone silent. Then Max broke the silence. "I'll work in Father's place."

The simultaneous "What?" from Alexandra and Marc was quickly extinguished as Max said more firmly, "I said that I will work in Father's place. I'm fourteen years old, and plenty of boys my age work hard. I can do it, and I will."

Marc shook his head. "That's very brave, but it's not like you imagine. The work is unlike anything I've ever experienced. I'm afraid it's just not possible. But it's a wonderful gesture."

Max grew defiant. "You can't stop me! I won't stand by and watch Father be hurt by all this." Max's voice broke and he covered his face with frustration.

Henry raised his hand, as if to say something, but couldn't make himself talk.

"Maybe Max is right, at least partially," said Honoria. The four of them turned to look at her.

"How so?" asked Marc.

"You volunteered to work double shifts. Perhaps Max could help during at least part of the extra shift. He is strong and his heart is good. That accounts for a great deal."

"See—she's right!" Max was defiant again. "I'll help."

"Max will help me," said Henry, forcing himself to sit up.

"Really, dear," said Alexandra. "You should lie down and rest . . ."

Henry put up his hand. "I'm still the patriarch in this family, so you will listen to me." Alexandra bit her lip, and Marc resolved to hold his tongue. "You are all correct. I should not be doing this. I'm too old and lack the proper conditioning. But I made a contract, and I can't back out of it. But if they will allow Max to step in for even a few moments during the course of my shift, I think it will give me the time I need to catch my breath."

"But he can spell me—"

"No!" said Henry. "I will not allow this to destroy your future, Marc. You are already working harder than you should. I know that you've been drawing double from the coal bunkers so you can send coal to my side of the floor so I don't have to turn and lift it myself. I also know that George Connolly sees you do it but allows it to happen. You're already doing more than your fair share. So you will let me and Max do this. He will support me, you will help us both, and together we'll make our way to Panama. Then we will reassess our strategy before going on to California." Even though he didn't have the energy to make the word *California* sound as if it was followed by an exclamation point, everyone knew that it was. Henry had spoken, and that was that way it would be.

Alexandra cast a quick glance toward Marc, who simply shrugged. On the one hand, she felt enormously relieved to think that Henry would get some help. Then she looked over at Max—a well-built young man, but still so very young. Now she'd have him to worry about, as well. She shook her head and bit her lip.

"You rest now, dear. It's going to be all right, after all." Henry fell back asleep almost instantly.

15—REPRIEVE

In the Caribbean—June 25, 1850

Looking up at the moon, Marc was startled by the sound of Gloria's voice. "It's really quite beautiful, isn't it?"

Marc turned and motioned for her to come join him at the rail. "It's the same moon that shines on England. And California, for that matter. It is a constant companion for us travelers."

"Quite poetic, my young coal-shoveler."

Marc shook his head ever so slightly. This woman was so far disconnected from what was happening on this ship and the impact it was having on his family that it would be irritating if it wasn't just naiveté. The last thing he had time for was romance. Right now he was worrying about how his father and younger brother would survive the next day, and her attempt at flirtation had hit a more sensitive topic than she realized.

"Not poetic—practical. I like to keep myself grounded, and the constancy of the moon helps with that."

"Ah . . ."

Marc had expected more words from Gloria, but she kept her thoughts to herself and simply stood by him. Now he felt as if he should say something, but he just stood there with his elbows on the railing, resting his head. He'd have to break this off soon because he needed rest. He'd only come up on deck because it was so stiflingly hot down in their cabin. Yet he enjoyed being with Gloria. She was more beautiful than ever in the new clothes she'd purchased in New York City. Perhaps these new clothes were more humble than the ones she'd brought from England, making her feel more like a person and less a social statement.

"I love opening the windows of my cabin at night and letting the light flood in, along with the air. I've never been in tropical waters before, and it's so . . . pleasant."

Marc's temper started to flare when he heard this, but he calmed himself down by forcing himself to see things through her eyes. How could she possibly be aware of the nightmare the rest of them were living? They'd decided early on as a family not to subject Gloria to the truth about their situation, since they didn't want to put an undue burden on her, too.

But even with the best of intentions, Marc couldn't stop himself from saying, "Don't get a lot of breeze down where my father and I work. Mostly just heat." He should have stopped there. "And Mother and Honoria don't get much of the Caribbean breeze in the laundry—just tubs of boiling water and hundreds of pounds of soggy bed linens."

Gloria caught her breath. She didn't say anything for a long time and just looked out at the sea. She moved away from him, which, of course, made him feel both vindicated *and* bad. Once again he was surprised that she simply absorbed his criticism. She had changed since that day on the dock of Liverpool. Life had opened her eyes in so many ways—had made her one of them in some aspects. But not in others.

Turning toward her, he said, "Listen. I don't mean to . . . I don't want to ruin . . . but things are very chancy for us right now. I didn't want to tell you . . . Father isn't doing well, and Max is going to have to help to keep things from getting worse. At any rate, I just came up for some air, but now I really need to get some sleep."

"Of course." He was startled to see the distressed look on her face. *Are those tears?* "I hope that your father does all right."

"I hope so, too."

"I should have done something for you, for him, so that he didn't have to do all this work . . ."

"What could you have done? You barely had the money to scrape together a regular fare, and we wouldn't have taken that from you. It's our problem, and we'll solve it."

Marc was flustered by this regret of hers, particularly since she acted so—he didn't know how she acted. *Strange?*

"Yes, well, it's awful what they're doing to him. To your mother . . ." She seemed to want to say more, but Marc was just too tired to stay.

"Yes, well, I guess I'll be off. I hope you have a pleasant evening."

"Thank you." She cleared her throat as if to say something more but then turned away to the rail. Marc walked off more confused than ever.

* * *

George Connolly shook his head. "This is completely irregular. He signed up to do a job, and he needs to do it!"

"You know as well as I do that he's not up to it. Now give the man some dignity and allow my younger brother to help. Plenty of fourteen-year-olds are working every day. They wouldn't turn him away at the Welsh coal mines where this black stuff is dug up, so why should it matter to you if he shovels it into the furnace? This way you get two good workers instead of one who struggles."

Connolly was furious. "This is what you get when an owner meddles where he doesn't belong. I told him not to hire you . . ." He hesitated. "Not you, you're a good worker—you've grown into it. But your father . . ."

"But Mr. Aspinwall did hire us, and now you need us. Please let this happen. It's the only way."

Marc was surprised at how hard he was pushing himself on Connolly. But the stakes couldn't be any higher.

Connolly turned and looked directly at Henry and Max, who were standing off to the side. Henry had planned to make the appeal, but Marc insisted that he do it instead. His fear was that Henry's pride would cause him to give up too quickly on the idea if Connolly hesitated in the least.

"Fine! Your brother can't do any worse and will probably do better. But all this ends in Panama. I'll make sure that no one hires either of them on the Pacific side—it's not fair to the line." The firm set of Connolly's jaw convinced Marc that this wasn't a point worth debating. Besides, the man was right. His father had no business shoveling coal. They'd have to find some other way to make money in Panama so they could pay for passage to San Francisco.

"All right, then. I'll get to work training Max right now."

Connolly chewed furiously on the end of the cigar that was ever-present in his mouth. "Chandler, Chandler Two, and now Chandler Three—what a disaster."

In spite of himself, Marc couldn't help but smile. The three of them were in it for the long haul, but they would do it together.

* * *

"Good afternoon, Gloria."

Gloria looked as if she'd been caught in the act of stealing a neighbor's watermelon. "Oh, why, hello, Mr. and Mrs. Chandler. I'm pleased to see you."

For the first time on the voyage, Henry had found enough energy to wash himself and clean up, and now he and Alexandra were out taking a stroll on the upper deck.

"It's really rather beautiful here," Henry said. "That island is so lush and green."

"Cuba, they tell me," said Gloria. "I'd hoped they'd stop in Havana, but the captain says that the urgency of getting all these gold rush people to California makes that impossible."

Henry raised an eyebrow ever so slightly. "You engage in conversation with the captain?"

"Yes, at dinner . . ." Gloria paused, embarrassed by the luxury in which she traveled. "You know that they were sold out of any second-class cabins, so I really had no choice but to purchase first class."

Henry picked up on her squeamishness. "No need to be embarrassed—we're glad you're having a pleasant voyage." When Gloria failed to respond, Henry went on as pleasantly as possible. "I too had hoped to make a port of call in Cuba. I've heard a great deal about it and always longed to see a tropical island. But now it appears we'll only see it from the ship. But even at that, it's quite impressive, isn't it?"

"Yes, it's very large. From here you could never tell it is an island. It extends as far as the eye can see." The mountainous island, draped in a canopy of tropical green, seemed to extend into infinity as they watched it from the railing. A rain squall darkened one segment of the sky, casting deep shadows on the lush mountain terraces, while the sun shone on a dazzling emerald spot farther down the island that led right down to the beach, making a marvelous contrast that couldn't help but please the eye.

"It's very good to visit with you again. It seems as if you are doing better. Marc . . . had led me to believe that you were under quite a strain."

Henry darkened. "I'm fine. We're doing very well, in fact."

Gloria dropped her gaze, embarrassed yet again by this inscrutable family. "Well, I'm afraid I have to be off. There's a group of us who get together every afternoon . . ."

"Of course," said Alexandra. "Please do have a good day."

After Gloria disappeared into the elegant salon toward the bow of the ship, Henry turned to Alexandra. "You seem very subdued, my dear. You hardly said a word to Gloria."

"Not really. I was being polite to let the two of you chat so amiably."

"Yes, well, I thought perhaps she had done something to upset you. It's just you are usually somewhat more chatty."

Alexandra was thoughtful. "Gloria desperately needed our help at one time. Now she doesn't and has returned to her proper place. I suppose I was reflecting on how different life can be depending on your circumstances. That's all."

Henry knew better than to press harder. Alexandra was worried about him, and he was very sorry about that. Henry sighed. But then he took a deep breath—the air was too pleasant for him to fret over it. Max had made a tremendous difference the past two days, and Henry felt he was finally starting to master the operation.

* * *

"You there! Chandler Three! Get a move on. At this rate we'll never make it to Panama!"

"Yes, sir!" shouted Max. The high pitch to his adolescent voice was so out of place in the engine room that it would have sounded funny had it not been so pathetic.

"You're doing fine," said Marc earnestly. But he knew better. Max had done heroic work the first two days, but by the third day the strain had caught up to him, and his stiff muscles and young frame were being taxed beyond measure. Coal shoveling was work for a man—a man in his prime, not one in his fifties nor one who was only fourteen.

"I'm trying." Max turned and lifted another heavy load—probably almost equal to his own weight. Pivoting to the furnace, he stumbled, the coal in the shovel tumbling to the floor.

"Blast you, Chandler Whatever Number!" Connolly started striding straight toward Max, apparently intent on striking him for his incompetence, but he was stopped in his path by Henry, who forcefully placed himself between the two of them.

"I'll take over now. The boy needs a rest."

Connolly raised his fist as if he was going to hit Henry instead. But then he withdrew. "One incompetent replacing another."

"I can do it," Max said defiantly. "I just stumbled, that's all." But Henry told him to go get some water, and even though the break had only been a few minutes for Henry, he started the laborious work of feeding the hungry maw of the boiler once again.

Marc shook his head in despair. He had no idea what to do next, and they were still at least three days from Panama.

* * *

When Alexandra and Honoria got back to their cabin, they found the three men sound asleep—Henry preferring to sleep on the floor since it supported his aching back, Max in a hammock, and Marc curled up on the ottoman.

"They make quite a sight," said Alexandra.

"I think Father's doing better, don't you?"

Alexandra nodded. "I hope so. It's been a real blessing to have Max working, even though the strain is hard on him." She was hopeful now, with Panama just two days away. She was so enormously proud of Henry for making it nearly two weeks at such incredibly hard labor. Reaching down, she stroked his face. He placed his hand on hers but didn't wake.

* * *

Gloria found herself irritated by the women's chatter. "It seems like we are going so slowly," one had said to the group, to which another had replied, "The last ship made it in less than fourteen days, and we're already past that. I don't know if they're scrimping on coal, but someone should do something about it." The final straw was when one of the women said with disdain dripping from her voice, "My husband tells me they just can't get good help anymore—all the regular crew members went on strike for higher wages, so they picked up some riffraff at the pier to act as stokers. I'm sure that explains why we are so frightfully behind schedule."

Gloria stood up so abruptly that it knocked her chair over. "That's enough! All this complaining when men are down there working themselves to death in unbearable heat and choking on coal dust! You should all be ashamed for their sakes!"

The women were so shocked by this outburst that they covered their faces with their Chinese fans, stunned that they were being attacked on such a frivolous topic.

"I beg your pardon," said the one who had used the "riffraff" reference. She wasn't really begging anyone's pardon, which would be admitting to a mistake, but her words were rather an indirect challenge to Gloria for embarrassing them.

"Yes, I'm sure you do. Well, just know this, ladies. You may think that it's steam that moves this ship forward, but the reality is that it's human toil and labor, and we should be grateful, not spiteful!" She swallowed hard to calm her voice and then, before anyone could respond, quickly added, "And now I will beg *your* pardon, but I need some fresh air. This room is far too *stuffy*." Everyone understood the slight. When no one said anything, she stormed off through the salon doors that led up to the next deck.

16—AMAZING GRACE

In the Caribbean—June 25, 1850

"Let me take my turn," said Henry to Max. "You've worked far too hard."

"It's all right," said Max, although his flushed cheeks suggested otherwise.

"I'm fine," said Henry. "You've given me the rest I need." As Max stepped to the side so that Henry could step forward, Henry paused just long enough to give Max a quick hug. Then he went to work with all the energy he could muster, shoveling the heavy coal into the open grate of the fire.

"It seems hotter than usual!" Henry called over to Marc, who was wiping his brow with the sleeve of his shirt. Marc noted that Henry's face was already red, even though he'd done less work than usual during this shift. But his condition had seemed so precarious for so long that Marc hadn't paid attention.

And then Henry stumbled and fell against the door of the furnace.

Marc was looking forward when it happened, so he didn't react until he heard Max shout out in alarm. Turning, he saw that Henry's face had struck the boiler and that his father was lying where he had fallen without attempting to get away from the heat. With an urgent cry, Marc threw down his shovel and dove to his father.

"Father! Are you all right?" he shouted, but Henry didn't respond. By this point, Max was at his side, shouting, "Papa, Papa!" but to no avail.

"What is it?" asked George Connolly. Upon seeing Henry limp before the boiler, he quickly told Marc to take him up to the open deck where he could get some air. Marc reached under his father, who was now quite light because of all the weight he'd lost.

As they reached the upper deck, Gloria raced to their side. "What happened? Can I do anything to help?"

Next came the captain, attracted by the ruckus. He had not been well-disposed to the Chandlers. "What's this all about, then?" he said impatiently.

"It's my father—he collapsed!" Marc said.

The captain reached down and felt Henry's pulse. "He is still alive, but I doubt he'll recover. He's completely overcome by the heat."

At this wanton lack of compassion, the captain found himself confronted by Gloria, who whirled on him in a fury. "How dare you dismiss this man so lightly—can't you see the trouble he's in?"

"My dear lady, what can I do? He made an agreement, and we've done everything possible to accommodate him. We've given him lighter duty than any of the others in his position and even allowed his son to help on his shift. I really don't see how we can be held to blame."

"It isn't about blame! It's about compassion." Tears streamed down Gloria's face. Seeing no response from the captain, who simply pursed his lips, she turned once more to Marc. "What can I do?"

"Go get Mother and Honoria—and quickly." Marc's voice was dark and frightened. Max looked terrified. Henry was breathing heavily.

"I should have told Mr. Aspinwall to shove off," said George Connolly. "I knew this would turn out bad from the beginning."

When the captain started to reprove him for speaking that way of the owner, Connolly's glare was more than enough to silence even his superior officer.

"Oh, my Henry!" wailed Alexandra as she and Honoria came running toward the spot where Henry lay. By now a crowd was gathering, and they had to force their way through. Kneeling, Alexandra cradled Henry's head in her lap. "Oh, my dear handsome man. Don't leave us—not yet."

"He was doing fine," said Marc. "Max had just taken an extra long turn and Father seemed as if he was ready to go. But as he stepped forward he stumbled . . . I thought he tripped on some coal . . ." His voice trailed off as Marc realized that instead of a stumble he was very likely having heart failure at that very instant. "He just fell forward against the furnace."

It was only then that Alexandra realized there was a bad burn on Henry's shoulder in addition to the cut on his face. The pain of that alone could cause someone to pass out, which gave her hope for just a moment that he might yet rally. But then he groaned, almost a rattle, and she knew that it was vain to hope.

"Henry," she said quietly, whispering in his ear. "Before you go, I want you to know that we love you. You are a brave and strong man who went beyond the limits of endurance for us. We love you." For just a moment his eyelids fluttered and opened and hope flared in her heart. Henry attempted to say something, but his voice was so weak that she couldn't hear it. Leaning down, she asked him to repeat himself and then put her ear close to his lips. The others could see that his lips moved, but to them he was still inaudible. Alexandra gulped and nodded, and glanced up at Marc, which frightened him.

Then Henry went limp. "Henry! Henry!" she pleaded, but to no avail. "Oh, Henry," she said more quietly. What a moment before had been the living, breathing soul of her husband, the man she loved more than any other person in the world, was now nothing more than an empty shell.

Looking up at her children, she choked back tears and said, "He's at rest now. His suffering is over." Honoria let out an inhuman kind of wail and slumped to the deck. Marc put his head in his hands, and Max fell to his knees next to his mother. Alexandra did not cry. Instead, she felt a numbness creeping up her body. "Oh, my dear Henry."

The captain motioned for the crowd to disperse as the family gathered by their mother. Marc looked up at the sky. *Dear Father, how can You let this happen to one as good as he?* It was a sign of his despair that he simply closed his eyes and rested his head on the shoulder of his mother.

* * *

It was Max, perhaps an hour later, who ventured to ask his mother, "What did Father say to you?" Alexandra motioned for him to come near and stroked his hair when he sat next to her on the bed.

"He said, simply, 'Tell Marc it is true—the pearl is worth the price.'" Alexandra worked to clear her throat. "And then he smiled." Alexandra turned to Marc and asked, "I think I know what Henry meant, but can you tell me for sure?"

Marc swallowed hard, embarrassed that his father had to make these his final words. "While coming from England, Father and I had a private talk about Captain Edwards's offer of an education at the university. I suppose I was feeling a bit sorry for myself that I couldn't take up his offer. Father told me that the gospel is the pearl of great price referred to in the New Testament and that perhaps one day I would appreciate it for what it is." Marc looked off into space. "Now he has sealed that thought as a final testimony." Marc found that he could not continue speaking.

Alexandra nodded. The image of Henry's coal-streaked face came into her mind. "And now we will go to Zion for you, my dear. Since the gospel is true, we must go."

17—ON TO PANAMA

June 25, 1850

"YOU HAVE THE PRIESTHOOD, SO please do this for me, in spite of your uncertainty."

Marc was very nervous. He did hold the priesthood but didn't fully know what it meant. His father had loved studying the gospel, but Marc was content simply to attend church out of duty. Now his mother was asking him to offer a blessing before Henry's body was sloughed into the sea. The captain had paused the brief memorial service and was doing his best to remain patient as these odd people struggled with the service. Marc nodded and stepped forward. Trying to remember what he'd heard Henry say at the gravesite of an elderly member of the Church, he invoked his priesthood, spoke in the name of Jesus Christ, and dedicated the spot as the final resting place of Henry James Chandler. Embarrassed by his clumsiness, yet moved by the feeling his words had invoked, Marc stepped quickly to the side, nodding to the captain as he did so.

"To the deep we commend this soul," said the captain in a sonorous voice, and then two crew members tipped the platform on which Henry's swaddled body lay. His remains went sliding into the deep blue waters of the Caribbean. Honoria sobbed quietly, and Marc did his best to hold back the tears that wanted to come. Max accepted a hug from his mother.

Off to the side, the women who had run afoul of Gloria clucked quietly that Henry had been a fool to sign up for such arduous work, thereby relieving themselves of feeling any guilt. Gloria stood off to the side, looking absolutely stricken. She quickly excused herself when the service was over, explaining awkwardly that she needed to return to her cabin.

As Marc started to turn to take his mother back to their cabin, which would feel empty the rest of the voyage, George Connolly approached them.

"Listen, Chandler—Marc—I'm sorry about this. I should have been more forceful with Mr. Aspinwall." He stopped and shuffled, aware that this was not the time to try to exonerate himself. "At any rate, I just want to say that your father was a very good man who tried harder than anyone I've ever known. I'm sorry this happened to him."

Marc was surprised to find that he held no animosity for Connolly. In fact, he'd felt all along that Connolly was right about Henry. "You were very fair to us, and Father had no ill feelings for you. He admired you for the excellence of your leadership. Thank you for giving us time for this memorial service."

Connolly stiffened, his surprise at this generous response evident in his face. "Yes, well. Take your time."

"I'll be to work as scheduled. Now more than ever we want to make it to Panama."

"About your brother . . ."

"He'll work in place of Henry," said Alexandra quickly. "My husband would insist that we do our part, and Max is ready."

Max nodded his agreement.

"Yes, well, that won't be necessary. With such a short distance left, I've asked the other men to lengthen their shifts just a little, and we'll make it without the boy." When Alexandra started to protest, Connolly held up his hand. "I don't want anything else on my conscience." Alexandra nodded, relieved beyond measure.

The crowd, which had been transfixed by this little drama, started to disperse. "Come on, then, Mother, let me take you below." None of them noticed Gloria standing in a shadow, watching as they made their way. Nor did they hear her whisper, "Why was I so selfish?" Of course it didn't matter now.

* * *

In Port at Aspinwall, Panama—July 1850

The Pacific Mail Steamship Company was the single most important entity in all of Central America in the summer of 1850, which is why the village at the eastern terminus of the Isthmus of Panama was named in honor of William H. Aspinwall. It was a dubious distinction, given the fetid condition of the place: raw sewage pouring into the streets, malaria and yellow fever periodically decimating the miserable residents who eked out a meager living by serving the needs of the highly stressed passengers that disembarked from the various steamships and sailing vessels that now appeared with increasing regularity.

The climate of the tropical rainforest made it easily one of the most beautiful places in the world, with a variety of lush tropical plants, birds, and wildlife that were magnificent to behold. But the price for such incredible beauty was some of the highest rainfall in the world, which, in the blazing tropical sun, led to almost unbearable humidity. With nothing to cool the daytime air, the choice was either to bake in the stifling heat of the sun or get steamed in the shade of the jungle canopy. This is why Panama was a favorite haunt for bandits and criminals—a place where they could slip out of sight with just a moment's notice and where civilized people chose not to come.

All of that changed with the discovery of gold in California. The mania that followed had made Panama, with its slender fifty miles of tropical jungle separating the Atlantic from the Pacific, the most prominent transit point in the entire world and the choke point for travelers wishing to make their way quickly from one coast to the other. It had become even more important with the recent victory of United States troops in the Mexican–American War, won at least in part by the grueling 2,500-mile march of the members of the Mormon Battalion through the desolate deserts of the Southwest leading to San Diego. What had been Alta California under Mexican rule was now a territory of the United States, and the people of California were anxious to link the two coasts together as quickly as possible. They needed to attract enough permanent residents to overwhelm the remnant of Mexicans and native Californians who might long for the old regimes. So Panama was now of vital interest to both the United States government and the more than 100,000 "forty-niners" who were desperate to reach California for gold.

For these reasons, the village of Aspinwall, a port that had been hard-pressed to service the needs of just *hundreds* of travelers, now struggled with thousands—tens of thousands—who arrived by boat daily with no greater desire than to quickly make their way to the Pacific coast and on to San Francisco. "It's just fifty miles to cross the isthmus, and then on to California!" many had exclaimed, few realizing the human toll in tropical disease and rain-soaked skin that would be extracted mile by painful mile.

"The usual way," said George Connolly to Marc, "is to take a tender to port and then to charter seats on dugout canoes that the natives will paddle up the Chagres River as far as possible. That will cover more than half the distance. Then you take mules down to Panama City, where, if you're lucky, a northbound steamship will take you on to California."

"But how much does the canoe passage cost?"

"It depends on the traffic. Our ship is bulging with people, so I'm sure the available spots will sell out quickly to those most willing to pay."

"And for those of us who may not be able to pay?"

Connolly shook his head. "I really don't understand why you came so ill-prepared. It seems completely out of character for the kind of man your father was."

"It's complicated. We thought that because my father worked for Cunard, we could get complimentary or at least significantly reduced fares to California. But that didn't happen, and so what few funds we have must be conserved." Marc did his best to conceal the desperation he felt.

"Well," said Connolly, "if ever there was a time not to scrimp, this is it. Nothing else you encounter will be as dangerous as Panama. Not only are there dangerous people here, but the climate is a bitter enemy to northerners who are not accustomed to the tropical heat or the diseases that infest this place." He looked across the horizon scornfully. "All the pictures that they paint on advertisements show it as a tropical paradise. But for my money, those pictures just conceal how alien it is to people of our background. You need to get through it as fast as possible if you are to survive."

Marc nodded uncertainly. "We'll do what we must, then. Do you know if there's work available for someone like me in Panama City on the Pacific Coast? If I spend all our money on the transit, I'll have to find some way to make funds over there to pay for our passage north."

Connolly shook his head. "I honestly don't know. At times there are as many as several thousand people stuck in Panama City waiting for ships to come into port. There was an incident last year where near riots broke out after more than a month of people waiting. When a sailing ship showed up from Peru, the captain had to stand offshore for fear of people mobbing his ship. As it was, he doubled his fares to San Francisco and still wound up with a ship that was overloaded by at least fifty percent. So if you get there when there are no ships waiting in port, that's the kind of competition you'll find for a job."

Marc sunk down on the bench that was lodged into the side of the deck railing. "I don't know what to do."

"The tragedy is that in a couple of years, they expect to have a railroad across this place. Then the passage can be made in a matter of hours. The wait will never be longer than a day."

"A railroad? Across *that*?" said Marc, pointing toward the low mountain peaks to the west. "Is that possible?"

"Possible? It's a reality. Work started last month. Of course, the grading will be backbreaking work as they cut through the highest parts of the mountain range to maintain an acceptable grade. And as hard as the grading work is, it may be easier than cutting out all of the trees, plants, and bushes. But once it's finished, all this misery will disappear behind the little steam engines."

"Amazing."

"Some even say a canal will be built. The French have already started digging what they hope to make as a sea level route that would take advantage of the Chagres River, but others say it will have to be made with locks and cuts to make it through the hills. That's not likely to happen soon. What's more likely is that someone will build a canal in Guatemala, and then Panama will be abandoned forever." Connolly looked at the tropical jungle shore, "And to my way of thinking, good riddance."

Marc sat quietly thinking through the money they had available, the potential cost of bidding against the first- and second-class passengers for passage up the Chagres, which almost brought him to the point of concluding they would have to take the old and over-grown Las Cruces jungle trail the entire distance, in spite of all the time and risk that entailed. Then a thought struck him. "You said they're starting work on the grading for the railroad right now?"

Connolly nodded.

"Do they need workers? Could I get a job?"

"Oh, Chandler—don't even think about it. You've nearly killed yourself on this run. Working in that jungle would be a new kind of misery you can't even imagine. Nothing personal, but you and your family are meant to be scholars or merchants, not hard laborers."

Marc smiled. "That's what you'd think. But unfortunately that's not an option right now. I have to make money somehow, and there might be less competition on this side than in Panama City. Besides, I assume they'd have to get me up to the work area, so maybe I could negotiate travel for my family at the same time."

Connolly pursed his lips. "I don't know what drives you, but if that's what you want, I know some people. I'll put in a good word for you."

Marc started to say thanks, but Connolly held up his hand. "Don't thank me, because it may be the biggest mistake of your life. You could easily die out there. So if you decide to do this, just promise me that you won't work for more than a few months. Every day you spend in that jungle increases the likelihood that you'll never come out of it. Once you've earned the money you need, move along. Do you understand?"

Marc nodded. "I'm sure I don't understand what's in store, but I've never been in better shape than right now, so I believe I can take it for a time." He looked up at George. "But I have learned enough to know to take you seriously. So if you say to move on as soon as possible, I'll make sure I do exactly that."

"I'll make the arrangements." Connolly turned to leave then hesitated. "I don't know what it is that's pulling you out to California, or wherever else it is you're going, but it had better be worth the price."

Marc was thoughtful. "I believe it is." He engaged Connolly's eyes again. "My father was convinced it is, so I'm going to go find out."

* * *

July 1850

It's not that any city smelled very good, but the odors in Aspinwall were more than some could take, and women were known to faint from the stench.

"We've got to get out of here," said Gloria desperately.

"Oh, we'll get out, but I'm not sure that what's waiting is much better," replied Marc. Miraculously they had managed to find a hotel room, although Gloria had to share it with them. The flimsy construction made it feel as if it could collapse under them at the slightest jolt, and it was unnerving to share space with so many people.

"I thought it was crowded on the ships, but nothing compares to this," Gloria said.

Marc nodded. Earlier that week Gloria had offered to pay everyone's way up the river by canoe, although she didn't say how she could suddenly afford that. It didn't really matter because two things made it impossible, anyway. First, when Marc heard how much the price of passage from Panama City to San Francisco had gone up, he knew that he'd have to earn more money than they now had even if the transit was free, and the railroad construction seemed the best way to do it. Second, by the time Gloria had gotten around to making her offer, all of the available spots had been sold out.

So now they were stuck until the railroad made arrangements to move them some ten miles inland, where the grading was taking place. The only reason the bosses at the railroad had acceded to his demands that they make a place for his family was that it was almost impossible to hire workers. Every healthy young man wanted to go to California to find gold before it was all played out. They were to set out the next day.

Talking about Gloria's offer of passage up the river, Alexandra had said, "I don't even think she has the money to do it; if she did, why did she wait so long to offer when we really needed help on the passage from New York to Panama?"

To which Marc had replied, "Even if she had the money, we couldn't take it. It's hers, and she will need it in California. Besides, I'm responsible for the family, and I'll take care of you."

You are proud, just like your father, thought Alexandra. But she said nothing.

18—WORKING ON THE RAILROAD

July 1850

THE IDEA OF A RAILROAD across Panama was not new in 1850. President Simon Bolivar of La Gran Colombia, which included the territories of Venezuela, Ecuador, Colombia, and Panama, had paid for an initial study as early as 1827, when railroad technology was brand new. But lack of funding and political turmoil made it impossible to pursue. President Andrew Jackson of the United States made a serious effort again in 1836, but the financial panic of 1837 brought an end to those plans. It was William H. Aspinwall who made the idea a reality after Pacific Mail secured the combined $500,000 route subsidy for steamship service to San Francisco. With predictable revenue for the steamships, he was able to raise a million dollars of capital in New York City to formally incorporate the Panama Railroad Company, with construction beginning in May 1850.

"You say they'll cook for the workers?" the railroad recruiter asked.

Marc nodded. Even with his inexperience, Marc could see that the camp could desperately use the service of women. Hiring people for the railroad was painfully difficult because so many wanted to hurry on to the goldfields.

"And you'll stay for at least six months? That's absolutely essential." The voice of George Connolly speaking inside his head urged three months, but the recruiter was wise enough to know that men would abandon the task just as soon as they had enough money, so they had imposed a minimum.

"I'll commit to six months."

"You'll forfeit your bonus if you don't. It will make up nearly half of your total income, so you'd be a fool to leave early."

"I understand—I forfeit my bonus if I leave early." Marc leaned forward, putting his arms on the table as he looked directly at the recruiter. "There's something you should know about me—if I tell you that I'll do something, I'll do it, no matter what the cost. If I say six months, it will be six months." A legacy left by his father.

"All right, then, we'll agree to your terms as well. Lodging for you, your mother, sister, and brother, as well as this other lady you mentioned." The sound in the recruiter's voice at the mention of Gloria irritated Marc, loaded with innuendo as it was, but he knew it would do no good to try to explain the relationship. *I can't explain it myself,* he thought. *Why she chose to stay with us rather than just go it alone with her own money, I don't know.* But stay she had, and now he was responsible for her as well.

"But the women have to work just like you and your brother . . ."

"They will—I told you that you can rely on our word."

"All right, then . . ."

"But my brother—he's just fourteen, and you agreed to find work that is suitable. No hard labor." Marc's voice had finality to it.

The recruiter shook his head. "You make a lot of demands for a person applying for a job. Usually it's the other way around."

"And usually you're not competing for men to work in a jungle when there's gold less than three weeks away in California."

The recruiter growled. "Fair enough. Sign here. You can make top money if you stay the whole six months."

Marc bit his lip and signed.

* * *

Panama—Late August 1850

"I don't know what I hate worse, the rain or the mosquitoes." Marc swatted at the cloud of insects buzzing around his head.

"That's easy—the mosquitoes. The rain cools you off, at least. The mosquitoes just suck you dry and fill you with poison," said Norman Bellweather, Marc's coworker, in a familiar British accent, every now and then bringing a wave of nostalgia with it. Of course, Norman was from a borough in London that was very different from the area where Marc had grown up, which meant it was almost as foreign as a separate nation. But at least the base language was common and not at all like the lazy-sounding American accent that was so hard to follow. Marc always had to strain to follow the instructions of Rex Spafford, chief foreman, who was from someplace called Atlanta. Spafford had a particularly troublesome accent that someone had called a drawl, and, boy, was it ever drawn out. It made Marc's head hurt just thinking about it.

"Well, we're going to have to move that whole darn mountain down here to fill in this swamp," Marc said. "I don't know how long I can go on shoveling dirt into three feet of standing water. My feet are turning into fins!"

Marc was pleased that Norman laughed. After three weeks on this miserable job, Marc found that he was happy. It made no sense, because the work was backbreaking. But while everyone else complained of the insufferable humidity, all Marc could think about was that it wasn't nearly as miserable as feeding the furnace on the steamship. The work was almost the same, except that they shoveled gravel instead of coal, but there wasn't the incessant roar of the fire and the swaying of the ship. Now you just stuck your shovel into the pile of gravel that was brought forward by the little tender engine and kept shoveling until the pile was gone. He liked the regularity of the work and the fact that he was able to provide for his family. His mother and sister seemed to enjoy cooking for the men, and they were treated with the greatest respect.

Gloria was an object of fascination for the men, because she was so beautiful, but it didn't take long for the others to figure out that she was strictly hands off—she had made that clear in a hurry. Most thought her stuck-up. For his part, Marc was puzzled about why she had become so quiet. He knew that she hated the kind of work she was expected to do, but it was more than that. Something fundamental was bothering her, but he couldn't tell what. He shook his head to clear his thoughts. He hated it when he found himself thinking of Gloria. At times she acted as if she really had a connection with Marc, but then she consistently pulled back.

To divert his thoughts, he said to Norman, "Kind of funny how we move out into the swamp to a soggy spot where you worry you'll never be able to pull your feet out of the muck, and then you start shoveling gravel until you build your way up onto solid ground for a time."

"And then the blaggards send you back down into the swamp!" Norman stretched his back. At this point they had reduced their pile and were waiting for the next train to come forward with a new load of gravel. It gave them a chance to take a drink of water, swat several hundred thousand mosquitoes off their face, arms, and other places, and just generally take a moment to recover their strength for the next round of shoveling.

"Y'all doin' all right?" Marc turned at the sound of Spafford's voice.

"As well as a person can do in a place like this."

"This ain't nothin'! Oh, it's hot, I give you that. But no hotter than Atlanta, and we got every bit as much humidity. And trees—you should just see all the wonderful trees we have back there. Not these pathetic ficus trees and palms that lie rotting everywhere, but good substantial trees like mahogany and magnolia."

"I'm told they have magnolia trees farther inland," said Marc, more to change the conversation than anything else.

"Ah've heard that too, but I'll have to see it to believe it. Meanwhile, we're in the swamps, and, not to disparage your fine work an' all, but this ain't no place for white people to be working. Back in Georgia we'd have our slaves at this, and they'd fit right in with this swamp. They'd love it. This place is probably just like Africa, where they came from."

"I'm personally glad that there aren't any slaves working here, since I wouldn't have a job, but not really sure why you don't employ indentured servants, since it's less costly," said Norman.

"Mr. Aspinwall is from New York—do I need to say more? A nice fellow an' all, but not always so practical."

Spafford was an extremely amiable fellow, a bit rotund and not well-suited to doing any physical labor himself. It was often a topic of discussion among the working men about why he had gotten the foreman's job in the first place. Most concluded it was likely he knew somebody in the company, and they found a spot for their friend. Still, he was a lot better than some of the taskmasters on other crews who drove the men with contempt. Spafford was both fair and reasonable in his demands.

"We abandoned slavery in England nearly twenty years ago," said Marc, surprised at himself for raising such a controversial topic. The last thing he should do was provoke his supervisor. But instead of shutting up, he found himself continuing. "I'm surprised that a country as civilized as America still allows it. After all, you're the ones who said all men are created equal." Marc knew that he was running a risk here, because Rex Spafford was a confirmed Southerner. *But you're the one who brought it up, and America's hypocrisy on the issue of slavery is a bit galling.* Marc braced for the reply.

"You're not goin' to bait me on that one, Chandler. Circumstances are different in the South than they are in England. It's cold where you come from, and our slaves wouldn't like it at all. But they like Georgia. It suits them just fine."

"I can't imagine they like being held in servitude, with their families broken apart whenever it strikes their owners' financial interest." Marc caught the warning glance from Norman but couldn't seem to stop himself. Apparently there was more of the idealist in him than he realized.

"There you go again, tryin' to get me riled. I know how you people see it, and I can even understand why you'd think the way you do. I'm more open than most Southerners. But the truth is that our 'peculiar institution' is just what's needed for our people. They're like children, really, and they need a guidin' hand. That's all. We spend a lot of money on our slaves, and the last thing we're gonna do is abuse them. Now how'd we get started on this anyway?"

"You said that this is the perfect place—"

"Oh, yes. Well, that was just talk on my part. The fact is that it's up to us to make it happen, since we have to do with what we have. I don't own no slaves; most Southerners don't, you know, maybe only five percent or something. So you're the closest thing I've got. Right now you work for me, and I see that there's another train coming." Spafford's voice had lost its warmth, and Marc knew he was in trouble when he saw the expression on Norman's face. It was stupid for him to have said what he said. After all, on something as controversial as slavery, it was unlikely that he could do anything to change Spafford's opinion, anyway. Spafford moved off a ways, and Norman sidled over to Marc.

"You should apologize," he whispered. "You had no right goading him like that."

"He has no right standing up for slavery—" Marc choked the words, afraid that Spafford would hear. "At any rate, I'm entitled to my opinion as much as the next man."

"Entitled, yes, but that doesn't mean you should be stupid. You'll get all of us in trouble, and for what?"

Marc was angry now, frustrated by his own inability to keep quiet and yet defiant that people should support slavery. Slavery was barbaric, no matter what the excuses given for it, and if people said nothing, then nothing would ever change. *Still, I need this job, and Spafford is the most decent foreman on the worksite, aside from this obvious difference of opinion.*

Marc moved closer toward Spafford. "I'm sorry if I provoked you. Sometimes I do that . . ."

"No, no. You were perfectly right to talk about it. I brought it up. The truth is that it's a big issue everywhere, particularly now that California has come into the Union. There's gonna be a big fight over that, I can promise you. There is many a Southerner who is gonna want to move out there to make their fortune in farming, and they'll want to bring their slaves with them. Meanwhile, our brethren in the North are gonna try to say no, and then there will be a fight. You can mark my words on that!"

"California? I had no idea that would be an issue."

"Well, it will be. Not now, not while gold is all the thing. But in time it will matter. The main thing is that we think people up North should keep their noses out of our business. We're smart people in the South, and we'll figure it out someday."

"Yes, sir. At the very least I shouldn't talk about such things on the job."

Spafford nodded. "Good advice for all of us, I suppose. Now let's drop it."

Marc marveled at the man's self-restraint and realized that he'd misjudged his supervisor. The slowness of his speech had made Marc prejudiced against him—judging that he must be slow-witted. But the truth was, the man was very broad-minded and tolerant and was undoubtedly better informed on many things than Marc was. He'd never thought about California having anything to do with slavery, after all.

"Well, right now I have to get ready to become waterlogged again," said Marc, as cavalierly as possible. "It's at times like this that I wish I could walk on water." He needed this job, and he didn't want to be on anyone else's crew. He hoped Spafford wouldn't hold a grudge. Fortunately, Spafford laughed. "We all need to be like the old water striders that skip along on the surface of the ponds back home. Skinny little bugs that can walk right on top of the water. Mean, though—they stick their little fangs into some other insect and just suck the life right out of it. We don't want to be like that, do we?"

"Sounds like mosquitoes, to me," muttered Norman, to which both Marc and Spafford laughed. Marc was grateful the moment had passed but shaken that he could see the world so differently from the way such an otherwise intelligent and informed man did. He realized that he had much to learn about American ways.

The train came chugging up, still some two or three hundred feet away, and Marc got ready to start the arduous task of moving the gravel forward to the end of the grade. Just as soon as they got the foundation secure, new tracks would be laid so that the next time the train could come even closer. It would be like that until they reached the edge of firm ground on the western side of the swamp, and then they'd start hacking their way through the jungle with picks while using their shovels to scrape out a level roadbed. Marc suspected they wouldn't be there by the time they got into the jungle, at the rate they were going. He wouldn't regret working in this place, because it gave them what they needed. But he wouldn't miss it, either. He hoped they would have enough money at the end of the six-month commitment to continue on to San Francisco. He caught Norman looking at him strangely out of the corner of his eye. *Probably thinks I'm daft for provoking the boss, and I probably am.*

* * *

Panama—Late September 1850

"A little lighter on the potatoes, if you don't mind. We have to haul them more than two thousand miles, and I don't want the men wasting them," Alexandra's supervisor said.

Alexandra nodded. She wasn't nearly as content in Panama as Marc was. Not that she minded the work. It was fine, and she liked the men. Even though they were a hard lot, they treated her and Honoria with respect, probably because they realized what a treat it was to have well-cooked food. It was the heat—the unbearable, always present, completely oppressive heat. She had no idea how very much she could miss England, where it was always cool, even in the summer.

"I can certainly give the men smaller initial portions and let them come back if they're hungry," Alexandra said to her supervisor, a man who had run the kitchen before she got there but who now pretty much trusted everything to her care.

"No, it's not that I want them to be hungry. We need well-fed crews so they can work hard. Just don't let them waste it. The cost of getting food here is staggering."

Alexandra nodded and returned to the boiling pot of turnips that would give the men iron. It was well-known to help women, as well, so she insisted that Honoria eat them liberally to build her blood.

"Are you doing all right, dear?" Alexandra asked her daughter.

Honoria wiped her brow. If the heat was bothersome to Alexandra, it was downright oppressive to Honoria.

"I'm fine." She tried to smile. "I just wish I could find a way to be a bit cooler."

"Don't worry," said Gloria. "It will rain soon enough, and then you'll shiver as you always do." This was not said unkindly, but Honoria interpreted it as a rebuke. Her mother noticed her bite her lip.

"Perhaps you could bring me that kettle," Honoria said to Gloria. Gloria sighed but delivered the kettle without complaint. At first Gloria had planned to just pay some money for her room and board while waiting for the Chandlers to accumulate enough to make their way across Panama and on to San Francisco, and she was dumbstruck when the railroad company said that they didn't need her money and that the only way she could stay in camp was to work.

Alexandra had not intervened when Marc suggested that she hire the natives to take her upstream and on to Panama City, but Gloria had insisted that she stay with the family. Now the adjustment to physical labor taxed her greatly, and occasionally she became exasperated. Alexandra wished that she could figure out why Gloria had chosen to stay with them—was she frightened to go it alone? Was she interested in Marc, which sometimes appeared to be the case? Whatever it was, Alexandra felt sorry for her because her life had changed so completely.

"You look quite nice in that dress," Alexandra said to Gloria to make conversation.

Gloria smiled a wan smile. "I'll have to throw this and the rest of my clothes out when we get to California. I hope I can find a good dressmaker in San Francisco. I wish I knew what it was like out there."

"I think all of us worry that we've left civilization forever," said Alexandra. "But something tells me there will be dressmakers and other amenities." She smiled. "It can't be worse than here."

Gloria returned her smile. "I have to agree with that!"

"Look, there's Marc and Max!" said Honoria with joy. "Their shift is over!"

Alexandra waved to Marc, who looked completely spent after another exhausting day in the sun. Max looked better, having spent another day learning how to run one of the small steam locomotives. In fact, he looked quite cheerful. Alexandra was grateful that the company men had proved true to their word and were training Max for work that he could do at his age. For their part, the company thought it a good idea to put a scrawny kid on the engine to free up a full-grown man for work on the roadbed.

"Have some water," said Gloria, taking a ladle over to Marc. "You need to rest." He slumped onto a bench in the kitchen.

"It smells wonderful in here!" Max said.

"I'm afraid it's mostly turnips," said Alexandra.

Marc laughed. "Just what a growing boy needs—it builds the blood, you know!"

19—CANDLE TO FLAME

November 1850

THE FAMILY GATHERED FOR THEIR evening meal. "Don't you think
you could go a little slower?" Marc asked Max. "It seems like we get
one load moved and there you are with another." He knew that this
would please Max, who took great pride in the fact that he could help
run a railroad locomotive. His job was assistant fireman, in which he
monitored the various gauges that gave them vital information like the
water level in the boiler and the steam pressure available to go to the
small pistons. Under the direction of the fireman, he could open the
valves to release more water to the boiler or open an escape valve if the
pressure built up faster than the pistons could draw it off. It was just
the kind of thing Max loved. He also helped throw wood onto the fire
when told, although the fireman usually did that. Typically the engine
had just two people on it, but his fireman had managed to convince
the bosses that with Max's help he could do the job enough faster to
justify Max's half-pay. The train itself wasn't all that much, usually
never more than two or three cars loaded with gravel, railroad ties,
and such. But it still took a full head of steam, and they were praised
when they could turn things around more quickly than another crew.

"You know I can't slow down deliveries," replied Max in a very
serious voice. "We've got to run as efficiently as possible." Marc
suppressed the urge to tell him that it was a joke, recognizing that
this was all very important to Max. In spite of everything the rest of
them had said to persuade him that he wasn't responsible for Henry's

death, Max continued to feel guilty that he hadn't been able to relieve his father of the duty completely. So now he worked even more diligently, taking virtually none of his payment in script for his own use but turning it in to the common fund to help the family make their way on to California.

"All right, then, but maybe if you tell me how the thing works, I can sabotage it so my mates and I don't have to work so hard." Max turned his head in alarm then finally laughed when he realized Marc was joking with him all along. "Seriously, I'd like you to tell me about how the thing works since it looks like you have a much more interesting job than I do."

"Really? Or are you still joking?"

"Nope, I really want to know. Tell me how a railroad locomotive works out here in the swamp."

Max was pleased to no end and started into a lengthy explanation of the inner workings of a railroad locomotive, right from the firebox to the steam chamber, then on to the pistons and the wheels. Before long he had all of them interested, not so much in the engine as much as how someone his age could master so much detail.

"And you're the one who makes it all go," said Honoria.

Max nodded in satisfaction. "Not completely, but I think I could run it if I had to. Tim, the engineer, said he'll let me try it in a week or two. He's started showing me the controls he uses. Pretty soon I'll know the whole thing inside and out."

"Good for you, little brother. But it keeps coming back to that gravel you keep shoving off on those of us with shovels. Don't get too good at what you do." This time Max laughed, secure that he was being taken seriously.

After four months, the small gravel hill to the east of Aspinwall had been pretty well moved to the roadbed that ran parallel to the Chagres River. The Chagres was an oddity of a river in that it's total fall from highest point to lowest was approximately 250 feet. At less than forty miles in total length, it didn't have long to think of itself as a river. But when the rains came, it carried a considerable amount of water, often flooding out into the swamps on the Atlantic side of the Isthmus of Panama. The employees' job would be less miserable if they could avoid the river altogether, except for the fact that it had managed to carve out the most manageable route through the foothills that, at their top, represented the Continental Divide between the Atlantic and the Pacific. So it made sense to extend the roadbed right from the ocean through the swamps and then up into the hills.

There was a lull in the conversation, and Marc turned to Gloria, who had been listening from a distance.

"Care to go for a walk?" he asked. It was evening, and the most intense heat had started to cool in the shadows.

"I'd like that."

Marc noticed Honoria roll her eyes at this, but he proceeded to take Gloria's arm anyway. They lived in two tents: one shared by the three women, Marc and Max in another with four other fellows, including Marc's working partner, Norman Bellweather.

Once outside the tent, he said easily, "This is probably the most beautiful place I've ever imagined, even though the weather is often unpleasant."

"It seems to me that this climate agrees with you. When I first saw you, I thought you a bit skinny, but now you're quite muscular and tan."

That pleased Marc. "Why, thank you. I had no idea you'd noticed."

Gloria raised an eyebrow but then simply fanned herself.

"Well, I guess I should say that you look—"

"Don't say a word," she broke in. "I look a mess. This place most definitely does not agree with me. My clothes are horrid, I've ruined every dress I own except for one that I'll save to the last breath, if for no other reason than I can be buried looking decent. And my hair needs attention. So don't you say anything about how I look."

"I was going to say that you look a little less stressed, of late. I was hoping that maybe you were getting used to things."

"Oh. I guess I am. I certainly appreciate the hardships our household servants endured back in England. I'm sure I'll never take that for granted, again—not that I'll ever have servants or the reprieve from hard work, for that matter."

At this point they had made their way to a trail that led into the jungle. There was just enough light that Marc felt they could make their way back, so he refrained from going under the thick canopy of trees. The ground around them was covered in ferns and various types of palm leaves, which proved endlessly fascinating to him with the unbelievable variety of colors and flowers.

"Have you thought any more about what you'll do when you get to California?" Marc asked. "If the people we've met so far on the journey are any example of what it's like out there, then it seems it will be totally foreign to what you must be used to."

"I've been thinking that maybe I'll open a dress shop. From what some of the men have said who have been there, San Francisco is growing rapidly, and now that Mrs. Fremont is living there, more women are being attracted to the place." By Mrs. Fremont, she referred to the wife of John Fremont, famous explorer and one of the wealthiest men in California. She was also the daughter of a United States senator, so she was very much at ease in the best society. "At any rate, I believe that I understand fashion as well as anyone, and it would be an honorable way for me to make a living."

Marc nodded. "That sounds like a good idea. You probably couldn't do that in Utah, could you?"

"Utah?" She stopped and turned to look at him, the shock registering on her face. "Who ever said anything about Utah? It's in the middle of a desert, for heaven's sake."

Marc blushed, which humiliated him even more. "It's just that we've gotten quite used to having you around. But of course that can't last forever."

"I thought you were going to stay in California—that your church was going to locate there because it's a more favorable place for colonization."

Marc shook his head. "Not from what I hear from the men coming back that way. There are Mormons there, but Brigham Young has called most of them back to Utah, making it clear that Salt Lake City and the huge territory surrounding it is where the Saints are to gather. So I suppose we'll have to make our way there."

"Oh. I didn't know that." Gloria went quiet for a time. "I guess I'd imagined that you'd always be nearby, in San Francisco."

Marc felt dispirited. He'd never felt comfortable enough to openly express affection for Gloria, but he also liked having her near him. He could be interested in her, but the difference in their social status would have made it very difficult for them in England, if she were interested in him, and he didn't know how to get around that, even out here.

"Well, I suppose we'll figure all of that out when we get to California." He laughed. "We certainly haven't been in too much of a hurry to get anywhere since landing here in Panama."

"No, we have not. I should have gone on ahead . . ." She hesitated. "Somehow I feel like I'm supposed to remain attached to you, at least for the present."

Marc decided that he liked that.

Gloria, her arm nestled in his while they walked, used her foot to swish a small iguana off the trail. Marc marveled that she thought nothing of doing that, while most wellborn women would have shrieked or fainted. "Well, I see that we're back at our tents. And you need to get up early to get ahead of the heat of the day."

Marc nodded. "Thanks for walking with me."

As she pulled her arm from his, he did something incredibly impulsive—he reached over and gave her a peck on the cheek. Stepping back quickly, to avoid the expected slap, he was surprised to hear her say, "Well that certainly took long enough," and then she laughed at the astonished look on Marc's face.

Before he could stay anything, she said, "Good night!" and then stepped inside the tent.

* * *

February 1, 1851

"We'll give you a raise and a spot in management if you'll stay. What's another six months?" Spafford said to Marc.

"I appreciate the offer," said Marc. "I really do. People told me this would be the worst job ever, but I haven't minded it. In fact, it feels pretty good to see what we've accomplished."

"See, then you oughta give it another six months. Besides, that little brother of yours can certify as an engineer, and think of what that would do for him." Max shuffled uneasily, knowing that the family needed to move on but tempted by the offer and gratified by the recognition.

"I just don't think we can do it, Mr. Spafford. It's been eight months since we left England, and my sister's health just isn't that good. We need to get her to a drier climate. Besides, we'll need time

in San Francisco before moving on to our final destination." He chose
not to mention Salt Lake City because of the odd reaction it sometimes prompted.

Spafford nodded. "Well, then, I guess it's time to say good-bye.
You've been a good worker. If things don't work out in the West like
you hope, come back this way and we'll put you to work again. At the
rate we're going, we'll probably still be at it for at least another couple
of years. You could easily become a supervisor."

"Thank you—who knows but that we might take you up on it
someday." Marc didn't think this likely, but it never hurt to have
friends. Spafford was about to turn and walk away when Marc
stopped him. "You know, just in case we do come back, maybe you
could write a reference, if it's not too much trouble."

"Not at all. And while I'm at it, I'll write one for your brother.
People aren't likely to believe that he knows as much about locomotives as he does, so we'll put it on official Panama Railroad statio-
nery—that way there can be no doubt."

Marc was pleased to see the grin this put on Max's face.

"Thank you, Mr. Spafford. That would be great," Marc said as he
put his hand on Max's shoulder.

"If you're not leaving until the end of the week, I'll get it to you
before then."

"That's when we start up the river." Now, with the resignation
accepted, a tinge of excitement found its way up Marc's spine. While
he appreciated the top wages he'd been earning, he was also restless
to get on with their lives. It really was important to get Honoria to
a better climate. She'd been wilting like a flower in a dry vase, and
Alexandra had urged him to get going as soon as possible. And as
excited as the family was, Gloria was absolutely ecstatic. After she and
Marc began testing the new ground of their feelings, she had rallied
and was once again her energetic self. Not that they had made any
commitments, but at least they could hold hands on walks and let
their guards down a bit.

As he and Max started their way back to their tent, Marc turned
to his younger brother and said, "Do you think you could get me a
ride on your locomotive? I need to go into Aspinwall and arrange for
travel to Panama City."

"I'm sure I can. We're not supposed to let people ride in the cab, you know, but I think they'll make an exception."

Marc smiled. "Of course they will. I'm related to a big shot, after all."

Max laughed. Having let go of his desire to stay and run trains, he too was excited to be moving on. They were about to start their biggest adventure yet.

20—UP THE RIVER

On the Chagres River, Panama—February 1851

COLOMBIA, OF WHICH PANAMA WAS a province, was still a very wild and unsettled land in early 1851. Nearly 200 years earlier, Spanish missionaries had made inroads with the native population, and their travels across the Isthmus had developed a number of trails—first the El Camino Real Trail and later the Las Cruces Trail. But then, as Spain's position in the New World declined, the trails fell into disuse and the jungle quickly swallowed them up so that it was difficult to even find a remnant. Cutting and hacking through the jungle was both dangerous and tiring work, so travelers avoided it by hiring natives to paddle them up the Chagres River almost to its headwaters, where the party could then follow a more developed trail down the mountains to the Pacific coast.

"Let me help you, Mother," said Marc. He took Alexandra's hand and steadied her as she stepped gingerly into the canoe. The Panamanian guides could speak passable English, Spanish, and French in addition to their native language. They were more international in their abilities than most of the passengers they carried.

Surprisingly, it was much hotter on the water than in the jungle, because there was no shade. The sun reflecting off the placid surface of the water created glare that was hard on the eyes, and it also intensified the exposure to the sun. "Be sure to keep your arms covered," said Alexandra to Honoria. By now both Marc and Max were pretty much bronzed from having worked out in the open for the past six months, so sunburn wasn't an issue. But the fair-skinned women, who had spent most days inside the cooking tent, were very vulnerable.

"Is it dangerous in the water?" asked Gloria. "You know, crocodiles and alligators?"

"There are crocodiles, ma'am, but no alligators," said the native guide with a thick accent. "You will see them as we make our way up the river." All the English passengers, including the men, noticeably stiffened and pulled their arms closer to their bodies. "But not to worry—we know how to spot them, and we will stay away. Just keep inside the boats and you will be fine."

"Do they swim up to the boat—how will we know?" Gloria didn't look comforted at all.

The fellow laughed good-naturedly. "No, you will not see them swimming. They lie absolutely motionless in the water with only their eyes above the surface. That's how they trap their prey—birds and fish are unaware of their presence until they are within striking distance, and then *whap!*—the croc lurches out and grabs them then forces them underwater until they drown." To illustrate the closing of the jaws, the native put his hands together and brought his fingers together in a quick, slapping motion.

Gloria was not the only one who shuddered.

"Again, you should not worry. Crocodiles seldom attack humans; we are too big. Besides, we are in a boat, which makes the croc think we are even bigger than he is. The only time a human gets attacked is when he is thrashing in the water, so we never do that. At least not until we get farther upriver."

"You thrash when you get upriver?" Honoria's eyes widened considerably.

"We get out of the boat sometimes to push when the draft is too shallow to row. Mr. Marc and Mr. Max will have to help us then."

"But the crocodiles . . ." said Alexandra, alarmed.

"The crocodiles like mostly salt water. When we get that far upstream, the crocs will be long gone. Besides, we only get out where it is shallow and they can't hide. Again, you should not worry."

When the group still looked dubious, the fellow added, "You see that I am very old—see how wrinkled is my skin? I look very much like a crocodile myself, don't you think? Yet I am still alive. So you will be fine. Just keep your hands inside the boat." He really didn't need to add that last warning since at this point everyone in the group had their hands so close to their bodies that they could have been wrapped in mummy bandages.

"Of course, there are the man-eating fish . . ." he said playfully.

The women dutifully gasped, but Marc interjected, "Piranhas are in Brazil, not Panama. He is just joking around with us now, aren't you, Ramon?"

"Oh, Mr. Marc, you spoil all my fun." He exaggerated a crestfallen look. "It is true there are no man-eating fish in Panama. But there are fish-eating men here, so the fish need to be more scared of us than we are of them."

Marc and Max laughed, but the women were still too traumatized at the thought of crocodiles to really enjoy any kind of banter, though they pretended to laugh to cover their discomfort.

Seeing the state of alarm his passengers were in, Ramon rested easily on the paddles for a bit and said, "No more joking. You are safe on the river. You can relax and enjoy our beautiful country. It's much more beautiful than your London, after all, and not nearly so cold."

"What do you know of London?" asked Alexandra. "Have you ever been there?"

Ramon nodded in a knowing fashion. "Why, yes, I have. Five years ago I go to London to learn your language better. We make our money from you good people, so I need to know how to talk to you. I went by sailing ship, working on the crew."

"And how did you like London?" asked Gloria, dripping from the heavy warm rain that was now falling on their canoe. The odd thing about it was that the morning sun was shining directly on them from a low angle while they were being drowned from a small cloud directly overhead. Even though they'd been on the river just a short time, they had gone in and out of several rain squalls by that point.

"How do I like London? Big, noisy, and smelly. Plus too much rain!" Ramon laughed easily at his own joke. "Seriously, I think it is a wonderful place. People looked at me funny, but that was all right. All those big buildings. We have nothing like that in Panama. But it was great to visit."

"It's the cultural capital of the world," said Gloria wistfully.

"The what—I don't understand the word *cultural*?"

"It is the center of great art and music and finance. And we have a great navy. England is the most powerful nation in the world! People everywhere are envious of our great wealth."

Ramon smiled again. "Yes, that's just what people said to me when I was there."

"And you don't believe them?" asked Marc.

"Oh, yes, I believe them. It's just that it's much simpler here. Without a great navy and big buildings we don't have to go to war with everyone. We just get up in the morning, pick the fruit we need for the day, go out and catch some fish, and every once in a while take good people like you up the river. We don't worry like people there. All I saw in London were people with worried faces. I think it comes from the cold. It is hard for us to worry when the sun is shining on us."

"I personally miss it," said Gloria. "I loved going to London. But it is hard to argue with someone who is so content."

"I think I could learn to like it here," said Marc. "Maybe I was supposed to be born in the Caribbean instead of England, and the old stork dropped me at the wrong spot."

"Marc, really," said Alexandra. "You know perfectly well you were supposed to come to our house."

"No offense, Mother. I love you and my family. But I do love it here. I like how the heat soaks into my bones and how we travel at the speed of canoe paddles rather than muscling our way through the water in steamships. If I were an angel and could pick anywhere to go, I think I'd come to the Caribbean instead of England."

"See! Mr. Marc understands," Ramon declared.

"Well, I'm looking forward to San Francisco," said Gloria. "I hope it has at least some kind of developed culture—and that people clothe their whole bodies!"

That amused Ramon, and he burst out laughing. "That's the other thing about London—everyone covered from head to toe in clothes. How do you ever feel the sun when everything is covered? Plus all the colors are dull—when we do wear clothes here in Panama, we like them to be bright and beautiful colors. Not black and gray and all those sorry colors that people wear there."

Marc laughed easily. He liked Ramon, who couldn't possibly understand Gloria's love of beautiful clothing. "Gloria hopes to open a dress shop in California, so it's important to her that people want to wear those head-to-toe clothes."

"Ah," said Ramon, "now I understand."

Marc allowed himself to drift off into a daydream, unthinkingly letting his hand dip down into the water. "That's not good, Mr. Marc," said Ramon. "This is the place where crocodiles like it the most, so better to keep your hand out of the water!" This time Ramon was serious, and Marc quickly drew his hand in. The women once again pulled their arms close, until they were as tight as a bale of cotton. Ramon looked forward and smiled.

* * *

The Western Slope of the Isthmus of Panama—February 10, 1851

"This is where we say good-bye," said Ramon. "It has been a pleasure to serve you."

Marc stepped forward and handed Ramon a tip, which would be shared with the others on the boat. Ramon smiled and thanked him.

"You and Mr. Max were very good on the river when you needed to get out and push. Better than most."

"And why is that? I thought we were rather clumsy."

"No, not at all. You were patient and good. The Americans are always impatient. They push too hard and cause more trouble. Americans are always in a hurry, and usually it ends up slowing them down."

"How is that possible?" asked Gloria. "If they hurry, they should get where they are going sooner."

Ramon tipped his head. "That's what you would think. But here in the Caribbean we know that you must take things as they come, and then everything works out. When you hurry, things break or people stumble. They get frustrated in the water and slip and fall, and then you lose lots of time pulling them out." He nodded his head knowingly. "No, Mr. Marc and Mr. Max understand—they worked with us, and it was better."

This pleased Marc. "Well, I'm glad to hear that. Thank you."

"You could be a Panamanian, Mr. Marc. It seems that you understand us. I don't say that to any other passengers!"

"Our good luck," said Gloria, "to be traveling with an Englishman who acts more like a Panamanian as he takes me to America!"

Marc and Ramon laughed heartily at that. "Well, I really would like to meet you again, someday," said Marc to Ramon. "But if we're lucky, we'll make it to America and then stay there."

"So perhaps I will need to come to America to see you. I like to travel," said Ramon. "I've never been to San Francisco, so who knows? Maybe I come stay with you!"

"You would be welcome anytime." The two men shook hands, and then Marc made his way over to the group of mules. The men in this group looked far less amiable than Ramon and his men. Ramon slipped up to Marc and said quietly, "Watch yourselves with these men. They are always in a hurry. They're not native, you know—lots of Spanish in them."

"Are they trustworthy?" asked Marc, in something of alarm.

"They will not steal from you or hurt you. But they will not help you, either. This is the time for you to act more like the Americans and hurry your way to Panama City. Don't spend too much time on the trail."

Marc nodded. "Thanks for the advice." He turned and impulsively stepped forward and gave Ramon a hug—a very un-British sort of thing to do. "Thank you for everything."

Ramon stepped back and smiled. "You can come back to my Panama anytime, Mr. Marc. We will make you—how do you say it—a native?"

"I would like that very much."

Marc extended his hand and Ramon took it cheerfully. And then, in an instant, he was back in his boat and the whole group was paddling quickly down the river, back toward Aspinwall.

Marc went over to the sullen fellow who was in charge of the mules. "Well, then, what do we do now?"

"Do now?" asked the man in a thick Spanish accent. "You bring your things so we can load them on the mules. Then we start down the hills."

Marc motioned for Max, and the two of them started assembling the small number of items they had left. All the steamer trunks filled with clothing and china that they had brought across the Atlantic had long ago been sold so they could lighten their load. Now all they had were bare essentials, and even at that it seemed like a lot. Fortunately, the mules were stout creatures and seemed not to care as they were loaded up with the few worldly possessions that were left to the Chandlers and to Gloria.

Quite roughly, it seemed to the ladies, the men on the mule team lifted the women up onto the sidesaddles of the mules. This was not entirely natural to Alexandra and Honoria, who had usually traveled by wagon or carriage. But Gloria took command. An experienced horse rider, she waved the man off with her hand and easily mounted the mule that had been assigned to her. It was obvious in a moment that she knew exactly what she was doing, and Marc was impressed. It clearly brightened her attitude—to return to something so familiar.

"Kind of small, aren't they?" said Marc as he settled himself uncomfortably on the back of the mule. "I'm sure I look completely foolish."

Honoria smiled. "Yes, you do, as a matter of fact." Marc was glad that his sister could joke. All of them were worried about her health, and this little sign of life was important.

"Well, then, I think we're ready," Marc said to the man in charge. With nothing more than a grunt, the fellow waved the two other men with him to move forward, as well as those in the "Marc Party," as they had been identified. The group included the Chandlers, Gloria, Marc's partner on the railroad, Norman Bellweather, and a local Panamanian named Guillermo (who carefully explained to Max that his name was pronounced "Heezhermo"). Guillermo said that he was tired of living in Aspinwall and was anxious for change in Panama City.

* * *

"These mules are uncomfortable," said Gloria miserably. The heat inland was stifling, particularly as the sun came out after three hours of torrential rain. "What I wouldn't give for a good horse and an open field." The entire jungle was steaming, and the random rays of sunlight breaking through the jungle canopy periodically blinded them as they moved in and out of shadows. But at this point, six hours into the journey, everyone else was simply too tired to even respond.

Marc and Norman had talked easily with Guillermo when they could and found him to be a charming fellow, if a bit radical in his politics. Guillermo thought that it was criminal for the Colombian government to give rights to the new railroad being built across their land to a United States business syndicate that would suck all the profit earned by the railroad out of the local economy and send it to the wealthy investment bankers in New York City. But he did express both surprise and admiration for the fact that Marc and Norman had worked on the roadbed for six months.

"Not many gringos can stand up to our heat," he said in lilting English.

"Marc here really likes it," said Bellweather. "If it weren't for his family, I think he'd take up residence here."

"Is that true, Marc?" asked Guillermo.

"You know, I think it is. I like the tropics, and I like the people here."

"So why not stay?"

"My mother and sister—the climate is too hard on them. And our religion. We're going to join a group of pilgrims in the western United States." He'd found it wise not to immediately disclose that he was Mormon—not out of embarrassment but more because most people did not know anything about the Church, and it was complicated to explain. Some even became hostile. So Marc was cautious.

"Ah. Not enough freedom of religion in the United States—your people need to go out into the wilderness? Like Moses?"

Marc laughed at that. Clearly Guillermo was a student of the United States and used this as a way to poke fun at them.

"Something like that. But I'm British, you know. At any rate, I'll be glad to get on our way to California when the time arrives, but I'll miss Panama."

Guillermo went silent, lost in his own thoughts. There wasn't really a lot to do on the trail down. The transit from the point where the canoes ended to Panama City was only some twenty miles and could be easily covered in two days. It was now getting to be late afternoon, and the winter sun was going to drop behind the horizon quickly.

"We'll make camp over there!" said the leader of the group. Surprisingly, he seemed to say this only after a subtle nod from Guillermo, even though Guillermo was just a passenger. No one but Marc noticed it, and the only reason he saw it was because he happened to have turned to Guillermo at just the precise moment. Marc didn't say anything, but he felt some vague unease in his stomach.

"So far off the trail?" asked Gloria.

"Under that canopy of trees," said Guillermo, pointing up. "To keep the rain off, if it comes."

Marc noticed an edge to Guillermo's voice as he said this.

An hour later, a fire was roaring away, and one of the guides was busy cooking a stew. For some reason, the guides seemed agitated. At least that's how Marc perceived it. After everyone had eaten a hearty dinner that was provided as part of the escort fee, the group settled under tents to fall asleep as early as possible. The sounds of the jungle were unusually subdued—at least compared to the camp they'd lived in up north on the Atlantic Coast. In a puzzling twist of geography, the Atlantic was to the north of Panama and the Pacific to the south, not east and west as one would suppose.

"Don't worry about anything," said the leader of the company in very broken English. "We'll take turns staying awake to guard the camp." For some reason, Marc found little comfort in this assurance. But it was dark and he was tired, and soon he and the others were fast asleep.

He was startled out of his wits sometime later to hear Gloria scream at the top of her lungs. Marc's body undoubtedly left the ground as he stiffened up, and for a moment it was impossible to tell if he was still dreaming—a nightmare to be sure—or awake. It took a moment to realize where they were, and then he bolted from under the little canvas canopy he and Max were sleeping under to find Gloria struggling with Guillermo while a number of other men stood by laughing. Of course his mother, Norman Bellweather, and the others were all awake at this point, as well, and the whole group came out. Seeing that the party was aroused, Guillermo slapped Gloria with enough force that it knocked to her to the ground, at which point Marc charged him with a tackling blow that sent them both tumbling to the ground. When Norman came flying after them, the night air was rent with the sound of a gunshot, and Norman went sprawling to the ground, crying out in pain as he landed. Honoria screamed, Alexandra grabbed Max and pulled him near to her, and Gloria started backing away from the group, still on the ground.

"Why are you doing this?" Marc shouted to Guillermo, who had now extricated himself from Marc. Of course it was a foolish question. They were being robbed, and Gloria had discovered the men in the act. But the shock of the shooting overwhelmed Marc and caused him to go on.

"He was unarmed! How could you do that?" He started to stand up as if to attack Guillermo again, but a swift kick to his ribs from one of Guillermo's men—it was clear Guillermo was the ringleader here—sent him back to the ground, groaning.

"You can have whatever you want," shouted Alexandra. "But don't hurt anyone else. We have nothing that is worth our lives. Please, let my son go."

"Marc," said Guillermo, "you will stay right where you are, or I will have to shoot you as well. Do you understand?"

Marc nodded, the adrenaline falling off, leaving him cold and filled with dread. He was in the middle of the jungle, surrounded by armed men, and the only other full-grown man in the party was now writhing in agony. He felt compelled to protect the women from these men but he didn't know how.

Once everyone was immobile, Guillermo motioned for Alexandra to go to Bellweather, which she did immediately. He waited for a few moments for Alexandra to assess his wound.

Looking up, she said, "It glanced off of his right hip. He's hurt badly but not fatally. I will need bandages." The anger in her voice tempered the good news in the report.

"Ah, Señora Chandler disapproves of us," said Guillermo, his easy style of speech returning. "But when one is fighting for a cause, unfortunate things happen."

He motioned for one of the men to give some fabric to Alexandra, and he allowed Honoria to join her mother in tearing the coarse fabric into strips that they used to staunch the flow of blood.

"Now, for an explanation. We do not want to kill any of you. We simply want your supplies. A wise person would let us do so without notice, but this stubborn girl objected. She's at fault here."

"I didn't shoot him—you did!" Gloria yelled.

Guillermo raised his hand again, and Gloria shrank back. Marc felt completely powerless, forced to sit on the ground, his legs open and apart as directed by Guillermo so he couldn't easily spring up.

"You are not a generous person, Gloria. You value your possessions too much. It's people like you who convince me that we must take control of our own country, rather than leave it to the British and the Americans to do with as they please."

"The British! What have the British done?" asked Gloria, more quietly.

Guillermo laughed. "Selfish and uninformed. Just last year your ambassador gave away Nicaragua—as if it was his to give. Yes, you colonialists are an indifferent lot. So, we must wage our little war quietly to make it too unpleasant for your people to be here, except as our paying guests."

"So you take our money to do it? You would leave us penniless?"

Guillermo turned to Alexandra. "Yes, I am afraid so, my poor lady. But you are just a few hours from Panama City, and you will find shelter there. We did not intend to hurt Mr. Bellweather—that was an unfortunate consequence of Marc's attack."

"But Marc and Max worked so hard . . ." The sound of resignation in Alexandra's voice expressed her grief.

"Yes, well, life is hard." Guillermo moved toward a bag that had been the source of the earlier struggle with Gloria. "No! Please not that bag. You can have all my money." Gloria carefully stood up. "Here, I have the cash right here." She made a motion seeking permission to move to another bag.

"Be careful, Gloria. Should you have a weapon, I would be forced to shoot . . ." He paused then pointed to Marc. "I should be forced to shoot him, and with no possibility of surviving." Gloria's eyes widened. "Yes, I thought you might care for him. So be careful."

Gloria carefully reached inside her bag and drew out a stack of British pound notes. Honoria gasped, and Marc shook his head in disbelief. Even Guillermo was impressed. "My, but this is our lucky day." He reached out and took the notes from Gloria.

"Now, you'll let us all go?"

"Of course. But that was my intention from the beginning."

"And my bag. You will give me my bag."

Guillermo laughed and reached down to pick up the bag, acting as if he was going to give it to her. "But of course I cannot give it to you without first inspecting it . . ."

"No!" said Gloria while lunging for the bag. "You said—"

"I said nothing," replied Guillermo, pulling the bag in such a way that Gloria went sprawling forward on her face. Quickly turning over on the ground, she had tears in her eyes as she rose again and pleaded with Guillermo.

"Not that. Please!"

Guillermo simply opened the bag and turned it upside down. Personal items came tumbling out, none of which had any great value. Except for one, and it caused the biggest gasp of all.

"What have we here?" asked Guillermo, reaching down to the ground.

"Please, no . . ." Gloria begged.

"Such a beautiful pearl bracelet. This is jewelry fit for a queen."

"It's the only thing of value I have," said Gloria bitterly. "It's all I have to remember my home by. Certainly you won't take this."

Guillermo shook his head. "I know I shouldn't, but we need this more than you do."

Gloria fell back to the ground, brought her face into her hands, and started sobbing. It was as if all of the suppressed emotions of their long ordeal finally forced their way to the surface, and she was inconsolable.

"Now we must be on our way. The rest of you, give me anything of value you have, and don't hold back or I'll have to follow through on my threat to shoot Marc here." Alexandra and Honoria quickly made their way to the tent, bringing out what little cash they had and some jewelry. When the women were finished, Guillermo pointed to Marc, who got up and went to the small trunk that was next to one of the mules. He reached in and brought out six months of earnings and brought it carefully to Guillermo.

"And that is everything?" Guillermo said as he took it.

Marc nodded. "Everything. So now you will leave us alone."

"Not everything," said one of the men in broken English. "There are women. It's been a long time since we had women." The look in his eyes sent a chill up the spine of everyone in the camp. But it didn't last long. As the man started toward Gloria, Guillermo kicked his knees out from under him. The man rolled over with fire in his eyes and made ready to attack Guillermo, but another kick sent him back down to the ground. The other men looked on and said nothing. "You can buy all the women who make themselves available to men like you from your share of this money, but you will not attack these women."

"And why not?"

"Because I am not that kind of man." Guillermo paused. "And because the authorities in Panama City will tolerate robbery on the trail. But if we do more than that, they will send out the army for us. They need the American trade and will not tolerate murder or other violations." He reached down and extended a hand to the man, who, though scowling, reached up and took it. Guillermo was clearly a leader to be reckoned with.

"Well, then, we will leave you," Guillermo said with a small bow.

"Can you at least tell us how to find our way to Panama City?" asked Marc.

Guillermo nodded. "You will see the trail in the morning. Just follow it down the mountain."

"And Mr. Bellweather?"

"Just help him onto a mule. It will be painful, but he will survive. There will be medical help when you get there."

Marc nodded, his lips pursed and face drawn. Guillermo motioned for the others to take off with most of the mules.

"Leave three," Guillermo said. "One for Mr. Bellweather, one for Señora Chandler, and the third for her daughter." Turning to Marc, he added, "The mules carrying your mother and sister can easily carry what possessions remain."

Marc couldn't bring himself to thank Guillermo, although he realized it probably would have been wiser for Guillermo to leave them with no mules at all. So he just nodded. Still Guillermo hesitated. He stayed behind while his men continued back up the trail. Then, impulsively, and out of sight of the others, he reached into his bag and pulled out the money that Marc and his family had turned over.

"I do this only because you like Panama and its people. I have plenty from the little queen, so you take this and make your way."

Marc's surprise was so complete that he couldn't say anything before Guillermo turned and quickly disappeared into the thick foliage, now a bit brighter with the coming of twilight.

When the bandits were gone, Alexandra stood up and Marc moved quickly to take her in his arms. Honoria stayed on the ground by Norman Bellweather, and Max moved in closer to hug his mother along with Marc.

Gloria remained on the ground, her crying now subsided. She simply sat there with a vacant stare.

Marc made his way to help her up, but Honoria jumped up suddenly and rushed with startling speed between Marc and Gloria, shouting with a firm voice, "No! You will not help her!"

"Honoria?" said Alexandra, shocked. Marc fell back a few steps, surprised to hear such an outburst from his usually taciturn sister.

"But she has been victimized just like the rest of us," said Marc. "Perhaps worse—she lost such a great deal."

"I just realized that she lost the money that could have *saved Father's life!*"

Alexandra gasped. "Oh, Honoria, you're not yourself . . ."

"Please be quiet, Mother," said Honoria firmly. "I am myself." Turning to Gloria, who now shrunk back before Honoria, she continued. "Father helped her in Liverpool when no one else would." Her voice caught as she thought of her father, but she quickly swallowed to regain her composure before anyone could interrupt her.

"But—" Gloria started to interrupt, but Honoria furiously motioned for her to be quiet.

"I will have my say. I've stood by you all these months treating you as a friend and feeling sorry for all that you have lost. But now I find that you could have easily saved my father's life. After everything we did for you, you selfishly allowed him to suffer at the furnace until it drew the very life out of his soul! How could you do such a thing?"

"But, Honoria, it was *her* money . . ." said Alexandra.

"Her blood money," replied Honoria. "This woman is selfish and cruel, and I hate her for it. Now she has lost her money and her jewelry, and she is finally just like us. We should not feel sorry for her—I know I don't."

"Honoria! That's enough!" said Marc.

"No," said Gloria, reduced to silent tears. "She's right. About everything. Your father was the kindest man I ever knew, and I should have helped him. But I didn't know . . ." Gloria's voice caught. "She's right. I could have made all this suffering go away, but I didn't . . . because . . . I feared I would die if I lost the money. You have your family—each other—to support one another. All I have is me. The money goes, and then . . . what next? In New York, Brandt said he'd sell me as a slave if I didn't come back to England with him. What if the money ran out and I would have to sell myself or work in some sweatshop or . . ."

Gloria began sobbing again as she had upon losing her bracelet. Marc knelt down to comfort her, even though this revelation was shocking to him too. By that point Honoria had retreated to her tent, and Alexandra returned to helping Bellweather. As they sat there alone, Gloria searched his eyes for understanding in the dim light of the campfire.

When he remained silent, she said quietly, "I was just so frightened. I couldn't imagine living life without anyone or any means to survive, and running away from home meant that I would never have my father to help me again. That cash was all I had, and it is what I hoped would get me started in business. I thought I'd need it. I had no idea that things would be so hard for your father and you. After you told me how much he was struggling, I even went to the captain and offered to pay, but he said they could not get by without the work, so he refused my money."

"That dirty, self-serving—" Marc had to bite his tongue to avoid saying what he *wanted* to say, which would have been offensive in the company of a lady. "And that's why you went so quiet on the ship."

She nodded. "I felt trapped. I should have told you what I'd done but was afraid of this very thing—that you would all hate me for not helping out from the beginning. Now your sister does hate me, and you must feel nothing but contempt."

Marc swallowed hard. Things could have been so different with her money. *How can I forgive her?* To gain time to think, he said, "Tell me about the bracelet."

Gloria swallowed and looked away. Marc felt her body trembling next to him. "It was my grandmother's. My father is a gentle man. In some ways he is like your father, though not nearly as well-read or passionate." She paused, thinking about the contrast. "He is meek, and my mother is domineering."

"Your grandmother?"

Gloria nodded, "His mother. She was the kindest lady I ever knew as a child. My mother didn't like her because she thought her weak, as well. But I loved her and she loved me." Gloria's voice trailed off. "The bracelet was my gift from her when she died. It had been her mother's and usually would have gone to my father's younger sister, but my grandmother had asked special permission of her daughter to leave it to me. So it was the most special thing in the world to me."

"I'm sorry you lost it."

Gloria successfully suppressed a sob then turned to Marc and said quietly, "If I could go back and undo everything that's happened, I would gladly spend all the money and the bracelet to pay for your father and your mother and all of you. I would have given up everything to make things different." Her breathing was fast and shallow. "But instead I was selfish, just as Honoria said, and now the bracelet and the money are gone, and they have done no good whatsoever. Had I shared them, everything would have been different, but now all is lost."

Marc shook his head. *It could have been so different.* As he thought about his father, he felt a sudden rush of feeling. *The real pearl of great price is what Father always wanted. Valuables and money only pale in comparison. Gloria knows that, and now so do I.* He realized that Henry Chandler had died full of hope and goodwill. *He would have forgiven Gloria—am I as good a man as he?* He struggled to contain his emotions.

And then he said softly, "Nothing is lost. We are all still here and alive, Guillermo spared you and the others from violation, and tomorrow we will make our way to Panama City."

"But your father . . ."

"My father died heroically." Now it was Marc's voice that caught. "Is there a better way to leave this world than protecting those you love?" Out of the corner of his eye he caught Honoria looking through the flap of the tent. She had heard everything they'd said. He wondered what she was thinking as her head disappeared again.

"I am so sorry, Marc! I am so very sorry . . ." This time Marc drew Gloria's head to his chest, where he cradled it with his arms, gently stroking her hair as she silently wept.

Marc shushed her and whispered, "You aren't alone, Gloria. You were never alone since you met us on the dock of Liverpool."

21—LOSS

Panama City—February 25, 1851

THREE DAYS AFTER THEIR ARRIVAL at Panama City, the *S.S. California* steamed into port from San Francisco. That in itself was a miracle, given how long some people had been waiting there. After explaining to the local authorities what had happened to them in the hills, the local constabulary said they would pursue the infamous Guillermo but doubted that there was anything they could do to recover the party's lost possessions. Apparently others had fallen victim to the charming Panamanian, and the fact that he now had trail crews in league with him complicated the task of bringing him to justice. He was a modern-day Robin Hood. The local people believed he was standing up for their rights against the domination of Europe and the United States.

Marc knew that getting any of their possessions back was hopeless but didn't say that to Gloria, who, in spite of her remorse for not helping the family, now faced life with a new kind of dread that she'd never experienced before—no money and no possessions. But she was coming more and more to understand that her new family was more valuable and provided more security than any kind of monetary wealth.

The Chandlers had been forced to face that when Cunard had disavowed them, and so their loss wasn't as great. Besides, because of the unexpected return of the family's money, they could afford to buy passage for everyone.

Marc was sitting on the porch of the small hotel they were staying at in Panama City when his mother came up and sat beside him.

He thought about what had been weighing on him since that night on the road to Panama City. "Do you think Honoria will ever forgive Gloria?"

"Here's how I see it, Marc," his mother said. "If we had never met Gloria, our outcome would have been the same. We were unprepared, that's all. When Cunard refused to offer us the discounts your father had counted on, the die was cast. He was set on going to Utah and would have made the very same decisions, and he would have suffered the same fate. So it's not her fault, and she shouldn't bear the blame."

"Have you explained that to Honoria?"

Alexandra nodded. "But the way we feel about things always comes down to the way we view them. Honoria sees what Gloria *could have* done, rather than the fact that for us the outcome was unchanged. But I think she'll come around."

"I suppose it won't matter much longer. We're just weeks away from San Francisco."

"And that bothers you because you care for her."

Before Marc could respond, Alexandra added, "For better or worse, Gloria has become part of our lives, and it does no good to nurture grudges. So you must forgive her and try to understand her. I will do the same."

"Well, our fortune will soon turn and we'll all be on our way to California." Marc tried to say this as brightly as possible to chase away the gloom he felt. It had shaken him to the core that he had been unable to defend his family out on the trail, and he felt guilty about many things.

"I think I'll go for a walk," he said.

"Perhaps Gloria will join you."

Marc smiled at his mother's suggestion. She was remarkable in her ability to move on and not let the past burden her.

"Yes, well . . ."

Just then Max came running out the door, crying, "Mother, come quickly! Honoria is sick—she needs you!"

"Of course. What's wrong?" Marc followed them through the door. One look at Honoria told them what was wrong.

"Malaria fever," said Alexandra, trembling. Marc pulled Max back, concerned about all of them catching the disease too.

"My dear Honoria," said Alexandra kindly.

"Oh, Mother, I'm so hot."

Alexandra motioned for Max to bring her the basin of water and a washrag. She started gently wiping Honoria's brow and hair with the wet rag, which brought a degree of relief.

"What can we do?" asked Max.

Marc shook his head. His poor brother had seen so much of the unhappiness of the world and now was about to see more. He contemplated whether to answer him honestly or to shield him for a few more moments. "There's nothing to be done. Some people suffer for a few days and get better, and others—" His voice cracked.

"And the others die," finished Max. It was pathetic to hear the sorrow in a voice so young. Marc nodded. Max walked quietly over to Honoria's bed and rested his head on his sister's stomach.

"Poor Max," said Honoria. "I love you, my dear. You know that." Max nodded without lifting his head. "I will tell Father hello for you."

Tears now streamed down Max's cheek.

"Don't talk like that, dear," said Alexandra. "You are strong enough to weather this storm. You've been through so much— certainly you can survive this."

Honoria smiled weakly. "You know I'm not strong. I never have been. The truth is that I have secretly wished for a release from all that we have gone through—must still go through."

Alexandra stroked her daughter's head with some fresh water. Honoria motioned for Marc to come over. There was a lump in his throat as he did so.

"I love you too, Marc. I'm sorry I hurt you the other day," Honoria said through tears.

"You didn't hurt me."

"Yes, I did, because you love her."

He bit his lip. It seemed so obvious to everyone else when it wasn't at all clear to him.

She looked deeply into his eyes. "I meant what I said. From my point of view, I meant it. But I may have been wrong. She tried to make up for it. Perhaps I can forgive someday." She struggled as a wave of pain crossed her face. "But I never for one moment felt anything but love for you. Please forgive me for being harsh with you."

"Of course."

"So when you think of me, you'll think of the happy times."

"I love you. And I always will—now, and many years from now, when we both die of old age."

Honoria smiled and put her hand on Alexandra's. "I love you most of all, dear Mother. You have been my friend as well as my mother." Alexandra bit her lip and let out a muffled sob. "Now I need to rest. I am so hot and tired."

Honoria closed her eyes. She lived another two days but never regained her consciousness. She was buried in Panama City within twenty-four hours of her death, as was the custom in this Catholic country. Marc and Gloria went into the wooded areas to find flowers to put around her body and in her hair. When the time came, Max was chosen to say a few brief words before Marc, now sadly more experienced, dedicated her grave.

"I shall never get over her loss," said Alexandra. The pain in her face was more than Marc could bear, and he closed his eyes. *And now You've taken another one from us, dear Lord. Where is the kindness? What is in store for the rest of us?*

22—THE CALIFORNIA FRONTIER

"I CAN'T BELIEVE HOW DESOLATE it is. I thought California was the land of milk and honey. Full of gold." Gloria held her face in her hands as she leaned on the railing of the S.S. *California,* an older steamship, now sailing north from Panama City toward San Francisco. After making sure that Norman Bellweather received the medical care he needed in Panama City and that he had enough money for his recovery, they paid a small premium to book passage on the next ship to California. Now they were passing just a few miles to the west of a small village that had recently been renamed Los Angeles. There were just a handful of adobe huts, and someone on board reported that members of the Mormon Battalion had camped there a few years earlier. From there the map showed the coast jutting far to the west before turning northerly again at Monterey and then to San Francisco.

"If we were on a sailing ship, we'd follow the trade winds to the Sandwich Islands, called Hawaii by the natives, and then circle into California from the north."

Gloria looked at Marc with a puzzled glance. "But that adds thousands of miles to the journey, doesn't it?"

He nodded. "It does. But when you are under sail, you have to follow the winds. With steam you can plow ahead regardless of how the winds are blowing. It just shows how much steam travel has changed the way people navigate. It has shortened the transit from Panama by nearly a month." He was reflective for a time. "I can't help but wonder if we should have chosen a different means to make our way to Utah. There were alternatives."

"Such as?"

"We could have gone overland by railroad to the Missouri River and then by wagon train to Utah. That would have taken three or four months, which at the time seemed way too long."

Gloria nodded. "Now it's been seven months, and this was supposed to be so much faster."

"Or we could have taken a sailing ship all the way around Cape Horn at the bottom of South America and out to the Sandwich Islands. That would have taken far longer, but the cost would have been less than half what we've paid for steamship travel." His voice caught. "And then Father wouldn't have had to work, and Honoria would never have had malaria."

Gloria knew that he didn't say this to hurt her, even though it did. She still felt guilty for Henry's death since she could have helped them financially. That Alexandra and Marc had forgiven her was completely foreign to the way she had been raised. She wondered how they could have such compassion.

"I sometimes think if I hadn't been there in New York City to burden all of you, none of this would have happened."

"The truth is that you had nothing to do with the decision to go by steamship," Marc tried to reassure her. "It was Father's choice. He was so anxious to make his way to join the other Saints as fast as possible. But now, when we land in California, none of us will have much money. The passage took most of what Max and I earned."

Marc and Gloria looked out to sea. Gloria finally said, "I do hope it gets a little less desolate when we get to Northern California. We could use a little hope."

* * *

San Francisco—March 10, 1851

Ninety thousand people called San Francisco home in 1851. Astonishingly, of that number, 60,000 men (and only 1,979 women) had arrived in the preceding twelve months. In the first days of the gold rush, almost no one stayed in San Francisco, which left ships abandoned in the harbor because their crews had made off for the gold fields. But that pattern had changed in the previous two years. While gold was still being harvested from the rich California foothills in greater abundance than anywhere else on earth in many hundreds of years, the image of one solitary man dipping his pan in the creek and making a fortune was now hardly more than a myth. Mining companies had been organized to take advantage of high-volume extraction techniques, including sluice boxes and hydraulic spraying of hillsides that could wipe out an entire mountain in very short order. In some places the magnificent forests of the Sierra Nevada looked like giants had stomped through the forest canopy leaving ugly scars of mud and toxic minerals. The effect was to reduce most of the forty-niners to employees of the great mining concerns, and the people in San Francisco who outfitted these men and provided the wide variety of entertainment venues to take away their hard-earned gold were the ones who prospered.

Into this rowdy and raucous world the S.S. *California* deposited its passengers in early 1851. There were more than 350 ships docked in San Francisco Bay at the time, which was evidence of the spectacular rise in San Francisco's fortunes. It had, overnight, gone from village to city, with all the growing pains that change entails.

"Who should we ask to find Elder Tyler?" asked Alexandra nervously.

"I don't know," Marc replied. "Maybe the first question is to ask a clerk or policeman if they know of any Mormon churches in the area."

"I think the first question we should ask is where we can find a hotel that is suitable for women," said Gloria. She looked anxiously about the place, well aware of the gigantic imbalance between men and women on the wharf.

"It is rather barren," said Alexandra. Except for a few forlorn eucalyptus trees that had been planted on the northernmost headland of the peninsula in an area the captain of the ship had called the Presidio, the city was nothing more than sandy hills with almost no vegetation. That seemed a little surprising, given that across the magnificent harbor were foothills that were clearly covered in trees.

"Yes," said Marc. He looked around nervously. "I think Gloria's right. I'll go ask the shipping company clerk where we can find suitable family lodging." He fretted that they had such little money, having heard that prices there were exorbitant because of the gold-fed inflation.

In a few moments an animated discussion was taking place. "I told you there are no good hotels with any vacancies. And no, I don't know anything about Mormons, other than that they are some crazy sect out in the desert."

"But what of Joseph Tyler? Have you heard of a Joseph Tyler?"

The fellow looked at Marc with contempt and said, "And that's because it's such an uncommon name, I suppose. Joseph Tyler—how many fellows do you suppose have that as their Christian name?" Before Marc could respond to the sarcastic comment, he added, "It doesn't matter, because I don't know one anyway. Now move along!"

Marc sighed and was about to turn back to the group when a thought struck him. "What about Sam Brannan? Have you heard of a Sam Brannan?"

The dock fairly well came to a standstill at this name.

"And what do you know about Sam Brannan?" asked the clerk, the tone in his voice of a much different quality now.

"I was told by my friend Joseph Tyler that if I could not find him, I was to look up Sam Brannan when I got to San Francisco. They are friends, and he said Mr. Brannan would help me."

The clerk pinched his lips. "Well, that's a little different, then. I do know Mr. Brannan—of course I do. Everybody in San Francisco knows him." He waved his arm in an arc to all the others standing nearby, and they all nodded. "So if it's true that your friend is acquainted with Mr. Brannan, then I'll tell you where you need to go."

"Thank you." Marc was so relieved at this glimmer of hope that his voice trembled. He motioned to his mother, Max, and Gloria, and they quickly joined him at his side. The fellow pointed up to Market Street, a major corridor running from the Embarcadero on the San Francisco Bay west toward the Presidio.

"Go to the corner of Fifth Street and then turn left. You'll find one of Mr. Brannan's main businesses in the middle of the block. If he's not there, they can tell you where to find him." The fellow hesitated. "And tell him that Will Bardell helped you out."

Marc unconsciously tipped his head back. Brannan must be an important character to have multiple businesses and to be a person whom the clerk would want to know he'd done a favor for.

"Of course, Mr. Bardell. You have been most helpful. Thank you."

They started to move off, but Gloria just couldn't resist asking, "And this Mr. Brannan—what makes him so well known?"

"What makes him well known?" The clerk's eyes widened. "He's the one who single-handedly created the California Gold Rush. He learned about it up at Sutter's Mill, came back, bought every shovel in San Francisco, and then started walking up and down Market Street shouting, 'Gold! Gold!' which caused an immediate sensation. He owned a newspaper, the *California Star,* which he used to stir up additional interest in the gold fields. But in some ways that hurt him since he was so successful in getting people worked up into a frenzy that all of his printers up and quit to leave for the gold fields. That left no one to print his paper. But he used all of those shovels to start stores up and down the American River to sell supplies to miners. Sam Brannan was the first California millionaire, and he didn't pan a single speck of gold to get it. And . . ."

"And?"

He looked at Gloria intently. "And nothing. That's all you need to know. If you really do know how to get connected to him, you can learn the rest on your own."

Gloria raised an eyebrow. "Fine. Thank you."

In a way Marc was glad to hear the old imperious sound in her voice. She had been so beaten down by the events in Panama that he thought she might have lost her natural confidence.

"Cab!" Marc knew it would look unseemly to show up at Mr. Brannan's with two women in tow and no one to help with their luggage, so he decided to splurge on the cost of getting help. He only hoped that Brannan was as good of a member of the Mormon Church as Elder Tyler had led them to believe and that he could help them find inexpensive and safe lodging. Glancing around, he couldn't help but be impressed by how many men there were for each woman—in fact, it was hard to even find a woman in view, other than the two he was chaperoning.

With the snap of a small whip above the heads of the horses, the cab lurched out onto the busy thoroughfare and quickly turned off into a residential district. The family stared at the homes they were passing. Compared to the solid mortise-and-tenon-joint homes of their native Liverpool, built with heavy oak beams fastened with dowels and faced with rock or brick, the clapboard houses of San Francisco seemed insubstantial and fragile.

"It looks like they would all fall down if a stout wind came up," said Gloria.

Marc nodded. While there were a few brick residences, the vast majority were made out of a very light timber, and they marveled as they went by a house being put up by nothing more than a two-man team of laborers.

"How is that possible?" asked Max. "It seems like houses being built at home have dozens of men working on them."

"It's called a balloon frame," said the cabdriver amiably. "We developed it here in America. It uses precut two-by-four studs, placed sixteen inches apart. Very light but very strong. We can put up a house faster than anything—and they're every bit as strong as all the old-fashioned houses in New England. We pioneered these houses in Chicago, my hometown."

"This truly is a remarkable place," said Marc, cowed at the ingenuity that was evident all around them.

After perhaps twenty minutes of driving, the cab pulled up in front of a large and handsome brick residence. It was a mansion compared to everything they had gone by.

"Here we are, then," said the driver. "Home of Mr. Sam Brannan, probably the second-most important man in all of California!"

"And who is the most important," asked Alexandra.

"Colonel John Fremont, ma'am. He's the fellow who won our freedom. And now he's a gold rush millionaire, just like Mr. Brannan. As soon as I serve out my contract here, I'm heading out to the hills, although it's a lot harder for an independent to make any good claims anymore. Still, I can make more out there than I can here—at least I hope I can."

Marc stepped out, helped the women out, and then tipped the cabdriver. "Will you wait until we're sure Mr. Brannan is here and that he'll see us?"

"Sure. I can do that." The easy tone of the man's voice had an unfamiliar sound to it—not at all like the Southerners they'd met, and different from the New York City accent.

"It's amazing how many different ways there are to speak English," whispered Marc to Gloria.

"Well," he said, taking a deep breath. "It's time to find out if Elder Tyler led us true." With all that had transpired since Elder Tyler had first come into their home in England, it seemed like a different century and a different world. Gathering up his courage, Marc knocked on the elegant bronze door knocker then stepped back to wait. In a few moments an austere man in a tuxedo stepped to the door, with a very formal and somewhat condescending, "May I help you?"

"Yes," said Marc. "I hope so. We are hoping to see Mr. Brannan. I know it's impolite to come without an appointment, but we just stepped foot off the ship . . ."

"And what business, may I ask, do you have with Mr. Brannan?"

When Marc hesitated at this seeming rebuke, Alexandra stepped forward. "We are here to see Mr. Brannan at the recommendation of Mr. Tyler. We have traveled a great distance and suffered much hardship, and we need to see him directly." The firmness in Alexandra's voice was unmistakable.

The butler stepped back. "No offense intended, ma'am. It's just that Mr. Brannan has many callers. Why don't you come into our drawing room, and I will tell him that you are here. That is, if you will share your names . . ."

Marc was very embarrassed that he hadn't introduced them to this man and quickly did so. "Perhaps I could go let the driver know that we're going in, and I can help him with our bags—"

"No need to trouble yourself," said the butler. "He works for Mr. Brannan, and I'll let him know that he is to wait for you. I'm sure Mr. Brannan would have it no other way."

Marc gulped. Gloria seemed absolutely at ease, and Alexandra seemed as if she was about to burst with joy. Max was, as usual, fascinated by the place and quickly lost himself in thought.

After just a few minutes of waiting in an elegantly appointed drawing room, with crushed velvet upholstery and beautiful oriental rugs on the floor, they were startled by a deep and mellifluous voice, "Good afternoon, ladies. Gentlemen. My butler tells me you have come a long way to see me." Standing up quickly, the family was greeted by a handsome young man, perhaps thirty or so, and dressed in an expensive waistcoat with vest and tie. He had dark sideburns that flanked both sides of his jowls, just touching under his chin, but no mustache, as seemed to be the habit in America. He seemed absolutely at ease in the relative splendor of his San Francisco mansion.

"Mr. Brannan," said Marc quickly, "please allow me to introduce my family."

"I'm delighted to meet them," said Brannan, who stepped forward easily. As Marc introduced Alexandra and Gloria, Brannan gallantly took their offered hand and gave it a light kiss. He shook Max's hand firmly, and then turned again to Marc.

"Yes, well," said Marc, "we are here because of Elder Tyler. At least that's how we knew him in England."

"I know Tyler," said Brannan. "A very good man who works for mc. Almost a year ago he told me that he had invited a family to visit us here, a family that he taught in England. But they never showed up, so we assumed they had either stayed in England or made their way to Utah by crossing the plains."

"Yes, that was us—is us. We came by steamship, but I'm afraid we encountered some difficulties along the way that delayed us."

Brannan bit his lip. "I noticed that you didn't introduce your father."

"He died on the crossing from New York to Panama," said Marc.

Brannan turned and expressed his sympathy to Alexandra.

"At any rate," said Marc, "we are here and I have no idea where to find housing for Gloria and my mother and brother. We hoped that perhaps you could give us some guidance. We were led to understand that you hold an important position in the Church . . ."

Brannan nodded. "I certainly am interested in members of the Church. I was set apart as mission president for California."

"That's wonderful," said Alexandra, hoping to learn more, but Brannan didn't volunteer any additional information, which left something of an awkward silence.

"We would need something modest but safe," said Marc, his cheeks coloring a bit. He hesitated, wondering if he needed to explain everything.

"You don't need to worry about that in the least." Brannan turned and motioned to the butler, whispered something in his ear, and then turned back to the family. "I understand that a cab is waiting outside with your things."

"Yes," said Marc, "your man told us it would be all right . . ."

"He was absolutely right. And I've just instructed him to arrange for an apartment that will be suitable for all of you. A separate room for Miss Palmerston, Mrs. Chandler, and a shared room for you and your brother. It is in one of my buildings, and you will be safe there and in a clean and friendly environment. In time we'll help you find something better . . ."

"But just until we go to Utah," said Alexandra quickly.

Brannan's demeanor darkened ever so slightly. "Of course, if that is what you want, but in the meantime I'm sure you'd like to spend some time getting acclimated to our Western air. You may find that California is an ideal place to settle." When Alexandra started to protest, he raised his hand. "But of course that is a discussion for another day. For now we will see you safely settled. And while I must beg your pardon now, since I have a pressing business engagement, I hope that all of you will join me for dinner on Sunday."

"Why, thank you," said Alexandra. "That would be lovely, I'm sure."

"Well, then, I will excuse—"

"There was one more thing," said Marc a bit desperately. "I was hoping that perhaps you could help me find a job. While we have enough money for some time, we will need more regardless of where we are to live. I know you have to go right now, but perhaps . . ."

Brannan smiled. "I'm afraid that I had already taken it for granted that you would want employment. My man will arrange it for you right away. California is booming and there is great opportunity for a smart and healthy man like yourself." He cast a glance at Gloria. "It's the perfect place to raise a family." If he was surprised by Gloria's lack of response, he didn't show it.

"Thank you, that would be great."

"And I'm hopeful," said Gloria quickly, before he left, "that you can find something for me to do. While I'm very happy to live with the Chandlers for the time being, I will want to find my own place."

Brannan raised an eyebrow. "Ah, that is unexpected. But I'm certain that a lady with your obvious breeding and culture can add a great deal of elegance to our rather rowdy city. Perhaps we can talk about that on Sunday. Are you able to wait until then?"

Gloria smiled, obviously relieved to think that she could end her dependency. "Sunday will be fine," she said in a smooth voice.

Brannan was not that much older than either Marc or Gloria, and
Marc felt his cheeks flush at the look that passed almost impercep-
tibly across Brannan's face.

But he was too polished to press for more information and said
quickly, "Well, I hope that settles you for the moment. I will be
off, but if you'll wait here for a few minutes, I'll have my best man
coming to gather you up and take you to your new home. And then I
will have the pleasure of seeing you all again on Sunday."

"Thank you," they each said almost in unison. Once Brannan
was clear of the room, they all sat down on the chairs without saying
a word. Then Marc sighed, definitely a sigh of relief, and everyone
laughed. The tension was broken, they were safe, and they were no
longer alone.

* * *

"I thought Mr. Brannan was charming," said Gloria. "He seemed quite
refined and genteel."

Marc nodded. He'd been quite taken with the well-dressed Brannan
and appreciated the very fine house with two bedrooms and a kitchen
that Brannan's man had arranged for them. It was far more than they
could afford, but Brannan's assistant assured them that they'd have no
trouble just as soon as Marc and Max went to work in one of his many
business ventures.

"You disagree with us," said Marc to his mother.

Alexandra looked up at him. "Why do you say that? I didn't say a
word."

"Which is why I assume there's something you don't like. You
almost always have something to say."

"Don't you be impertinent, young man. I'm still your mother."

"Sorry. But you do disagree."

Gloria looked down at her knitting.

"It's just that he was so evasive when we asked him about the
Church. He didn't seem at all interested in Utah and even changed
the subject when I mentioned it. That seems a bit odd for one who
claims to be the mission president for this area."

"Maybe they don't have enough members to form a congrega-
tion."

Alexandra harrumphed, laid down her knitting, and looked up at him. "You don't know any more about it than I do. We do know that the Mormons were among the first to find gold at Sutter's Mill and that Mr. Brannan went out to meet them. Besides that, we know that the Mormon Battalion came through here. And if there's a mission, there must be some members to populate it." She looked to the side and then back. "I'm just not sure I trust him."

Marc nodded. "That part did seem strange. But given all he's done for us, I can't help but feel indebted to him. As for the Church, I'll see Elder Tyler tomorrow, and he can clear it up for us."

Alexandra nodded. "It will be good to see him again. But he does work for Mr. Brannan . . ." Marc noted that she did not call him Brother Brannan or President Brannan as he would have expected.

"For my part I can't wait to get a job and start earning some money. Then we can figure out how to get on to Salt Lake City," said Marc.

"You're still resolved to go to Salt Lake?" asked Gloria. "It's so mild and temperate here; for April the weather is practically perfect. Mr. Brannan said that Utah was cold and desolate." She looked quite earnest when she said this.

Marc shook his head slightly. How could he argue with both of them?

* * *

"So where do the local Mormons meet?" Marc asked Elder Tyler.

"Don't worry about that. Right now you need to get your feet under you. This is a great job," said Elder Tyler. "So don't fret about things."

Marc shrugged, because it was a great job. Sam Brannan had instructed Elder Tyler (who said he now preferred to be called Joe Tyler since he wasn't on a mission anymore) to give Marc and Max jobs at his warehouse down on the Embarcadero, where tons of dry goods landed regularly for distribution through Brannan's extensive network of stores all up and down the American and Sacramento Rivers. The warehouse was a wonderland of supplies for the army of carpenters and contractors who were building the stores, warehouses, and homes that were needed for such a dynamic and growing population. Marc and Max would work hard but be paid top dollar in the warehouses. In time, they would even be allowed to make deliveries, which would give them a chance to get out and into the air.

"All right. When do we start?"

Tyler laughed. "You start right now. Nothing waits in San Francisco. There's too much work to be done. I'll drive you over there right away."

Marc and Max piled into the back of the wagon that Tyler had acquired, and it started making its way noisily toward the wharves. Apparently Joe Tyler was a favorite lieutenant of Sam Brannan, as evidenced by the great respect with which the other men treated him.

"Did you think Joe Tyler's remarks were a bit odd?" Marc whispered to Max.

"What do you mean?" said Max.

Marc blanched and leaned over to tell him to quiet down. He didn't want to be overheard.

"I mean whenever I asked him about the Church, it was like he didn't want to talk about it. Back in England, it was all he could talk about. Sometimes he used to make me a little crazy—now it's like it means nothing to him."

Max shrugged. He had been just a kid when the missionaries taught the family and hadn't really paid attention. "I don't know. Maybe."

Marc let it drop. In some ways he really didn't care. After all their trouble getting this far, all he wanted right now was to earn enough money to pay the rent and save some money for the trip to Salt Lake. He assumed they'd be going to Salt Lake since he was convinced his mother would sooner die than not complete the journey, and he owed it to Alexandra to see her dream fulfilled. The other thing he knew for certain was that he didn't want to leave Gloria in San Francisco, but he doubted that she would choose to go with them. So, as usual, he was stuck.

"Here we are, then," Joe said as he brought the cart to a halt.

Marc looked up at a huge wooden structure, built right down to the water's edge, with a pier extending out into the harbor. Glancing past the building into the bay, he saw a small island.

"Mind if I ask what that is?" Marc asked, pointing out to the island.

"It's called Yerba Buena Island—that's what the whole of San Francisco was called until a few years ago. Some of the early settlers felt that it wasn't an American enough name for a grand city like this one is going to be, so they changed it."

"And over there, across the water?" The bay was really huge—larger than any he'd ever seen.

"Contra Costa, although a lot of folks call it Oakland because of all of the trees they harvest on those mountains."

"Contra Costa?"

"It means 'opposite coast.' It's eight miles by water."

Marc nodded. He thought the bay was big, and eight miles of fully protected water certainly qualified.

"You'll be going over there to help load lumber onto the ferry boats. It's usually eight to ten degrees warmer than here."

"I like that. I've kind of grown accustomed to heat and being on the water."

Tyler smiled. "Listen, it's really good of Sam Brannan to give you two such great jobs. There will probably be some people who resent it because he passed over a lot of men who have been working here."

"We didn't—"

"Don't worry about it. He knows me and trusts me and is glad to do a favor for friends. But just do two things for me, all right?"

"What are the two things?" Marc asked.

"I want you to work hard—not so hard that it makes the other workers mad at you, but pull your weight. Mr. Brannan will take notice of that. The second is that you don't ask him a lot of questions about the Mormons. It's kind of a tender subject right now."

"But why?"

"It's kind of a tender subject with me, as well." Tyler set his jaw. "I'd prefer not to explain."

Marc cast a quick glance at Max, who shrugged.

"Okay," said Marc. "We'll do both of those things."

Tyler brightened immediately. "Good! Well, it's wonderful to have you here. I can promise you that San Francisco is going to be one of the greatest cities in the world. And we're right here where we can help it grow. Mr. Brannan is a generous man, and at some point he'll help us start buying and developing our own land, if that's something you want. I think we could all get quite rich here. In the long run, it will be in your best interest to stay in San Francisco."

That will never happen, thought Marc. *Not as long as my mother is alive. But we'll leave that for another day.* Marc remained puzzled about all the intrigue around Sam Brannan and the Mormons.

23—THE GREAT FIRE

San Francisco—May 1, 1851

"Sand. That's all this place is made of. Sand and wood. The buildings are made of wood. The wharves are made of wood. Even the sidewalks are made of wood. You'd think they'd want something a little more permanent, like brick and stone." Marc looked off into space. "Like in England. I guess for the first time since we left, I miss England." He looked forlornly at his feet. "It's been one year since we left—one year to the day . . ."

"I don't miss it," said Gloria. "I like the weather here, and I like being away from all the drudgery of structured English living." She turned and looked out at the San Francisco Bay, certainly one of the most scenic settings in all the world. "It's been a very hard year, particularly for your family, but now that we're landed and stable, I think California is refreshing. And as for wood, I'd hate to walk on the streets without sidewalks when it rains. It comes in such torrents. I'm afraid that people would lose their shoes in the muck and never be able to pull them out. At least the sidewalks allow the water to drain off."

Marc nodded. She was right, but after three weeks of unloading cut timber from the small steamer that plied the bay between San Francisco and Contra Costa, and then reloading it onto horse-drawn wagons, he hated wood. Every night his mother had to help him pull out slivers before they became infected. An infection was a quick way to lose a hand or even your life.

"I heard a little bit more about Sam Brannan," said Marc, changing the subject. He stood up and made his way to put his dinner plate in the sink to be washed.

"Well?" asked Alexandra. "What about Mr. Brannan?"

"He's very successful financially, but we knew that. Lately he's been meeting with some of the other leading citizens in an attempt to bring some kind of order to the city. There's talk about forming a vigilance committee. It's all very secretive, but Joe told me about it in confidence. I think he'll be involved."

"A vigilance committee? What's that?" asked Max.

"It's people who become disgusted with the lack of law and order," said Alexandra, "and who then take the law into their own hands. Sometimes they turn out to be worse than the people they're supposed to protect against."

"They say Sydney-town is the worst," added Marc. "There are some very hardened Australians who came here for the gold rush. Australia was founded as a penal colony, you know, so many of the people immigrating here from Australia come with criminal backgrounds. At any rate, murder and burglary are rampant, and men like Sam Brannan are fed up with the civil authorities who do nothing." For whatever reason, he felt he should defend Mr. Brannan from his mother's suggestion that a vigilance committee is bad. As the one in the family who worried most about the women's safety, he too was concerned about the crime.

"It's not that there weren't lawbreakers in England," said Gloria, "but nothing like here. Men can be so rude to me at the restaurant, saying the most outrageous things, even though I'm well dressed and proper. And it's supposed to be one of the finer establishments—I can't imagine what it's like in shabby places that cater to the lower class." She noted Marc's face color at the mention of men flirting with her. An almost imperceptible smile showed that she rather enjoyed that sign of jealousy on his part.

"I think it has to do with the place," said Alexandra. "There are very few native people here, with immigrants from all over the world. The men are less inhibited because only adventurers have the courage to come here. And with so few women to provide a civilizing influence, you get rough behavior, like from the Australian men."

"Well, people are getting fed up, and I think that some of the leading citizens are going to take matters into their own hands," said Marc. "And I understand why they feel that way."

Alexandra shook her head. "Personally, I can't wait to make our way to Salt Lake City. I can't help but feel that an entire community devoted to a set of shared religious values will make for a more civilized environment. I wish we could start right away."

"Two months is what experienced people tell me," said Marc. "They say that even in the first of June, many of the high mountain passes are closed because of snow. So we'll have to wait it out. Besides, we can use as much money as Max and I can earn."

If Gloria felt offended at being left off the list of workers earning money, she didn't show it. After all, she had expressed no commitment about going to the Great Salt Lake. When the topic of religion came up, she usually excused herself. While not particularly religious, she expressed loyalty to the Church of England. She had surprised even herself by being remarkably efficient as a hostess, managing to help the patrons feel valued while directing the flow of customers to the tables. It was the first time in her life she'd done anything like that, and she remarked more than once that there was much that she enjoyed about it. She was earning enough money in tips that she would be able to find her own apartment before long, and that suited her very well.

"Well, whether one or two months, we won't be here long enough to worry about how San Francisco residents choose to manage their affairs, nor how they choose to build their buildings and sidewalks, now will we?" said Alexandra, bringing the discussion to a close.

* * *

May 4, 1851, was a day just like any other San Francisco day. It started with fog, which burned off around noon. The weather was cool, perhaps in the low seventies, and the sky was a wonderful shade of blue. The smell of cooking fires from thousands of boarding houses filled the air but was quickly blown inland and out across the bay by the strong ocean winds. A haze that was somehow typical of the California coast left the air feeling heavy, even in the absence of fog.

It was a busy day for Marc and Max, who got to take their first trip across the bay by steamer, where they worked on the docks in the full glare of the East Bay sun, loading timber from the nearby hills while it was still wet and heavy with sap. Max was proving to have a much stouter build than either Marc or their late father.

"You don't complain a lot, do you?" Marc had asked him once, when Marc himself was almost at wit's end from exhaustion.

Max just shrugged. "Don't see what good it would do," which showed the maturity that life was forcing on him, even at his young age.

Alexandra spent her day volunteering at the National Theatre on Washington Street, where the celebrated pianist Henri Herz had performed when they first arrived in the city. The National was one of the serious theaters in the city compared to the bawdy saloon performances that were far better attended up and down the wharf. Alexandra loved the theater with a passion.

And Gloria had spent the evening working at the restaurant.

"Mr. Brannan himself came in tonight," she said as the group relaxed at the end of the day. "He was in particularly good spirits." She paused and then added, "And he commented on the good work you two are doing. He said you've made a positive impression on the supervisors." She was pleased to see the effect this had on Marc especially.

"Well, I'd love to stay up and talk," said Marc, yawning, "but I just can't keep my eyes open. I'm tired right down to my bones." With that, he and Max excused themselves and went to the bedroom they shared. Alexandra tidied up the kitchen, and soon she and Gloria were sound asleep in their bedroom.

Alexandra awoke first. At first the orange glow through the high window didn't seem alarming; there were often fires burning in barrels on the street as shopkeepers disposed of their trash. But as she rubbed her eyes and watched for a few minutes, Alexandra could see that the dancing images and shadows from the reddened glow were much brighter than usual. And then she heard muffled shouts and commotion.

"Gloria," she said gently. When the younger woman simply rolled to her side, Alexandra tried a second time, more forcefully. "Gloria! Wake up. I need your help."

Gloria stirred and rolled to her side. "What is it? What's wrong?"

"The window. Look at the window. Does that seem entirely right to you?"

Gloria rubbed her eyes and looked up, then she sat bolt upright in the bed. "It's a fire—a very big fire!" Fear now filled her voice. "I was very nearly burned to death when a barn near our home caught fire. This is very much the same." At this point, Gloria was up and out of bed, reaching her hand out to Alexandra. "We've got to wake the men and go out to see what's happening. We're on the third floor, for heaven's sake!"

Alexandra was unnerved by the urgency in Gloria's voice. "Yes, let's get them up right now!" Pulling on a housecoat that had been carried at great sacrifice across the Atlantic and up the Pacific, Alexandra raced out into the kitchen and opened the door to the men's bedroom. It was an interior room with no window. "Marc! Max! Wake up! There's a fire!" By now, Alexandra could hear a kind of roaring sound that unnerved her.

"What?" asked Marc sleepily. Max didn't even stir.

"You've got to get up!" shouted Gloria. "Right now! There's a fire!"

With that, Marc jumped right out of his bed. Looking past them, he saw the reddish orange glow through the window and pushed Max until he groaned himself awake.

"Get up, Max! We've got to get out of here!"

"I've got to get dressed," said Alexandra.

"No, Mother, we've got to get out right now." Recognizing the stridency in his voice, he said more quietly, "But get your good shoes and the things you'll need most urgently."

"You don't think our building is going to burn down. Certainly the firefighters . . ."

"I don't know. I just know we have to get out now. The last thing we want is to be trapped on the third floor of a building."

Gloria nodded. "Marc's right, Alexandra. We really need to hurry."

Marc and Max both pulled on shoes over their pajamas, and they all grabbed wool jackets then made their way into the halls. Marc was surprised to see that they were the only ones. "Perhaps we're overreacting . . ."

But from the end of the hall, Gloria said, "No, we're not! It's coming straight this way." She turned with a look of horror. "We may not make it; the fire is leaping from building to building as ashes fall on the wooden roofs."

"Quick, Max! Run up and down the hall pounding on every door. Shout *fire!* and then move on." Turning to the women, he said, "Go down to the lobby while I knock all the doors on the second floor. We'll be down in just three or four minutes."

Without hesitation, Gloria nodded and put her arms around Alexandra's shoulders to help her find her way to the stairwell in the dark.

"Hurry, Marc," Gloria said with a look of dread on her face.

Max was already halfway down the hall, so Marc ran down the stairs. There were some people stirring on the second floor, and he quickly urged them to leave all their belongings and get down to the street. He ran up one side of the hall and then back down the other side, pounding on doors and making such a commotion that he heard people stirring, some cursing, before they figured out what was happening. As he made it to the second floor landing of the stairway, he was relieved to see Max come bounding down the stairs, taking two at a time.

"Let's go!" Marc shouted as he joined Max on the stairs. There was a great deal of confusion in the lobby, and Max and Marc had to push their way through the crowd of first-floor residents, who had been more reactive to the noise outside. Once they got to the door, they pushed through and found Alexandra and Gloria across the street looking to the northwest.

"It's awful," said Gloria, pointing. Marc finally had a moment to turn in the direction of the fire, and what he saw was horrifying. It looked like the whole city was ablaze, although he knew that wasn't true. But the wood buildings, many of them still filled with sap because they had been cut green, were literally exploding as the heat set them afire. All the moisture in the sap would superheat and then explode, sending up great showers of burning embers that fell in cascades on the buildings that were downwind from the blaze. With abundant oxygen from the winds, the fire seemed to take on a life of its own, traveling from one building to the next in a mesmerizing dance of red, yellow, and orange, accompanied by the most horrific roar as the heat of the flames sucked air in from the dry, sandy mountains to the west. The Pacific Ocean was more than willing to oblige the demand for air, and the breeze was now almost like a tornado as fresh winds were sucked up into the sky by the heat of the blazes.

"We've got to get down to the wharf!" said Marc urgently. "We've got to get to the water!"

"But the flames are moving faster than we can run." There was an almost preternatural calm to Gloria's voice as she coolly analyzed the situation. She held her arm aloft. "I think we should move to the southeast, since the wind is blowing almost due east. There will be enough obstacles to slow the fire down that we can work our way south of its natural path. I think that's the best course to follow."

"But we need to get to the water—that's the only safe place!" said Alexandra.

Marc took a deep breath. He had no time to decide. He declared, "We'll go southeast. I believe Gloria is right." He hated the frightened look that crossed his mother's face, but he had to follow his instincts. He pointed to the south and started pushing his way through the crowd, making room for the others to follow. It was difficult, because most people were going the other way so they could negotiate an eastern turn to the waterfront.

"Marc, are you sure?" asked Alexandra in a desperate voice. Of course he wasn't sure—how could anyone know the direction a fire of that magnitude would take? But he had made a decision and now felt it right to follow through.

Fortunately, the crowd quickly dissipated in the direction they were going, and they were able to make better headway. From behind them they heard screams, undoubtedly the call of people who were trapped in upper floors of buildings that had been swept up in the conflagration. It was an awful, nightmarish sound, and Marc regretted having heard it. There was a loud explosion directly behind them, and the force of the blast knocked Alexandra to her knees. The heat wave was remarkable in its ferocity, and for a moment Marc thought his clothes may have caught on fire.

Quickly kneeling by his mother, he said, "Let me carry you." She started to protest but thought better of it. He picked her up—she weighed hardly anything—and they started running as fast as they could.

"It was whiskey barrels that went up," said Gloria, occasionally able to turn and glance over her shoulder. "That huge explosion was a saloon."

"See," said Marc rather breathlessly to Max, "I told you that alcohol was dangerous to your health!" He was pleased that Max laughed at the foolish joke.

"There's a large pond just two blocks farther," said Gloria. "I remember passing by it on my way to work one day. Perhaps we should go there. We could wade out into the water, if needed."

Marc nodded. The strain of running while carrying his mother was difficult, particularly since the smell of smoke and embers was now an ever-present reality that tortured their lungs.

"There it is!" shouted Gloria. "There are people there, but I'm sure we'll find room."

"There aren't any buildings close by—the open air should give us a chance!" said Max, who was now rushing ahead of them. It was because of his determination to get to the clearing to find a spot for the rest of the family that Max completely failed to see the team of wild-eyed horses pulling a fire wagon as it emerged from a north–south street just as he entered the intersection. There was really nothing the driver of the team could do—the weight of the huge steam boiler that powered the water pump was simply too great to slow quickly. Alexandra shrieked as Max went down under the hooves of the lead horses. It was disorienting enough to the horses that they veered ever so slightly, which is why the wheels of the heavy wagon managed to miss Max by a matter of just a few inches.

"Max!" shouted Marc as he started to run.

"Put me down and go to him!" said Alexandra.

Marc set his mother down as gently as he could and then sprinted to the intersection, where some others in the crowd had started to gather round the boy.

"Max!" cried Marc as he reached the spot, shoving some men out of the way to reach him. Kneeling down, he found Max lying in the street, an ugly gash across his head and a wet stain on his pajamas in the area of his ribs. "Oh, Max." Marc leaned down and put his ear directly to Max's mouth. He felt warm but labored breathing. Looking up desperately, Marc asked the crowd, "Is there a doctor? A nurse?"

A plain-looking woman stepped forward. "I'm a nurse. I'm not sure if there are any doctors." When no doctor stepped forward, Marc asked, "Can you help us?"

She kneeled down and felt Max's chest. "From the sound of his breathing, I'd say he has a broken rib and that it may have punctured his lung. We need to get him into the light where I can take a better look." By now Alexandra and Gloria had caught up.

"We need to get out of this street," said Gloria. "I hear another wagon coming."

Marc looked up and to his left, and sure enough, perhaps a block away, another wagon was approaching. "I'll carry him." As gently as he could, he put his arms under Max's limp body and lifted him. Even though he'd just turned fifteen, he was much heavier than their mother. "Let's go—you lead the way." Marc couldn't sort it all out and was happy to simply be the beast of burden.

"This way," said Gloria. "Quickly!"

Marc allowed her to pull him along, her hand on his sleeve. "Is Mother coming?"

"I'm right here," said Alexandra. "I'm fine."

They managed to clear the street in time and then made their way to the edge of the pond. It was an artificial reservoir, dug out to capture the rain water so people would have a place to do their laundry. The crowd parted so that the refugees could make their way right to the water's edge. "The nurse?"

"I'm here. Lay him down gently and then take off his shirt and jacket." Marc did as he was told, and he could see immediately that the nurse's original diagnosis had been correct. "What do we do? It sounds like he's drowning."

"He will if we don't get his lung reinflated."

"How do we do—?"

"Shush! Listen to what I tell you. Do you have a sharp knife?"

Marc nodded and reached down to his belt to unsheathe the six-inch blade he'd inherited from his father. "Good. Now go down to that pond and bring me a couple of reeds. I need to make an incision into the side of his lung, and then you will insert the reed and blow air into the lung to reinflate it."

Marc's eyes grew wide. "I don't know if I can do that . . ."

"There's no time for nonsense—just do as you are told."

Marc handed her the knife and raced over to the small reservoir, where he found some hollow reeds. Pulling them from the mud, he washed them off and then raced back to where Max was. He got there just in time, because the nurse had already made a cut in Max's side—a very deep cut that made Max squirm, even though unconscious. Marc swooned a bit at the sight of blood oozing out of the new wound.

"You've gone pale," said the nurse. "I need someone reliable." She started to turn toward the crowd, but Gloria stepped forward.

"I'll do it." She quickly kneeled and, following the nurse's instructions, forced the reed into the opening, pushing very hard to get it to go through the tissue of the lung. Unfortunately, the reed buckled.

"That's all right," said the no-nonsense nurse. "I'll make a deeper cut."

She did this with a firm and quick hand. Marc passed out as he watched her work. Luckily he wasn't conscious to hear the laughter of those who were looking on. Fortunately, this time Gloria was able to insert the reed and then to blow with what required a great deal of pressure. Max suddenly started coughing as the lung reinflated, and then his eyes popped wide open.

"Max!" said Alexandra. "You've come back." But he hadn't really. His eyes were glazed, and it was obvious that he still remained unconscious—at least unaware of what was happening. But in the act of opening his eyes, he struggled to sit up, which the nurse helped him to do. In a moment everyone could see both sides of his chest inflating and deflating as he labored to breathe. The surgery was a success. Max then started coughing again, which concerned Alexandra, but the nurse assured her it was normal. The coughing subsided after a few moments, and his eyes fluttered closed again.

"Now we have to close up the wound. Do you have a thread and needle?" the nurse asked around.

Alexandra seemed stunned and embarrassed that she didn't. At the moment her son needed her most, she felt she had failed him. But a woman in the crowd stepped forward. "I was working on some embroidery—I couldn't sleep—and I just pushed it in my pocket when I ran out the door." She handed a needle and some coarse thread to the nurse, who went to work stitching up the hole she'd made just a few moments earlier. Again Max winced slightly as the pain drew him back toward consciousness.

"I think he'll be fine now. His rib will take time to heal, but there's nothing to be done for it except to limit his movement. The main danger is pneumonia, but the moist air here should help with that."

For the first time since the surgery, Marc stirred, and Gloria turned to him. Lifting his head into her lap, she stroked his hair. That inspired him to open his eyes.

"What? What?" Marc sputtered.

"You say that a lot, don't you?" said Gloria.

Marc shook his head. "Max? The fire? What's happened?"

"You fainted. But it's all right. They've done what they can for Max. As for the fire . . ." She turned and looked in the direction of the city. "As for the fire, I believe we've managed to escape it. It's heading east, driven by the winds, and we're safely to the south."

Safely was a relative word, given the smoke and embers that drifted down on them. But there were no buildings that were going to go up in flames around them, and for the moment they were in as good a spot as could be hoped for.

"Thank you," said Marc, sitting up. "I'm very embarrassed."

"Don't be. He's your brother." She waited while Marc rubbed his temples. "And you should probably stay away from medicine as a preferred profession."

Her attempt at humor took a moment to register, and then he smiled. He reached up and kissed her. She resisted only a little until fully embracing the kiss and making it her own.

* * *

San Francisco—May 8, 1851

"We need to make a poultice to draw out the infection." The nurse who had helped them at the scene of the accident was a thorough individual, and now she was visiting the tent where the Chandlers and Gloria had found refuge. The fact that there was an urgency to her voice was even more alarming than the red streak that was extending down Max's side from the site of the initial cut. "We need some slippery elm and charcoal."

"Charcoal will be easy to find, but I don't know about slippery elm," said Gloria, who was standing next to the cot where Max was lying and above the chair where Alexandra had been for the previous twenty-four hours at Max's side.

"Then we'll start with just charcoal. I need charcoal, water, and muslin, and I need it quickly. There's a doctor two tents down who should be able to help with the muslin."

Alexandra started to get up, but Gloria put her hands on her shoulders. "I'll go."

"But you'll be late for work."

"Work will have to wait. Now you stay here with him in case he happens to wake. He'll need you."

Alexandra patted Gloria's hands, and then Gloria was out the door. She ran to the tent indicated, but the doctor had moved on. "I need muslin—do you have any?" The nurse shook her head. With so many burn patients, everything that could be used to treat the burns had already been consumed. "Oh . . . I'll start with the charcoal." Gloria made her way out into the midst of smoldering cinders and tried to find wood that might have been from a tree, rather than a building. Spotting some scorched weeds, she made her way over there and found a large piece of a branch that had once been part of one of the few trees in the area. She picked up a couple of pieces and quickly made her way back to the tent, where she borrowed a bowl and paid for some extremely precious water that was so hard to come by. It cost her a dime, which was an outrageous amount to pay in any other circumstance, but she was assured the water was clean and fresh. Making her way to Max's bed, she set the bowl on the ground and started rubbing two of the branches together to form a fine black powder in the base of the bowl. When finished, she poured in some water and started stirring with a relatively stiff piece of charred wood. When it formed a paste she motioned for the nurse, who had been tending to another injured patient.

"The paste looks right, but what about the muslin? We need bandages to apply this to the wound."

Without a word Gloria tore off the left sleeve of her dress and quickly tore the sleeve into strips that could be used as bandages.

"Gloria!" said Alexandra, but Gloria put her finger to her mouth to show she didn't want to talk about it.

"It's a good muslin dress, and this is the best I can do."

Even the nurse seemed touched. She quickly took a wide strip and started ladling the paste into the bandage. "We can't apply the charcoal directly; we need to isolate it between layers."

Gloria did her best to help and, before they were done, had torn her right sleeve to make up the bandage and the strips that wrapped around Max's chest to hold it in place.

"Will this do it? Should we try to find that slippery elm you talked about?" Alexandra was nearly frantic. "Shouldn't he wake up?"

"This will help. It's all we have, so it will have to do." The nurse's voice was calm and steady. She'd seen too many people die after making what appeared to be a full recovery to ever make promises. The risk of the infection spreading was high, and if it reached his heart, it would surely kill him or leave him crippled. Standing up, she left a few final instructions and then made her way out of the tent to tend to other victims.

"He has a fever," said Alexandra as she stroked Max's forehead.

"From the infection, I'm sure. But I'm told the fever is beneficial in that the heat kills off whatever it is that causes the infection in the first place."

"I hope so. At least I find it comforting."

"We used poultices all the time," said Gloria, trying to sound reassuring, "on animals and people. They are extremely effective in drawing out infections and other irritants. I can't help but feel this will be effective . . ."

"But charcoal? Who ever heard of using charcoal?"

"My father used it quite often. The main thing for a poultice is that it be warm and dry so that it pulls moisture from the affected area. The charcoal is very dry, and it will certainly have a strong drawing power as it starts to dry further in the air. In the process, it will absorb more moisture from the infection."

The two women were silent for a time. Then Alexandra convulsed into sobbing. "I just don't think I can stand it!" said Alexandra. "First Henry, then Honoria, and now Max. I really don't think I can stand this!"

There are times when words are more discouraging than silence. Gloria simply rested her hand on Alexandra's shoulder as the older woman sobbed.

* * *

"You there, Chandler?"

Marc turned at the sound of Sam Brannan's voice. The city was a disaster, but Brannan was in top form. He'd waded into the reconstruction with a gusto that was amazing, ordering his warehouse to remain open around the clock as wagonload after wagonload carried new wood into the burned-out zone to start new buildings. Just as soon as a site was cleared, the carpenters moved in like an army of ants.

"Yes, sir!" Marc responded.

"How's your brother?"

Marc was amazed that in the midst of all this, Brannan would remember to ask about his brother.

"Still very sick, but he woke up today for a few moments. My mother was sleeping when he opened his eyes and spoke, and it startled her so badly I thought she'd have heart failure. But he seemed lucid."

"Well, that's a good sign," said Brannan. "Any idea when he'll be out of the woods?"

That was a phrase Marc had never heard before, but he picked up on Brannan's meaning. "We finally had a doctor stop by. He said the nurse who helped us the night of the fire most certainly saved Max's life. He's still in grave danger, and we won't know the outcome for at least another day or two. To me it looks like the streak of infection has diminished, but the doctor says the problem is that if the infection reaches his heart, it could weaken him forever. Perhaps even be fatal."

Brannan looked around at the scene of devastation surrounding them. "Rather a poor welcome to America for all of you. Wish it could have been better."

"Yes, well," said Marc, his voice tightening up. "This isn't the worst of what we've experienced. I lost—" He stopped.

"You lost?"

Marc could not say why he was opening up to this man. But something about Brannan made you want to talk—his affability and charisma were trust-engendering. "I lost my father and my sister in Panama. Exhaustion and malaria."

"Ah." Brannan nodded his head. "Well, if there's anything I can do . . ." He hesitated. "If you need to go to help your brother . . ." Marc knew that was the greatest sacrifice. With the needs that came with reestablishing order in the city and the ability to sell an almost unlimited amount of wood and hardware, Brannan would not only help the city to recover but would add to his fortune while doing so. To offer Marc time off to be with Max was a huge sacrifice, and he was grateful for it.

* * *

"I'm thirsty. Can I please have a drink?" Max asked in a hoarse voice.

Marc smiled. "Of course you can! Not that we haven't been giving you drinks for the past four days . . ."

"Four days? What happened?" Max looked around, trying to sort things out.

"You got tangled up with some horses. Broke a rib and collapsed a lung. Then a little surgery."

"Enough of that, Marcus—he doesn't need to know everything all at once." Marc was grateful to hear that confidence had returned to Alexandra's voice.

"I was run over by horses?" said Max, bewildered.

"Yeah, but you're a tough little guy. It would take a lot more than that to knock you down. It might have been even more of a challenge if the wheels of the fire wagon had gone over you."

Max smiled. "A fire wagon?"

"Go get some fresh water, Marc." Alexandra said this in an authoritarian voice, even though Marc knew full well it was her way of conveying confidence to Max.

"Yes, ma'am. And if it's all right, I'll go tell Gloria that he's awake. She certainly played a part in his recovery."

Alexandra nodded. "She certainly did. I don't know how I could have gotten by without her."

Turning to Max, Marc said, "You'll need to be getting up and about soon enough—you've missed out on rebuilding nearly half of San Francisco as it is. I keep making excuses for you to Mr. Brannan and Joe Tyler, but they won't put up with this malingering forever! And I'm tired of doing the work of two men."

Max smiled. "Thanks for covering for me."

Marc had never felt so relieved and grateful in his life. Leaving the tent, he glanced up to heaven. "Thank you! Thank you for my brother." It was a very different prayer from the ones he had said when Henry and Honoria died.

* * *

May 14, 1851

"Forty percent of the city burned to the ground." Marc read this in the newspaper. "That's the official assessment—and more than four million dollars in damages." It had been just ten days since the fire. Remarkably, fully one-fourth of the buildings that were destroyed by the fire had already been replaced by new ones. Marc had been working fourteen-hour days, bringing more lumber across the bay. Such was the energy of this robust young city.

"Four million sounds like a great deal," said Alexandra. "But I still don't understand dollars and how much they're worth. I'm afraid I think in British currency."

"Something like a million British pounds," said Marc.

Alexandra's eyes widened at such an astonishing figure.

"And a very small part of the four million dollars is everything that we own," said Alexandra, her voice weary.

"But we're all alive," said Marc. "And we didn't have that much to lose."

Alexandra shook her head. "No, we'd given up most of it already, hadn't we?" She looked tired. "I so wish we could get out of this city and move on to Utah. I'm convinced that's where the Lord wants us."

"I've made some progress on that front," said Marc, putting the paper down.

"What does that mean?" asked Max, who after ten days was feeling well enough that he was restless and bored. After his fever had broken and the infection had receded, he'd made great progress. The doctor said it was still too early to tell if the infection had caused any damage to his heart, but that would come out in due course as he started to work again. But he was young and strong and had healed remarkably fast.

"It means that one of the men at work pulled me aside and told me that there's a fellow named Porter Rockwell who is coming into San Francisco next week. Apparently he was bodyguard to Joseph Smith and now to Brigham Young. At any rate, he owns saloons on the American River, and he comes to San Francisco to buy whiskey. But this fellow told me that Rockwell will be going back to Utah soon and that he sometimes helps groups of Saints find their way. I guess he's very skilled."

"How can you meet this Mr. Rockwell?" asked Alexandra urgently.

"The fellow told me where the Mormons meet but asked me to keep it quiet from Joe Tyler and Mr. Brannan—he didn't want it known that he was talking about the Church. Apparently he used to be a member."

Alexandra shook her head. "I still don't know what all this is about. I wish I knew what happened to Elder Tyler."

"Yes, well, it's awkward. And I don't want to bring it up with him. But I do think I can steal away to church this Sunday and perhaps meet this fellow. If so, we'll know what we're facing in making our way to Salt Lake City."

Alexandra nodded, obviously relieved. "Marc?"

"Yes?"

"What about Gloria? Has she said anything about Utah?"

Marc's face colored. "I've never found occasion to bring it up. She's always talking about how happy she is here. I just don't know what awaits us in Utah."

Alexandra bit her lip. "I think you may underestimate Gloria. I think she's waiting for *you* to start the conversation."

"I don't know what her feelings are for me. She is not a member of the Church, and I think that's an issue for her, as well."

"But you have feelings for each other. There's no ignoring that."

Marc nodded. "No, there isn't."

"So what are you going to do?"

"We'll have to see what Brother Rockwell says, and then I'll talk with her." He was very much afraid to do so, for fear that she would choose to stay. It was much easier to simply avoid the subject and pretend that they could stay here forever.

Picking up the paper, Marc read on. "It's the worst fire in the history of the city, and the mayor and other officials are calling for the formation of a true fire department with a superintendent paid from public funds."

"I should hope so," said Alexandra. Fortunately, Marc had managed to bring their money with him when they escaped the doomed apartment building, so they had enough for the basic necessities of life. But they'd lost pretty much everything else.

"And others are calling for brick buildings—something I've said all along. You just can't have a city this populated without permanent buildings, streets, sewers, and waterlines. And fire hydrants." Glancing up, Marc noted that Max had again fallen asleep—something he did quite often in his recovery, and Alexandra seemed lost in her knitting. *We lost everything and nothing*, he thought to himself.

Maybe Gloria's right—there is a freedom that comes from being without material possessions. Then he thought of Gloria and the trip to the Great Salt Lake. The thought of confronting her about her decision gave him a stomachache.

24—THE EDUCATION OF MARCUS CHANDLER

May 1851

"HE IS A DISTINCTIVE FELLOW, isn't he?" remarked Alexandra.

Marc nodded and then swallowed hard. Of average height, Porter Rockwell didn't look all that unusual except for his remarkable beard and uncut hair. For church, it was pulled into a ponytail, but it still made a profound impression. As did his great barrel chest, which gave him the appearance of a strong, muscular bull.

"Excuse me," said Marc nervously, "but I understand that you are Brother Rockwell?"

Porter Rockwell turned and looked at Marc with steely gray eyes. "And who might be inquiring?"

Marc felt his legs go weak. He'd never seen eyes like that, and their intensity was unnerving. "Marcus Chandler, from Liverpool, England. I'm here with my mother and younger brother, Max, as well as a friend of ours. We are hoping to go to Salt Lake . . ." Marc felt embarrassed, having given Rockwell probably more information than he would have liked.

Rockwell's eyes seemed to dance, as if he recognized how intimidating his presence could be. "So you are members of the Church?"

Marc nodded.

"Well, then, introduce me to your family." Marc shook his head to clear it then stumbled on his words as he brought Alexandra forward and then Max.

"My son says you are a businessman," said Alexandra formally, but with an earnest sound in her voice.

Rockwell smiled. "A business some people question—but it fills a need for people. Now, you said something about Salt Lake City?"

"Yes," said Alexandra, taking charge. It was her family, after all. "My husband and I were converted to the gospel in England, and he was determined to immigrate. We came by steamer to New York and then here via Panama. My husband and our daughter, Honoria, passed away en route. Now we are here and wish we were in Salt Lake City. Can you help us?"

It was clear that Rockwell was a hard man, based on the roughness of his hands and the weathered look of his skin. Which is why Alexandra was so surprised by a tear that rolled down his cheek. "I'm sorry about your loss. I've lost people who meant a great deal to me."

"The Prophet?" asked Alexandra. "I understand that you knew him very well."

Rockwell nodded. "From the time I was a young boy until he was murdered in Illinois. But there have been others. Too many others."

"Brothers and sisters, we'd like the meeting to come to order!" The voice from the small portable pulpit at the front of what the night before had been a saloon, but was now serving as a makeshift chapel, was pleasant but firm.

"We better take our seats," said Rockwell.

"But about Salt Lake City . . ."

He smiled. "If you want to go to Salt Lake City, I believe we can see that you get there."

Rockwell was invited to go to the front of the room, where he sat down next to the branch president. Alexandra, Max, Marc, and Gloria took their seats toward the back. "It feels good to be in church again," said Alexandra.

"Not much of a church," said Marc, looking around.

"Don't be so critical—it's the best these good people can do."

Marc nodded. He wished that he would think before saying things. He really hadn't intended to be disrespectful. *The truth is, it feels good to be with people who understand what brought us here.* In just the few minutes that they'd had to shake hands before the service started, he'd felt a great deal of warmth and concern.

"You'll sing with me?" asked Alexandra.

"I'll sing with you." The truth was that both Marc and Max had very fine singing voices, although it was apparent that Marc would spend his life as a tenor, perhaps sometimes going as deep as a baritone, while Max was destined to have a marvelously resonant bass voice. As Marc sang, he happened to glance sideways at Gloria, who registered her surprise that he could sing so well. *Good!* he thought. *It's all right that I can still surprise you.*

After the singing, they had prayer and then a sacrament service. Marc didn't know if he should take the sacrament after all this time, because there had been many occasions when he doubted his faith and even more when he'd found himself angry and discouraged. But when his mother saw him hesitate, she put her hand on his and whispered gently, "I think it is fine. Perhaps for your father." Marc was surprised to feel his throat tighten at the thought of Henry, and he did as he was prompted.

"Now, brothers and sisters, many of you know Brother Porter. Others of you do not. I am pleased to tell you that as the ninth person baptized in the Church, he was a friend to the Prophet from the earliest days. He has consented to talk to us now and to tell us some of the things he knows about this Church and what it means in the modern world. Brother Rockwell."

Alexandra, who was seated between Max and Marc, reached out and took Marc's left hand in her right, and Max's right hand in her left, and gave them a squeeze. As Marc turned and looked at her, she smiled. Then they listened, entranced, as for more than an hour Porter Rockwell recounted stories of the Restoration as he had heard and experienced them firsthand. His learning was not from great books, as was Henry Chandler's, since Rockwell could neither read nor write. But experience had been a sometimes harsh and demanding teacher, and it was apparent that Rockwell had learned a great deal. His testimony of the Prophet Joseph Smith left a burning sensation in the heart of all who heard him preach that day.

After the meeting, Rockwell met up with the family for a just a few minutes. When he asked what experience they had on the frontier, he shook his head to learn that it was limited to the time they'd spent in Panama as part of an organized group.

"Do you know how to shoot?" asked Rockwell, to which Marc shook his head. "Then we should do something about that before we leave. Can you meet me at the southern end of town next Thursday evening?"

"I can. But I don't have a gun."

"I can probably do something about that," said Rockwell.

"So when do you think we'll leave?" asked Alexandra, almost too excited to contain herself.

"Four weeks. You'll need to meet me in Sacramento, since I won't be coming back to San Francisco. Can you do that?"

Marc nodded. They would take a river steamer.

"Good. Thursday night. I'll tell you what you need for the trip across the mountains then." Rockwell left.

"Rather like a force of nature, isn't he?" said Marc.

"He's a very remarkable man," said Gloria. "I've never heard anyone preach like that. If what he says is true, it would change everything . . ." Wisely, neither Alexandra nor Marc pressed her. Authentic spiritual feelings needed time to grow and shouldn't be hurried.

* * *

"Never held a gun?" Porter asked.

Marc shook his head. "Almost no one in England owns guns. Not even our policemen. Only the military while on active duty and wealthy landowners who hunt for game."

Rockwell nodded. "I wasn't skilled with a gun until a group of Missourians forced my father and me at gunpoint to take them across a river to raid Mormon villages. I never felt so naked and helpless in my life, and I vowed that I never would again. So I bought a pistol and went out practicing until I can hold my own with pretty much any man."

"I've heard some stories . . ."

Rockwell shook his head. "Don't believe everything you hear."

Marc closed his mouth and pursed his lips. The last thing he wanted to do was aggravate the man who was going to help them get to their final destination.

"Here's a well-balanced pistol that can see you through pretty much anything we'll encounter between here and Utah. You'll need a rifle to bring down game, but this works just fine for varmints. And if we encounter any outlaws along the way, it will make them think twice."

"I know a little something about that," said Marc. "I could have used this in Panama." Before Rockwell could question him, he continued. "How much do I owe you?" Even though he tried to say it in a perfectly steady voice, the precariousness of their financial state caused his voice to tremble ever so slightly.

"Let's call it a 'welcome to America' gift."

"No, really, I can pay. I should pay."

Rockwell fixed his gray eyes on Marc. "When a man offers you a gift, you should accept it."

Marc nodded. It was going to be tough figuring out exactly how to relate to this fellow. Marc was sure that he was overly intimidated by Rockwell's reputation, which many of the men at work had been willing to talk about when they learned that Marc was meeting up with him. The consensus had been that Marc couldn't have found a better mentor as he prepared to adapt to living in the West.

"All right," said Rockwell, handing Marc the weapon. "You want to learn to balance it like this . . ."

* * *

By their third lesson, Marc had improved considerably, and the pistol felt quite natural in his hand. "I never thought I'd hold a gun in my life. Now it seems it will be part of everything I do."

"Not necessarily. Most folks who work in Salt Lake City don't carry a gun. It's only when you're out on the trail or hunting that you need a weapon. I carry my guns all the time because I'm a deputy marshal, and I never know when I'll need one. Besides, a lot of gunslingers looking to make their reputation want to challenge me, and I have my small arsenal to discourage them from trying or to reprimand them with when they do try."

"I've been told that you've killed a lot of men." Marc felt more comfortable with Rockwell now that he'd spent time with him and realized that his rather curt replies were more a sign of shyness than arrogance. Porter warmed up considerably as he got to know a person.

"There's nothing exciting or gratifying about killing a man. I try to avoid it whenever I can. But some people are fools and decide to take their chance with me."

"Can I ask you a question?"

"You can ask me anything. I may not answer."

Marc smiled. This was such a typical response. "It's about Sam Brannan. He's been very good to me and my family, but everyone tells me I shouldn't ask him about the Mormon Church. Yet when we were in England, we heard that he was an important leader. In fact, the missionary who taught our family now works for Brannan, and he seems disaffected as well. Do you know what happened?"

"He defied Brigham Young, so now he's lost the Spirit. It won't be long before he takes himself out of the Church."

Marc waited, hoping for more explanation. When none came he decided to press it. After all, it was he who was caught between the proverbial rock and a hard place. "How exactly did he defy Brigham Young?"

Rockwell, who had been pointing his pistol at one of the targets, brought his arm down and went over and sat on a large rock. "I don't like to talk about men. But Brannan had an idea that all the Mormons should come here to California to settle. He brought a group of Saints on the *Brooklyn,* a sailing ship that went around Cape Horn to Hawaii and then back here to San Francisco. He's so taken with the place that he made a trek out onto the plains to tell Brother Brigham about it. But Brigham settled on Salt Lake City. That put Brannan off. Then, when gold was discovered, President Young sent one of the apostles here to collect tithing from the men. The Church needs tithing money to survive. I came with him. When we got here, we found that Sam Brannan had already collected the tithing. When we asked him for it, he said no. When we said it was God's money, he said, 'Then have God sign a note telling me he wants it. That's the only way I'll give it to you.'" Marc's eyes widened at that impertinence. "The truth is that Brannan used the tithing money to buy all of the supplies that got him started in business. You could say that every brick in that mansion he built is because of tithing money that he stole from the poor Saints in California. So that's why Sam Brannan and I aren't on good terms."

"Seems like God would strike a man down for something like that."

"My experience is that God lets things take their course. But in the end there is always a price to be paid, and Sam Brannan will pay that price. You can be sure of that." Rockwell fixed his remarkable eyes on Marc. "And what if this missionary you placed such great trust in decides to leave the Church, as well?"

Marc thought about it. "I guess it wouldn't be real faith on our part if we believed only because of him." Rockwell seemed satisfied by this, and from the firm set of his jaw Marc could tell that they were done talking about this subject.

"What's next in my training?"

"Rifles. I don't have one to give you, but I'm going to teach you how to shoot, regardless. That way you can help me feed the party as we make our way through the High Sierras."

Marc gulped. As a city boy, he had never hunted for food. His life was taking such a different direction from anything he could have ever imagined.

25—SHADOWS ON SAN FRANCISCO

June 1, 1851

"GLORIA—CAN I SPEAK TO you for a moment?" Gloria could not possibly have imagined how fortunate she was to be summoned by Sam Brannan at precisely that moment. His premium restaurant, the Brannan House, had been spared by the fire and was now even more central to the cultural life of the more civilized elements of California society than before because his main competitors had burned to the ground. Business was always brisk, and Gloria had managed to meet all of the prominent citizens of the city. At first it had bothered her to be in a position of servitude, since that would have been unheard of for one of her social standing back in England, but what she found here in America was that nearly everyone in San Francisco had come from far more modest backgrounds than she and had simply made their way to the top by enterprise or the luck of striking gold.

There was one exception—Mrs. John Fremont. Mr. Fremont was the man credited with conquering California from the Mexicans, and Mrs. Fremont's father was a prominent senator back in Washington D.C. John Fremont had made a fortune in gold, and now the Fremonts owned a grand house in the city. It was widely rumored that Fremont would become the next governor, or most certainly the first United States senator, when California was granted statehood. Mrs. Fremont had taken a liking to Gloria and often stopped to chat with her.

"Perhaps you should own your own business," Mrs. Fremont had said to her one day.

"I hope to. But first I have to earn enough money. I'm afraid I lost my small inheritance to thieves in Panama."

"I had a terrible experience in Panama, as well." That had forged an even stronger bond, and Mrs. Fremont had promised to talk to her husband about backing Gloria for something more suitable to her background, perhaps a fine ladies' dress shop. "You certainly have the taste and style." Of course, that's what Gloria had been thinking, and it flattered her to be recognized for her good taste.

"Mr. Brannan?" said Gloria as she stepped away from the hostess reception area.

"Ah, yes. I'd like you to meet a newcomer to San Francisco and to help her feel welcome."

Gloria smiled at the middle-aged woman who had made her way with her husband from India, of all places. Brannan, the woman, and her husband chatted amiably, with Brannan offering Gloria's services to help Mrs. Caldwell adjust to life in their new surroundings. That he would do so was a sign of his growing reliance on Gloria in a wider role. For Brannan, it was a way to ingratiate himself to the successful businessmen with whom he could do future business by having Gloria help their wives get settled. That way Brannan and the newcomer could immediately begin to focus on their commercial activities.

During this interlude Gloria's eyes wandered. Casting a glance toward the hostess table, she spied two men, rather dark, handsome, and slick in their appearance. *The type of men who cheat at cards and charm wealthy women. The type who irritate me.* Still, such men were common enough on the frontier, and she let her eyes drift out to the dining room. But as her mind processed what she had seen, a cold electric shock ran suddenly from the back of her neck right down to her toenails and she jerked her head back to the table.

"It's him!" she said out loud. "It's him."

"What was that, Miss Palmerston?" asked Sam Brannan, annoyed at her outburst.

Gloria's eyes darted back and forth, and she moved so that Brannan stood between her and the two men.

"Nothing, Mr. Brannan. I'm sorry. I just recognized someone, and it surprised me."

"Well. Perhaps you can check in with them after you seat Mr. and Mrs. Caldwell." She'd obviously spoiled the magic that he had been weaving with the new couple.

"Uh, that's all right. Of course. Let me find one of our best tables . . ." She fumbled with the menus lying on a table next to them. "We can go this way." She desperately wanted to regain her poise, but it was impossible. *Geoffrey Brandt!* her brain screamed. *It's Geoffrey Brandt right here in San Francisco!* Her legs felt much like jelly as she led the Caldwells to a table near a window. Her sole objective was to seat them as far away from Brandt as possible so that he couldn't spy her. Mrs. Caldwell, completely unaware of the horror that Gloria was experiencing at the return of the man who had nearly sent Marc into exile and her back to England, chatted away amiably as Gloria did her best to respond with some degree of tact. *What on earth am I to do?*

* * *

Alexandra looked at Gloria intently. "It seems impossible. Are you certain it was him?"

Gloria nodded. "I'm sure. His is not a face that I'll ever forget."

Alexandra shook her head. "It seems as if our nightmares will never end."

"And you don't think he saw you?" asked Marc.

"I don't think so. But I was rather loud when I realized it was him. At least some of the diners turned our way. Hopefully he was too involved in getting seated to notice."

"We'll have to confront him. I don't see any other way."

"But Marcus, perhaps he's about to board a ship for Panama, and there will be no need for a confrontation." Alexandra said this as hopefully as possible.

"The risk is too great of him finding Gloria alone," Marc said. "He's already kidnapped her once. He'll certainly do it again."

"But maybe he's decided to live in California, and he won't be interested in Gloria," said Max. "A lot of people have come here to stay."

"That could be," agreed Gloria.

Marc pounded his fist on the table. "The point is that we shouldn't have to sit around wondering. This man very nearly ruined our lives once, and I won't let him do it again."

Gloria stood up from her chair. "I can't let you put yourself in danger again. It's me he's after, not you, so it shouldn't involve you."

"Do you *really* feel that way?" asked Marc, barely concealing his fury. "Do you really mean to say that after everything we've been through, you are still nothing more to me than an acquaintance?" He bit his lip so hard it started to bleed.

"No, it's not . . . it's just that I don't want to . . ." Gloria looked around the room helplessly. Max averted his eyes, Alexandra looked stricken, and Marc just stood there clenching his fists, his face flushed.

"Fine—" Marc started to say, and then he turned to storm out of the room. But Gloria was quicker. She managed to come between him and the door, and rather than say anything, she put both her hands to his face and pulled it to hers in a long and passionate kiss.

After perhaps a full minute, the two pulled apart. "Does that answer your question?"

"I guess . . . I guess . . . I guess it does," said Marc, staggered.

Gloria stepped back. "I only said what I said because you are too hard to read. I think you love me, but you've never come out and said it. If I'm to stay here by myself, then I need to deal with this problem on my own. But if you are to be part of my life, then we'll face it together."

Marc was speechless. Instead he pulled Gloria into a full embrace and kissed her with abandon.

* * *

"You're not experienced enough—not if this man has practice shooting at people. It's a lot harder than you think, and even a moment's hesitation will be fatal."

"I hope it doesn't come to that—I hope he just leaves us alone."

Porter Rockwell shook his head. "Do you think that's likely?"

Marc shrugged. It was not likely.

"I could do it for you. I'm not a lawman here, but I could let my reputation resolve this. He's not likely to take me on."

Marc shook his head. "I can't do that. What kind of man would I be?"

"A live one."

Marc smiled but quickly clouded up again. "I have to be the one to protect my family. My girl. Now that I know how Gloria feels about me, I have to protect her. If I back out this time, who can say if I'd ever have the courage to face up to whatever else might be coming?"

Rockwell had a surprisingly soft voice for one so tough. "You have courage. You told me about Panama and about how you outwitted this man in New York. You'll do all right. But we're going to practice drawing until you can do it without thinking. When you confront this man, you cannot have your hand on your gun. And if you don't want to face a hangman's noose, you'll have to wait until he draws. Then it will be in God's hands. I'll do everything I can to get you ready, but then it will be up to you."

"Thank you," said Marc quietly. He felt a lump in his throat. "I consider it a blessing that I met you, because otherwise I'd be a dead man for sure." He hated the fact that he was emotional, but the truth was he was frightened beyond measure. *But I have to do this! I have to be the one.* He thought about Gloria and the joy he felt when she acknowledged that she loved him. More than anything in the world he wanted to spend his life with her. The paradox is that it took a challenge like this—one in which he could very well lose his life—to finally gain the courage to discover her love.

26—THE SHOWDOWN

June 1851

MARC HAD HOPED TO CONTROL the time and place of his inevitable meeting with Brandt. Placing a few discrete inquiries through friends at work, he discovered that Brandt had arrived in California nearly three months earlier and that he had then gone up the Sacramento River to the gold fields. It was difficult to find out exactly what he was doing, because he wasn't the type to share his plans, which meant that the messages were mixed. Some reports suggested that he was going to stay in San Francisco and start a detective agency. Certainly the population was growing fast enough to support such an enterprise. Others thought he was going to return to Liverpool by steamship. Virtually no one had heard him inquire about Gloria. All of which led to confusion.

Marc had gone to the restaurant to escort Gloria home. It was late, there were no street lamps, but the walk back to their tent was through a relatively safe part of town. Once they left the shadows of the buildings, they would be out in the relative open where a bright moonlit night substituted nicely for the missing street lighting.

As they came around a corner there was a rustle of noise that made the hair on the back of Marc's neck stand up.

"Did you hear that?" asked Gloria urgently.

"It probably wasn't anything." Marc strained to see the street in front of them, but all was shadows. Just as they reached the center of the block, with the promise of an open field enticingly close in front of them, two men stepped from the shadows. Marc came up short and put his arm in front of Gloria's waist.

"So, Mr. Chandler, we meet again." The deeply resonant voice of Geoffrey Brandt was very much like the rumble of a black panther, causing an involuntary shiver in anyone whom he took by surprise.

Marc didn't even try to play dumb. He knew who it was and acknowledged him. "We heard you were in town, Mr. Brandt. Hopefully you're here in California to make your fortune."

"I'm glad to know you are concerned about my welfare." Brandt stepped out into the middle of the street, where the moonlight fell directly on him. He was an imposing figure with a lean, athletic build and was much taller than the average man here.

"I may indeed come back and start an agency here—I do like the weather."

"We do too, but we're not staying here. We plan to move on."

"And by 'we' I assume that you and Miss Palmerston have some kind of agreement with each other."

"We love each other." Even in this terrifying situation, he felt warmth course through his body as he declared his love publicly.

Brandt nodded. "I kind of thought it would end up that way."

"Which means that you can leave us to our own future!" said Gloria, her voice hardly betraying the fear she felt.

"You know, as a romantic fellow I would really like to do that. But as a man whose reputation has suffered at your hands, I just can't see that happening. I made a contract to return you to Britain, and I need to fulfill it. Plus that business of buying out Billy Call's debt was a very serious blow. He made it back to England, and I had to pay a pretty stiff bribe to keep his family quiet. So you can see why it's so important that I take you back."

"So you'd kidnap me again?"

"I will escort you. To your mother, in fulfillment of this warrant. It seems that you've been charged with stealing some fine jewelry from her, and it is her right to have you returned to face justice."

"My MOTHER!" Gloria exploded. "My mother pressed charges against me for me taking that which I had properly inherited from my father's mother? It never belonged to her."

"I suppose that's a civil dispute that will have to be resolved by British courts. Naturally, if you are found innocent, you'll be free to do as you please."

"I will not go back . . ." Gloria started to say at precisely the same moment that Marc started with, "She is not going back to England with you . . ."

"Listen," said Brandt in a more even tone. "I am a man who deserves much of the censure that is directed against me. People hate me for the line of work I'm in. But I really don't have any reason to keep you two apart, nor any desire to make your lives miserable. But I do need to convince you to go back to England. Once I've fulfilled my contract, I'll see to it that you have a choice as to whether to stay or leave. I can be a formidable enemy, but I can also be a powerful ally. Your mother is despicable, and I'll help you get away from her, if you like. But the warrant is genuine, and the reward is worthwhile."

"So you'd let us buy you out of the reward?" said Marc, a glimmer of hope emerging.

Brandt shook his head. "I wish I could. It would be a lot simpler. But the truth is that I still have an active business there, and I can't be known to sell out a contract."

Marc took a deep breath to calm his nerves. This was the moment of truth. At least he thought it was. But before he could say anything, he very nearly got bowled over as Gloria started charging toward Brandt, cursing as she did, with threats that she was going to personally strangle him. Marc reacted immediately and ran after her, grabbing her by the waist and physically pulling her back.

He whispered to her furiously, "Don't do this, Gloria. If he gets you, he'll put a gun to your head, and then there will be nothing I can do. Let this be my fight."

She retreated with him, the four of them standing in the deserted street. "You'd be wise to let her come," said Brandt. "I don't want to kill you. And I'm being honest when I say the two of you can work this out in England and come back here or wherever it is that you intend to go. But I will have Miss Palmerston return with me. That much is certain."

"But you know that my mother will see to it that I never get to leave!"

"Perhaps, but it remains that if your gallant Mr. Chandler here interferes with the lawful processing of a warrant and gets killed doing so—well, I'll be sorry, but it will be a price you chose to pay."

"A British warrant has no validity in California, and you know it," stated Marc.

"It does as far as I'm concerned." Brandt pulled back his overcoat to reveal a holster and a very shiny, expensive pistol. "And I'm going to enforce it by whatever means necessary."

Marc took a deep breath and pulled back his coat, showing his modest pistol. But it was reliable, and Porter Rockwell had assured him it was the finest weapon a man could have when defending himself.

"Ah," said Brandt with a big grin. "Mr. Chandler has learned to use a handgun?"

"I have. And I'll use it on you, if that's what it takes to get you to leave us alone!"

Brandt looked around. "Listen to me well, Chandler. I don't want to kill you. But you are no match for me. And even if you were, you're no match for the two of us." At that point, Brandt's man stepped forward and showed his pistol. "Between the two of us, you will certainly die—and Miss Palmerston will go with us to England. That is unless she's killed in the gunfight. That's what almost always happens when guns start blazing. So I advise you to step aside right now."

"Two men are not a fair fight," said Gloria with contempt.

"And who said I was ever interested in a fair fight?" Brandt stiffened. The moment was at hand. "Now don't be a fool and take on two men when you most certainly will be killed!"

Marc was sweating and not because of the heat. His heart felt as if it would pound right out of his chest. But he had to face up to this. He motioned to Gloria to move to the side of the street, "Get out of the way."

"Marc, there are two of them. It's hopeless."

Suddenly, there was a noise from behind them. "We don't fight that way in America," said a low voice. "We keep it fair."

"Who's there?" shouted Brandt, unnerved to see another fellow emerge from the shadows behind Marc.

"The name's Rockwell. Porter Rockwell. And I don't like the odds you've given my friend."

"Rockwell!" The tone in Brandt's voice changed dramatically. "I've heard of you. You're the gunslinger who has never lost a fight."

"I guess that's right," said Rockwell thoughtfully. "Never lost a shooting contest, and never lost in a gunfight."

Brandt spat on the ground. "So you're going to take this fellow off the hook? If you do, we'll find him someday when you're not there."

"Marc Chandler has to fight his own battle. I won't stop that. But I will take out your man, and that is a 100 percent certainty. If you and Chandler want to fight, so be it. But you will not double up on him." With that, Rockwell brought his pistol, which he'd had hidden under his vest, into plain sight and pointed it directly at Brandt's associate.

The fellow shifted uneasily. "I didn't sign up to go against Porter Rockwell. I'm not up to that!" And with that the man turned and fled down the street.

"Now it looks more even," said Rockwell, stepping to the side.

Brandt shook his head. "This really is something. I've tried to be reasonable." He stammered a bit, stomped his foot. But he kept his hand away from his holster, which meant Marc couldn't take any action. Finally Brandt smiled. "This just isn't worth it. There's no reason either of us should die over some stolen jewelry . . ."

"I didn't steal it! It's mine by inheritance!"

"Alleged stolen jewelry." He looked down at his feet. "So I guess you've bested me yet again, Chandler."

"I haven't ever tried to *best* you or anyone else. I just want to be free."

Brandt waved him off. "No more talking. I'm going to leave, and you can go on your merry way."

With that, Brandt turned his back to Marc and started to walk away.

Hardly believing his good fortune, Marc started walking toward Gloria—a move that might very well have been the end of him had Porter Rockwell not shouted, "Marc!"

Acting on pure instinct, Marc subconsciously noted that Brandt was wheeling, his intention now obvious. All the training and practice that Marc had spent under Rockwell's tutelage now asserted itself, and without even thinking about what he was doing, Marc whipped his pistol up and out of his holster and fired directly at Brandt. As he did so, he was stunned by an incredibly sharp, stabbing thrust to his shoulder that felt like a red-hot poker piercing right through him and sent him reeling to the ground in agony.

As he lay on the ground, trying to twist in such a way as to take pressure off the wound, he spied Brandt lying on the ground, and it dawned on him that the reason he was hit in the shoulder, rather than in his chest, was that *his* bullet had hit Brandt a fraction of an instant before Brandt had pulled the trigger. Marc's shot had been both faster and more accurate, hitting Brandt directly in the chest, which knocked him off balance just as he was firing. Brandt got off his round as he started to fall. But he was dead before he hit the ground.

27—UNTIL THE JOURNEY ENDS

The Sierra Nevada—August 1, 1851

"THE SUMMIT!" SAID ALEXANDRA WITH a touch of pride in her voice. "There's a great deal more in store, according to Brother Rockwell, but we have climbed to the highest pass we need to go through between California and Salt Lake City. There were times I didn't think we'd make it."

"And we did it riding men's-style on the horses," said Gloria, stretching her legs and back. The group had dismounted and was watering the horses in an open clearing.

"I think Brother Rockwell was right on that count," replied Alexandra. "I don't know how we could have ever kept our balance on some of the grades if we'd attempted it sidesaddle."

Gloria nodded and then lifted her head to sniff the air. "The trees are so wonderful up here. The smell is absolutely invigorating."

"Pine trees, hemlock, and firs," said Max, who had made it his passion to make a pencil sketch of as many of the flowers and trees as he could at the end of each day, hoping that he could match them to known samples once they reached Salt Lake City. "I wish we could have seen the giant sequoia; those are best of all—at least that's what I've heard." Attention to such detail was just one of the ways he took after his father.

"I'm still a little unsettled that Brother Rockwell left us while he went to meet the westbound group. I know we're in the middle of the wilderness and perfectly safe with Mr. Hendricks and Max, but it's still unsettling." Gloria shivered, even though the air was pleasant and warm in the midday summer sun.

"And what about me?" asked Marc, coming up behind Gloria. "Aren't you safe with me?" He put his arms around her waist from behind.

"My roughneck cowboy?" she said. "Of course I feel safe with you. But you are still impaired, at least a little. It's only been two months since you were shot . . ." She regretted saying that as soon as the words came out of her mouth. No one had worked harder to rehabilitate himself than had Marc after his left shoulder was wounded by Brandt's bullet. "I shouldn't have said it that way—I really intended to compliment you on how much progress you've made."

Marc nodded. If his feelings were hurt, he didn't show it. "I agree with your first sentiment. But I seem to be getting by, and we've made it this far."

Gloria smiled bravely but still regretted her words. She led him to a fallen log and motioned for him to sit down next to her. "So how are you doing?"

Marc wiped his brow and sighed. "It hurts a great deal of the time. I'm beginning to doubt that I'll ever be able to raise my left arm any higher than my shoulder. That's going to put a crimp in whatever work I hope to do in Utah." He paused and sniffed the air. "I could never have pictured such a wondrous place in all my dreams. I thought I'd miss England, but these mountains are magnificent beyond imagination." He then added, "But Utah may not be so beautiful."

Gloria smiled. "If a year ago you'd told me that I'd be riding a horse through some of the most rugged mountains in the world while making my way to a desert with a family of scholars-turned-outdoorsmen—well, I'd have urged you to commit yourself to an insane asylum." She turned and took his hand. "But here I am. And having made it this far, I think I can take whatever Utah has to offer."

Marc patted her hand in return and then stood up. "I want to have Max practice his shooting. He's got to get better at his shooting. I know that Porter is just three days away, but it's up to us now. Brother Hendricks is very good with a gun, but his son—not so much. So Max and I need to be prepared."

Gloria watched as Marc made his way over to Max, who put down his sketchbook—the one indulgence he'd been allowed to bring with him from San Francisco—and together they made their way to the edge of the clearing, where Marc started setting up a series of targets for Max to shoot at. Gloria's mind wandered back to the events of that night when Marc was shot and when he killed Geoffrey Brandt. At first she was terrified to think that Marc had been killed, and for a few days that was a real possibility. But Porter Rockwell had given him a blessing—something Gloria had never witnessed before—and from the moment he did, Marc had started to improve. Then there had been a trial after Marc submitted himself to the local marshal, at Porter's recommendation. It was in this venue that Rockwell and Sam Brannan had discovered each other's interest in the family, and while Brannan was disappointed that Marc and Gloria were going to Utah, he stood by them in the trial, attesting to Marc's character. With two witnesses testifying that Marc had acted in self-defense, a claim bolstered by the fact that Marc himself had been shot, the trial was quickly concluded with the judgment that Marc was innocent of murder.

From that point on, the family had made it their primary mission to get ready to accompany Porter Rockwell and a small group of Mormon Battalion holdovers who wished to make their way to Utah. As Gloria basked in the mountain air, they had now been on the trail for nearly three weeks, painfully making their way up the western slope of the Sierra Nevada mountain range. Although she had not joined the Mormon Church, Gloria had accepted Marc's proposal for marriage, which they agreed would take place after they settled in Salt Lake City.

Gloria got up and made her way back to the group, where the small company formed to eat a light lunch before moving on to find a suitable camp for that evening. In all, there were eight of them, now just seven while Porter Rockwell was off exchanging mail and information with a group of Mormons sent by Brigham Young to check on the Saints in California. They had met the lead scout earlier that day, and Porter had taken off immediately, assuring the group that under Marc's guidance they could continue on the path without Porter, promising that he would catch up with them by the end of the week.

Finishing Max's lesson, Marc walked over to Leandro Hendricks, a member of the group they were traveling with, and said, "I'd like you to follow at a short distance behind us to warn of any danger." Hendricks was an experienced veteran of the Mormon Battalion who had volunteered to be one of the men to stay in California when gold was first discovered. Many Battalion members had wanted to go on to Salt Lake City to be reunited with their families, even at the expense of giving up their share of the easy-to-pan gold, but Brigham Young had sent word that food supplies in Utah were too precarious to support that many additional mouths, and so some had stayed behind. Now that the Saints were more fully established, Leandro and his teenage son were on their way. His wife had died in Missouri before the trek west.

"Of course I'll follow," said Hendricks. "I'll leave Jake with the ladies while you lead out." Jake was Hendricks's son. By rights it was Leandro who should be leader in Porter's absence, based on his experience in the Battalion, but he was an unassuming fellow, and Porter's earlier experience with Marc had caused him to get the responsibility.

"All right, then, another four hours of travel and we'll make camp for the night." As they started down the trail, following the natural line of the creek, Marc felt exhilarated at the change in his life. He was facing down the wilderness of the great American West, and it was thrilling.

* * *

"Yes, I heard it." Marc motioned to the group to continue chatting, as if nothing was wrong. He got up and stirred the camp fire, then sat down next to Leandro Hendricks. "I'm quite sure someone is out there," said Marc quietly.

"I agree," said Hendricks, fingering his rifle.

"Why don't you get up and act as if you're going out into the woods to relieve yourself. Then find a tree to hide behind where you can keep an eye on the camp."

Leandro nodded. "It may be nothing, but that's a sensible plan. What about Jake?"

"Leave him where he is, but have him ready to fire if need be."

Hendricks got up and stretched lazily then excused himself. Marc went back and sat down by Gloria. He slipped her the extra pistol that Rockwell had left them. Gloria had practiced just once or twice and was clearly made nervous by this turn of events.

Turning to Max, he dropped his eyes to Max's rifle, and was answered by the slightest nod of Max's head. Max was loaded and ready. Marc couldn't use a rifle at this point, because of his injured shoulder, but Max was proving himself to be quite a good rifleman. His only problem that he was so deliberate in setting the shot up that animals often moved on before he could get the shot off at them.

"So, discover any new trees today?" Marc asked casually, in an ordinary voice.

"A couple of new flowers that I haven't seen before," replied Max, his voice slightly wavering.

"Kind of late for flowers, isn't it?" Marc asked.

Max's voice betrayed his anxiety. "These were kind of grayish—probably from the lack of rain."

"That is one of the big surprises here, isn't it? After all the rain in England and Panama, it seems hard to believe that all of this can grow without any rain for weeks on end. I guess it comes from all the snow in the winter." Marc's heart was racing, because he'd heard at least two or three more sounds of something moving in the bush, but the hundreds of reflective surfaces in the area made it difficult to pinpoint exactly where the sound was coming from.

Just when he thought the wait would prove interminable, a man stepped out into the clearing. Marc pulled up his pistol, but the man raised his hands. "No need to be hostile," the fellow said. "I'm just a little cold and hungry. Hoping you might lend me your fire for a few minutes."

Marc lowered his hand but kept the pistol pointed at the intruder. "You and who else?"

"Just me," said the fellow easily. "I know it probably sounds strange that I'd be out this late in the season, but my horse came up lame, and I saw the smoke from your fire, so thought I'd come seek some company."

It was a lie, of course, because Marc had distinctly heard rustling from more than one spot. Porter Rockwell had been training Marc and Max almost constantly since they'd left San Francisco, perhaps gratified at the earnestness of Max's study, and aware that Marc needed to be trained for an occasion just like this.

"Well, you can come a bit closer, but we don't have an extra horse or a lot of food. You found us a long way from San Francisco."

The fellow moved closer toward the fire but did not sit down on the log to which Marc pointed. Instead, he rubbed his two hands together then rested them down at his side. Marc knew what was coming next. Without waiting for the fellow to speak, he raised the angle of his gun slightly, a move that did not go unnoticed.

"So you don't really buy my story, do you?"

"Not for a second! What do you really want?"

The fellow smiled, a very crooked smile that revealed an extremely weathered face. "Well, if it was just me, there wouldn't be anything, because you've got at least a couple of guns trained on me." He spat out some chewing tobacco. "But since my boys are standing out there in the woods, I guess maybe we'll have to go through your things and take whatever can help us in San Francisco."

Marc bit his lip. He'd been through this before. "I'm afraid you won't find much. We've been swindled in New York City, robbed in Panama, and burned out in San Francisco. There's really nothing left."

The fellow motioned, and two other men emerged from the trees. "Sounds like a very sad story. But I guess you'll want to let us be the judge of that. This here is *some* of my boys . . ." Of course they had emerged into the clearing with their guns already raised and pointed, which put Marc at a complete disadvantage, even more so since he was sitting down. Without disturbing the gun in his hand, he slowly rose to his feet, which was difficult without using his arms to brace himself. To his surprise the fellow allowed him to stand. Marc glanced down and saw that Max was still sitting but that he had his rifle positioned in such a way that he could fire on at least one of the intruders.

"It appears that you probably have an advantage on us," said Marc quietly. "But things aren't always as they seem."

"No, they're not. You have two women with you and three men. It was four, but one left a while ago."

Marc had to shake his head to think about that. *Obviously they've been observing us, but his count is off. There are four men, five counting Porter. Did he just say it wrong, or is he really unaware of Leandro?*

"So," the fellow continued, "you and the two boys are it. And you are no match for us. Besides, you don't know what's in the wilderness and we do. I've been at this long enough that I never show all my strength, so you'd be wise to believe me when I say there are others." He made a motion with his hand, and Marc heard rustling from a number of different points. This guy really wasn't bluffing. "So you have to ask yourself if it's worth the fight."

Marc scrambled to think what to do. He had to bluff them out of this. One thing was certain if he didn't—he was not coming out of this alive. The two women were too big a temptation. Unlike their experience in Panama, where the trail was just fifty miles from coast to coast and the banditos were in something of a steady business, here in the Sierras it could be days or weeks, maybe even months, before anyone happened to this particular spot. In Panama the local authorities would make apprehending outlaws who violated women their top priority. Out here it was such a massive country that these bandits could do whatever they wanted and disappear into the forest without ever being discovered. They would kill Marc and the men first, have their way with his mother and Gloria, and then kill them as well. *That will not happen!*

Marc measured his words carefully. If he could convince them that the cost would be too high for them, maybe he could talk them into a retreat.

"You can outgun us. But you have to know that we'll kill at least a couple of you. I can't see that the pittance of money that we have makes it worth that. We really have suffered from everything we told you. So why don't you let us give you some food and you be on your way." He had managed very slowly to swing his gun to a firing position where he knew he would at least kill the leader, even if he got shot in the process.

"You'd risk losing your own life over some money? You'd let all of these people die? That doesn't make sense."

Marc slowly tipped his head forward. "If that's all we were talking about, I'd give you the money in a second. But you know as well as I do that there's more to it than that. These ladies are under my protection, and I won't back down. You've got to understand that I won't back down! Now if you leave, we won't say anything to the marshal or others. It will be just a group of men meeting on the trail and then going on their way. Otherwise, guns are going to blaze and a lot of us on both sides will die for no good reason."

He saw the fellow hesitate, turn to his side to see what his men were thinking, and Marc had the sense that maybe he could pull it off.

That's when young Jake Hendricks had to say, "You better listen to him—if you don't, Porter Rockwell will hunt you down!"

Marc rolled his eyes. *Not Porter Rockwell! Why did you have to tell them about Porter?*

"Rockwell! What's he got to do with this?" said the fellow harshly. Then it dawned on him. "He's the one who left camp." It only took a couple of seconds for the significance of this new information to register with the guy, and he responded exactly as Marc had thought he would—and it was bad news that he did. "That means that you have Porter Rockwell's saloon money. You folks have got a fortune!"

"He has it with him. You don't think he'd trust it to us, do you? Porter Rockwell is no fool." Marc felt sick to his stomach, knowing that Porter had indeed left a saddlebag with him for safe keeping. He hadn't even thought about it until this moment, but it was undoubtedly filled with a great deal of money. He knew that Porter often took the entire proceeds back to Brigham Young to use as he saw fit to support the Saints in Utah.

"He does not have it with him. I saw him ride off without his saddlebags," the bandit said.

This was the worst of all outcomes. Whether they had Porter's money or not made no difference now. These crooks would be so tempted that they'd have to find out. And they'd do the search even if it meant a couple of the outlaws themselves were killed—every man would bet it would be the others who went down. *Worse, once they start shooting, they will have to kill everyone in the camp so that there will be no witnesses—otherwise Porter will track them down and kill them. These robbers have to understand that.*

"And Rockwell's coming back," said Marc, now stalling for time. "Which means it's even more important for you to get out of here and leave us alone. He's not the type of man you want for an enemy."

"But he won't be back for a few days, at least. And when he does, he won't find anyone to tell him what happened."

This was it. The overwhelming greed was evident in the three men's eyes, and the one on the right was the first to surrender to it. As he started to raise his arm to shoot, Marc swung on him and fired then quickly pivoted and fired on the leader. Such was his training that he got off both shots before either of the outlaws could even discharge their weapons. But he wasn't fast enough for the third fellow—nor the fourth or fifth who came charging out of the brush behind them, their guns blazing. Instinctively Marc dropped to his knees, trying desperately to sort the situation out. From behind a nearby tree he heard Leandro Hendricks's weapon fire and saw a nearly simultaneous muzzle blast from Max's gun. *That's two shots for three men.* Two of the outlaws fell. *But those aren't repeating rifles . . .* The third man came charging directly for Marc, raising his pistol as he came. Marc started to swing his gun toward him, but another gun went off before he could fire, and he watched in amazement as the last man fell to the ground, right at Marc's feet. *Are there others? Gotta breathe.* He quickly pivoted in each direction in case there were more, but the forest was deadly silent, with even the animal noises that make up the background chatter of the wilderness temporarily subdued.

Heart pounding, Marc swung to his right just in time to see Gloria drop her gun and then fell to the ground, weeping. As Marc made his way toward Gloria, he heard yet another sound, a gurgling, unnatural sound that was horrible to hear. Turning around, he heard an anguished cry as Leandro Hendricks made his way to the spot where his son Jake lay dying. At least one of the many shots loosed by the thieves had hit Jake. The young man would probably never know that it was his impulsive words that had led to this bloody and tragic outcome.

Marc was shaking as he approached Gloria, but Alexandra got there first, putting her arms around the younger woman's heaving shoulders. "It's all right, dear. You saved my boys!"

Marc slumped down beside Gloria and his mother, the horror of the scene in front of them with six men dying or dead. He had protected his family but at a terrible cost. *How did it come to this?*

28—ZION IN THE DESERT

Utah Territory—September 1, 1851

"Is there anything else like it in the world?" asked Marc as he and the family gazed south across a vast sheet of dazzling white salt crystals. "It appears perfectly flat for as far as the eye can see."

"We call it the Salt Flats," said Porter Rockwell. "It's the residue of an ancient lake that covered this whole area for as far as you can see. When the lake evaporated, it left this! As we get closer to Salt Lake City you'll see the shoreline of the lake and just how deep and large it is."

"But why salt?" asked Max.

"Evaporation takes out all of the water, leaving only the minerals that have washed out from the mountains over the course of many years," replied Marc.

"Well, it makes my eyes hurt," said Alexandra. "There is nothing out here—even the mountains are barren. I'm tired of the desert." For one who was usually optimistic and curious, this negative reaction showed the bone-numbing fatigue that the party felt after being so long on the trail. "First we had to endure the more than 100-degree heat near Sacramento, then climb up the western face of the Sierra Nevada mountains until our horses were dead tired, and then cross the endless desert of Nevada. Will it never end?"

Marc understood how she felt. Nightmares had awakened him many of the nights since the attack in the mountains as his mind struggled to cope with the senseless and horrific violence. With many hours of tedious plodding, he'd replayed the scene a hundred times before finally praying for relief. After that the daytime visions faded, at least until today, and the nightmares had become less frequent.

Porter Rockwell remained quiet, simply squatting by the small fire he'd built. The smoke from the fire was pungent and strong with the smell of sagebrush, a grayish bush that was among the only plants hearty enough to survive the harsh environment.

"Why don't you let me cook dinner tonight," said Gloria. "I know that's a frightening thought, but even I can boil some water to reconstitute the beef strips."

"That would be nice," said Alexandra. "Thank you." That Alexandra would yield the cooking to another person proved that she was exhausted. "Not a lot for me. I'm too tired to be hungry."

"What about water?" asked Marc of Porter Rockwell. "It seems like this whole journey has been a dangerous game of hoping the water holes haven't dried up. I'm sure we'd have all died from thirst if you hadn't been here to guide us."

"More than one man has died out here for lack of water. But the path we took is calculated to always bring us to a well or small spring. The fools who travel across the salt flats to cut down the distance are the ones who end up dead or delirious."

Marc slumped down on his haunches. After riding on a horse all day, it felt good to stretch his muscles that way.

"You've been awfully quiet," said Gloria. "It was a hard day—I thought the heat would kill me—but no worse than yesterday. Is something bothering you?"

Marc shook his head then realized that it was wrong to deceive her. "I've been thinking again about the men we buried up in the mountains. I find myself dreaming about it, and I'm revolted by what happened."

"There are bad men everywhere. Geoffrey Brandt in England, the people who killed your Joseph Smith, which seems to have permanently affected Mr. Rockwell. Human beings can be cruel and foolish."

Marc nodded. "I know that's true. It's just that I've never had to be the one to do something about it."

Gloria extended her arm to help Marc into a standing position. Then she rested her head on his shoulder. "I had to shoot one of them, as well. But it was worth it to save your life."

"And I had to save you from Brandt." Marc took a deep breath. Unlike some of the others in the party, he liked the smell of the sagebrush fire. "Well, it is done and we can't change it. And we're still together and alive."

"I think the worst is over. None of us get to choose what circumstances we're given—we can only decide what to do with them. And I think we've chosen fairly well." She took his hand and squeezed it, looking into his eyes with something that can only be described as reluctant joy.

"Fire's ready," called Rockwell. "If you want to help with dinner, now's the time."

Gloria smiled. "My work awaits me. Promise you won't laugh if I somehow ruin the stew—particularly since it's almost impossible to ruin a stew."

Marc laughed. "I'll enjoy whatever you put in front of me. The truth is that I'm both hungry and tired." The seven hundred miles they had to cover between San Francisco and Salt Lake City was now down to less than one hundred, and, according to Rockwell, most of that was on level ground. That would be a welcome relief after the rugged mountains they had covered. And, as foreboding as the Great Salt Lake Desert was, it had more vegetation than the vast untamed miles of sun-bleached desert in Nevada.

"If we ever find water again, I'm going to go swimming and never get out," said Max with a sigh as he pulled the boots off his feet. That made even Alexandra laugh, and the group settled in for a quick dinner and early slumber.

* * *

The Great Salt Lake valley—September 20, 1851

"Just two more miles to go!" said Porter Rockwell amiably. "You can see the City of the Saints there in the distance." The group had travelled north of the Great Salt Lake, the sight of which had caused an audible gasp of admiration from the tired travelers who were stunned to see such a large body of water in the middle of a barren wilderness. Porter suggested that after getting settled, the family should take Max out to the lake for the swim he'd so earnestly wanted, with the promise that it would be impossible for Max or anyone else to sink because of all the salt. This was met with a whoop from Max.

The northern route allowed the group to follow a course that connected them to watering holes at strategic spots along the way. It also meant that they had passed by the small settlements of Ogden and Brigham City and were now rounding the bend by the Wasatch hot springs to the north of Salt Lake City. "This is where you should go swimming," said Rockwell to Max. "The water is an almost perfect temperature, particularly in the winter. It's heated deep in the earth. People really enjoy it." Max wanted to stop right then and there, but the group was not in the mood to wait any longer. The thought of finally reaching their destination was a great source of motivation to press forward.

As they reached the outskirts of the city, Gloria raised an eyebrow. "We spent the last year coming to this?"

Marc turned to her. "Not such a grand city—but it is in a mighty impressive setting."

She nodded her agreement. "It really is spectacular. The mountains here are even more dramatic than many of the Sierra Nevada because they rise up right from the valley floor."

"Do you see the distinctive line that runs all along the mountains to the east?" asked Porter. "That's the ancient shoreline I told you about back by the Salt Flats. Pretty impressive to think that the Great Salt Lake was once so deep. The old shoreline goes for more than a hundred miles both north and south of here, and it's almost all sand from the valley floor up to the line."

Marc shook his head. The valley was spectacular. But Salt Lake City was still developing—not nearly as glamorous or bustling as San Francisco seemed to be. At just more than 20,000 people, it was more like Salt Lake Village than a city, but it was a very orderly place, with wide streets and well-built homes. A number of business establishments stretched down what Porter called Main Street. Marc missed their temporary home in San Francisco but felt a certain peace here that wasn't existent in the California hub.

Porter turned and pointed to the top of a small promontory to the north of the city. "Do you see that spot?" The group nodded. "It's called Ensign Peak, and shortly after arriving in the valley, Brigham Young and a few of his companions went up there to survey the scene. Brigham had a vision while up there, and he told us that he could see a day when people filled this valley from north to south and east to west. He said that this would become one of the great cities of the world. So he didn't lay out these streets for the handful of people we have here today but for the millions who will eventually come here."

"A vision," said Marc. "Father always said that Joseph and Brigham were both prophets and seers. Perhaps this is evidence that it is true." That led to a short discussion of the difference between the gift of prophecy and that of being a seer.

"It's getting late," said Porter, "So I'm going to take you to Brigham Young's home next. He's the one to assign you a piece of property and to help you get established. I'm sure he's already made arrangements for you to stay with some of the Saints tonight and for as long as needed to put up your own place."

"And the people will help us with that?" asked Marc.

"Of course. All we had when we got here was each other, so everyone gets help when they need it. People will be glad to meet you."

As the group started trotting on their horses, Gloria said quietly, "I hope they're glad to meet me."

"You're worried because you're not a Mormon?" asked Marc.

"A little."

"Porter said you'll be fine. And I think he'd tell you otherwise if it was true."

Gloria nodded, but it was clear that she was still anxious.

A short while later Rockwell said, "We're here!" He dismounted and helped Alexandra and Gloria to dismount their horses.

"What's he like?" asked Alexandra, anxiety evident in her voice.

"Brigham Young?" Porter smiled. "In their daily walk of life, the people call him Brother Brigham, not president or anything formal. They love him. He has a great sense of humor, although he can be quite intimidating to those with whom he has a quarrel."

"Henry and I received a witness that he is a prophet, and now I find myself quite frightened of the thought of meeting such a man."

"You shouldn't," said Porter. "I told him all about you when I rode ahead a few days ago. He's anxious to meet you and to perhaps offer some comfort about your husband and daughter."

Alexandra swallowed hard. "Well, we've waited a long time for this . . ."

Porter motioned for them to follow him as he stepped onto the porch. A young girl opened the door and invited them into the parlor. When the women were seated, and while they were waiting to be summoned to meet the prophet, Porter motioned Marc to move to the side where he said, "Perhaps you should become a lawman. You have a quick hand and good judgment. You would do well at it."

"I'm not sure about that. Killing those men was very disturbing to me. Even though they attacked us, it is an awesome responsibility to take a man's life."

"I understand that better than anyone. But what you may not know is that being a good marshal is not so much about how fast you are with a gun or how brave you are in battle. The best way to resolve a situation is without guns. You have to be smart and quick-thinking, and you have proven to me that you have those qualities."

Marc nodded. "It's something to consider. I'd be pleased to serve with you, of course. But I think I'll see what President Young has to say. My mother and father have accepted that he is a prophet, so who better to give me advice about how to support my family?"

"But you haven't accepted that he is what he claims?" asked Porter.

"What?" Marc felt his face redden. He hadn't intended it to come out that way, but perhaps it was the truth. He really didn't know. Sometimes he believed and felt that his prayers were answered, and other times he felt as if it was just his emotions making him want to believe.

"I guess I just don't know. I wish I did, but I don't."

"I think that will be all right. You'll find out what you need to know soon enough." He paused. "But no matter what happens, you are very well suited to life here in Utah and more than capable of protecting and providing for your family. You're welcome at my house, my hotels, or my saloons any time you like. I'll make sure that word goes out that you are a friend of Porter Rockwell. In some quarters that will make a difference."

"I suspect it will make a great deal of difference," said Marc. "Thank you for all you've done for us."

Porter shuffled on his feet and then said, "Well, I guess I should be on my way home. It's been a long time since I've seen my wife and daughters, and I miss them."

"Of course," said Alexandra, rising. She gave Rockwell a small hug. Porter tipped his hat to Gloria and then shook Max's hand. Finally, Marc moved closer and accepted Rockwell's outstretched hand.

As Rockwell made his way to the door, he turned and smiled mischievously. "Perhaps Brother Brigham will perform your wedding," he said, and then he was out the door.

As they sat in the foyer, Marc said quietly, "It's been almost a year and a half since we left England and finally we're here."

"And only because of your fortitude and bravery," said Alexandra.

Marc smiled. "I think there's been more than enough courage to go around." He looked at the two women he loved and then at his younger brother who was now a man. "We did all right, I guess, didn't we?" It was a question that answered itself, and everyone fell into silence as they waited quietly.

In a few minutes they were ushered in to meet the famous Brigham Young, revered as a prophet by his followers and as a scoundrel by nearly everyone else. Relatively short in stature, he had a powerful, stocky build. "Please sit down and tell me about yourselves," he said simply.

Unlike Sam Brannan, President Young had a clean-shaven face, long hair that rested over his shirt collar, and, the women later agreed, he looked very handsome for a man of fifty. Powerfully built with dark, penetrating eyes.

"This is the culmination of a very long journey," said Alexandra tentatively. "My husband, Henry, died during the crossing but made us promise to persist until we made it here to join the Saints."

"He was true to the restored gospel to his very last breath," added Marc, hoping that there was no bitterness in his voice as he said it.

"Then he is in the care of the angels," said Brigham Young quietly. He was reflective for a moment. "I'm sorry to say that I know something of loss and death. The man I loved more than any other in the world was felled by assassin's bullets at far too young an age. So I know that you grieve, even as you have faith that your husband is in a marvelous place . . ."

"You speak of Joseph Smith," said Alexandra anxiously. "I so wish we could have known him."

"Well, perhaps you can know him through me. While I want very much to get to know each of you, let's take a few moments for me to tell you about Joseph Smith and the cause that he died for. Perhaps it will make what you have suffered seem worth the price." With that he motioned for them to take a seat in the comfortable chairs that stood in stark contrast to the modest home in which they met the president of the Church, and then they listened intently as Brigham Young recounted the story of meeting Joseph Smith for the first time, of sitting with him in council, and of returning to Nauvoo after his death.

"Now, please tell me about you, your hopes in this place, and how I can be of service to you." Before they could speak, he turned to Gloria. "My friend Porter tells me that you are not a member of our church but that you are a friend of the Chandler family."

"Yes," said Gloria, after clearing her throat. "That's all true."

This may well be the first time I've ever seen her flustered, thought Marc. *That, in and of itself, tells you something about the presence of this man."* The truth was that Marc had been skeptical, feeling that perhaps his mother had built up Brigham Young to the stature of some kind of mythological godlike figure as she had imagined this moment. *While he certainly isn't like that, he is remarkable. Utterly self-assured, with no pretense whatsoever.* Marc thought about what it was like to be in the presence of this man as President Young chatted with Gloria, who now seemed quite taken with him. *Father would have liked him.*

"Now, then, what about you, Mr. Chandler? It is likely to fall to you to support this family. What kind of work are you suited for?"

Marc bit his lip. "I'm suited for almost anything, sir. I've shoveled coal on steamships, hauled lumber for Sam Brannan, and fought off thieves in the Sierra Nevada."

Brigham Young smiled. "So Porter tells me. Said he left you on your own and came back to find that you had acquitted yourself quite well against very tenuous odds."

Marc nodded, his mind recalling all that had transpired, and how much he and his life had changed in the past year.

"But I suspect there's more to you than all that." President Young looked down at his legs for a moment then stood up. "Ladies, perhaps I could meet with Brother Chandler alone for a few moments. I'd like to get a sense of what the Lord has in mind for all of you, and I need some information before I ask Him about it. Would you excuse us?"

"Of course," said Alexandra. Her reaction to Brigham Young was quite different from when she met Sam Brannan.

When they were alone, Brigham turned to Marc. "There is something else you would like to do—I can see it in your face and I feel it in my heart. Tell me what it is that you gave up to come here to Utah."

Marc swallowed hard. And then against his will a single tear welled up and tumbled down his cheek. "I don't know that I can . . . it all seems so far away now."

And with that, Brother Brigham reached out and put his hand on Marc's knee. "You tell me everything . . . including the anger that you feel for what has happened."

With that Marc tasted blood in his mouth from where he bit his lip so hard to keep it steady. He had said nothing about anger, and yet this man somehow knew. "It started in England—in Liverpool . . ."

* * *

Thirty minutes later, Marc and President Young emerged from the room. President Young's secretary could not be more relieved, given that the president was now late in leaving for an important meeting. "Ladies, and young Max, I must excuse myself now. But I think you're going to like what we have in mind for all of you. I'm grateful you have come and hope you find this place all that you have hoped that it will be." The genuine warmth in his voice made it very clear why the Saints all called him "Brother Brigham," because his love for people he had barely met was evident.

After they shook his hand, Brigham Young and his secretary departed, leaving them alone in the drawing room to collect their thoughts and things.

"Well?" asked Alexandra. "What did he tell you to do?"

Marc shook his head slowly from side to side. "I don't know what to think. It's such a surprise . . ."

"Well, what is it?" asked Gloria, rising from the chair and moving over to take Marc's arm.

Marc turned to her and smiled. "He said that after we get Mother and Max settled into a comfortable home that you and I should go to Massachusetts, where a member of the Church can help me get admitted to one of the great polytechnic universities. He said he would arrange some financial assistance to help me gain my education."

Alexandra and Gloria gasped at the same moment. "What? He said you should go where?" asked Alexandra, even though she had heard perfectly.

Marc found himself quite emotional. "He said that Father was right all along, that God would bless me for my obedience and that in the long run Salt Lake City desperately needed well-educated men who could help build the infrastructure of a great city. He said that they need mechanical engineers and that the best way I could serve the Church was to improve my skills. He envisions a day when railroads will come to Utah, and steam-powered sawmills and mines." Marc shook his head to steady his thoughts. "Apparently he plans to send other men to Paris to study great art so they can decorate the great temple that is to be built." Marc put his arm around Gloria's waist. "He truly is a remarkable man with a great vision of what this place can become."

"What a wonderful tribute to your father," said Gloria.

Marc nodded, working hard to suppress the emotion he felt as he remembered the man who had inspired him. "Father was, indeed, like the merchant who recognized the pearl of great price when he saw it. He knew the gospel was worth any price that one must pay." And in the very instant that Marc Chandler said that, he received a confirming witness that all that his father had felt and known, all the things to which he had testified of—testified with his very life—were indeed true. "A prophet of God walks upon the earth today," said Marc quietly. The sound of his own voice saying those words surprised him. He turned and smiled at Gloria, who returned the smile with a hug.

ABOUT THE AUTHOR

Jerry Borrowman is a best-selling, award winning, author of ten published books—four co-authored biographies from World War II and Vietnam, including *A Distant Prayer* with Joseph Banks; *Three Against Hitler* with Rudi Wobbe, and *Beyond the Call of Duty* with Colonel Bernard Fisher, USAF retired, and recipient of the Medal of Honor. He co-authored *Stories From the Life of Porter Rockwell* an icon of the old west, with John W. Rockwell. He has also written six novels from World Wars I and II and the Great Depression, including *One Last Chance*. To learn more, visit www.jerryborrowman.com